Shaking the Nickel Bush

By RALPH MOODY

Illustrated by Tran Mawicke

University of Nebraska Press
Lincoln and London

First Bison Book printing: 1994

Library of Congress Cataloging-in-Publication Data
Moody, Ralph, 1898–
Shaking the nickel bush / by Ralph Moody; illustrated
by Tran Mawicke.
p.   cm.
"Bison book editions."
ISBN 0-8032-8218-4 (pbk.)
I. Title.
PS3563.05535S48   1994
813'.54—dc20
94-14503
CIP

Reprinted by arrangement with Edna Moody Morales
and Jean S. Moody.

The University of Nebraska Press is grateful to the
Lincoln City Libraries for assistance in the reprinting
of this book.

∞

TO

ANDY

Contents

SHAKING THE
NICKEL BUSH

1

In a Bad Way

NOBODY likes to go back to his home town dead broke, but I'd made up my mind to do it anyway. That was in St. Joseph, Missouri, on the night before the Fourth of July, in 1919. And that's why I was lying flat in a ditch in the freight yards, a couple of blocks beyond the passenger depot.

At the beginning of World War One I'd been old enough for the draft, but the board in Medford, a suburb of Boston where we lived, had passed me by because I was the head of our family. Then, when I tried to enlist, the doctor turned me down, so I went away to work as a carpenter at a munitions plant. By working seven days a week I made enough money to support our family and buy half a dozen fifty-dollar Liberty bonds. But during the summer and fall of 1918 I lost so much weight my clothes looked as if they were hung on a fence post.

When the armistice was signed and I went home, Mother sent me right up to see our family doctor. Dr. Gaghan was a gruff, blunt old Irishman, and the best doctor anywhere around, but he wouldn't tell me what the trouble was until he'd put me in a hospital and had me examined by several specialists. Then he pulled a chair up beside the bed, sat down, and looked at me over the top of his steel-rimmed spectacles.

"Son," he said, "you know me and you know I don't shilly-shally around. You've got diabetes, and when a lad of under twenty years gets diabetes he's in a bad way. These specialists think you can't make it for more than six months, but I don't hold with their notion. There's few things that God's good sunshine and fresh air—with a bit of common sense thrown in—won't cure for a lad. Why don't you go back to Colorado where you were raised—or better still, to Arizona where 'tis warm weather all the winter long? Wear as little clothes as the law allows and let the sunshine at your body; there's no end to the wonders it works. Fetched up as you were in a saddle, you could likely enough make your way at some easy job on one of the big cattle ranches they have out there. Only the other day I was reading about one o' them in the newspaper. I'll be dropping past the house and having a talk with your mother, and I'll write out a diet for you to follow. 'Twon't be tasty, but what's the odds if it does the trick? Now get your clothes on; 'tis no good it'll be doing you to lie abed."

My mouth went as dry as dust when Dr. Gaghan told me what the specialists thought, but before he was through talking I was all right again. Maybe it was because he said I should go back to Colorado; I'd been homesick to go back ever since we'd moved East, the year after Father died. Then too, Dr. Gaghan thought I could make it, and I had more trust in him than in all the specialists in the world.

He must have driven straight from the hospital to our house, and the talk he had with Mother must have worked about the same way as the one he had with me. When I got home that afternoon her eyes were red from crying, and she couldn't talk without choking up, but by the time the three youngest children came from school they couldn't have guessed there was anything wrong. Then, when Philip came in from his job, she seemed almost happy. "Ralph has decided to go back out West for a while," she told him. "Isn't that nice? You know, he has missed his cowboy friends ever since we moved here, and working on a ranch again will do him a world of good. I'm sure that within a few months he will have gained back all the pounds he's lost. He is going to Arizona for the winter, then back to Colorado when spring comes."

I think that's all she ever said to the younger children about it, but Grace, my older sister, knew. She'd already gone to Boston for gluten flour and other things on the doctor's list before I got home from the hospital.

That evening Mother sent the others to bed early, and she and Grace and I stayed up till nearly midnight. While Grace darned my socks, mended my underwear, and packed my suitcase, Mother cooked things I'd have to take with me, and she hardly stopped talking for a single minute. I think most of it was to keep Grace and me from worrying, but some of it was to keep herself from being afraid.

"Now you must not let yourself worry about us a particle," she told me as she mixed dough for gluten bread. "Dr. Gaghan tells me that fear and worry are the very worst things for diabetes, and we shall be perfectly all right. Philip will finish his apprenticeship in the spring, and as a full-fledged cabinetmaker he will earn us a good living. Gracie, would you bring that little notebook from the upper drawer of my dresser, and the postcard Dr. Gaghan left?"

While Grace was gone Mother slipped two loaves of gluten bread into the oven, put a dozen eggs on to boil, and told me, "Wherever you are, you must go to see a doctor every week and take him a sample—the first in the morning—then have him mail a postcard of his findings to Dr. Gaghan. In that way I shall feel as safe about you as if you were under his personal care. Gracie will write you out a whole stack of cards with all the questions on them, so the local doctor will have only to fill in a few check marks and figures."

When Grace brought the notebook, Mother had her write down the recipe for making gluten bread and a list of the things I could and couldn't eat. In between, she kept talking to me, trying to make the diet sound better than it really was. "This recipe is a very simple one, and I'm sure you'll find that any housewife or ranch cook· will be able to make you excellent bread by it. I suppose Dr. Gaghan told you that you must eat nothing that is either sweet or starchy. But you may have any sort of leafy green vegetables, fish, chicken, milk, eggs, and tea or coffee without sugar. No red meat, and nothing fried. But stewed or fricasseed or roasted chicken is very nice. And you remember what delicious trout you used to catch in the Platte River. Broiled trout are marvelous, and they're almost as good poached as fried. Then, you can have almost any kind of nuts. That should help a lot, for nuts are very nourishing—and easy for one to carry in his pocket."

The last few minutes of going away from home are never easy, even if you know right where you're going and when you're coming back. I thought it might be harder that time than ever before, but it wasn't, because nobody said good-bye.

I was taking the morning train from Boston, so Mother woke me quietly just before daylight. She and Grace must have been up for an hour or so. Breakfast was on the table when I came downstairs, and my suitcase and a big basket of things I could eat were set by the front door. During breakfast Mother kept talking about friends we used to have in Colorado, and telling me things to say to them when I saw them, but she never mentioned diabetes. Grace didn't talk at all; I think she knew that Mother had to. And she didn't go to the door with me either. As I was leaving the kitchen she just squeezed my arm, real tight and only for a second, then turned back toward the stove.

I thought Mother might break down when we reached the front door—and I was a little bit afraid I might, too—but neither of us did. When I stepped out onto the front porch she took the little notebook from the front of her dress and slipped it into the breast pocket of my coat. "It has always seemed to me that one is never alone when he has his Bible with him," she told me, "so I put the little one your father had when he was a boy in your suitcase. I've jotted down in this little book a few of the verses that have brought me comfort when things seemed darkest." She started to say something else, then turned back quickly and closed the door.

Mother had wanted me to cash my Liberty bonds before I started West, and to take the whole three hundred dollars with me, but I couldn't see much sense in that. It isn't safe to carry much money in your pockets when you're traveling around, and besides, I was sure I'd need only a few dollars more than my train fare to Arizona. Even if I did have diabetes I wasn't sick and, though I wasn't quite as strong as I had been the year before, I was a long way from being puny. Then too, I wouldn't be going West as a tenderfoot. By the time I was ten I could handle a horse and a rope better than some of the cowhands I worked with, and the summer I was twelve I'd had a job at full cowhand's wages. I knew exactly what I'd do when I got to Tucson: I'd go down to the stockyards and help some of the cowhands who were bringing cattle in. As soon as they saw how well I could handle a rope, some one of them would get me a job with his boss. That's why I cashed only two bonds, and took only twelve dollars in my pocket.

When I reached Tucson things didn't work out just the way I'd thought they would. The stockyards there weren't nearly as big as the ones they used to have in Denver; there were only a few cattle in the pens, and only a few cowhands hanging around—every one of them out of a job. When I borrowed a throw rope from one of them and tried to hindfoot a steer, I found that I'd either gone rusty or forgotten how. The loop would close before the steer could step into it, or I'd toss it clear up against his hocks. The nearest I came to making a catch was when I snagged a cow by the tail, so I decided I'd better not try for a top-hand's job till I'd got back into practice. I'd just take any sort of ranch job I could get hold of—even mending fences—and I had a pretty good idea how to get hold of one.

I knew that in every cow town there were employment offices that made a specialty of furnishing ranch help, but a fellow didn't have much chance of getting a job at one of them unless he could lay five dollars on the line. With only twelve dollars in my pocket I didn't like the idea of spending five for a job, but it seemed to me that I'd better hunt up one of those offices and do it. That morning I'd finished the last scrap of the food Mother had packed for me; that is, all but the five-pound sack of gluten flour she'd put in the bottom of the basket. And, of course, I couldn't eat that till I'd found a job where there'd be a cook to make it into bread for me. Then too, I hadn't brought a bedroll, so I couldn't sleep outdoors, but would have to rent a room. And between room rent and meals a fellow can run through five dollars pretty fast.

I didn't have much trouble in finding an employment office, but when I stepped in, my mouth went dry for a couple of seconds—the way it did when Dr. Gaghan told me the specialists didn't think I could make it for more than six months. There were at least twenty cowhands sitting around that office, and half a dozen or more had real good rigs lying at their feet; saddle, bridle, bedroll, and a good fat war bag. Men like that might be drifters, but they're top hands or awfully close to it, and they're not dead broke.

Between the time I stepped through that doorway and the time I reached the counter at the back of the room I did some fast thinking. Every man in the place had "working cowhand" written all over him. They were as stout and tough as range bulls. The sun wrinkles were deep around their eyes, and their faces and hands were as leathery as tanned cowhide. I could barely scale a hundred and two pounds—with my shoes on— and was as pale as skimmed milk. Even though I was wearing a blue shirt, jeans, and the old Stetson I'd had ever since I was a kid, it would have been hard to find a tenderer-looking tenderfoot. If jobs were scarce enough that men like these were sitting around an employment office, I was really in a bad way.

Of course, I still had two hundred dollars' worth of Liberty bonds at home. But Philip couldn't make a living for the family until he'd finished his apprenticeship in the spring, and Mother would need that money to keep from going into debt. Besides that, even if I did sell one of the bonds, it would take at least a week to get a letter home and the money back. Unless I got a job right away I'd go broke.

I was so busy thinking that I didn't notice the big man behind the counter till I was right in front of him and he said, "Hi'ya, stranger."

It's funny how the sound of a man's voice and what he says can take you back ten years or more in a half a second. Hi Beckman, foreman on a ranch where I was waterboy when I was nine years old, had a voice exactly like that man's. And no matter how well Hi knew a man, he'd say, "Hi'ya, stranger," when they met.

It's funny, too, how a long-forgotten sound like that will bring a picture back into your head. For a split second I could almost think I was a kid again, sitting by Hi's elbow in the old bunkhouse on the Y-B ranch while he was playing stud poker. The cowhands on the Y-B didn't play a very big game, and the bets were usually a nickel or dime—or sometimes a quarter— but Hi had been losing all evening and was down to two cart-wheels and a couple of quarters. I watched as he turned up a corner of his hole card and peeked; it was the four of spades. Then he drew a six, and stayed when Tommy Brogan bet a dime on a king up. On the next round Hi drew another four, but Tommy drew another king and bet another dime. There was already a four showing in the hand to Hi's right, and a six in the hand to his left. But he sat for a full minute or more, seeming to study every one of the seven hands. Then, without saying he was making a raise, he shoved a quarter into the pot.

I knew there must be some pretty good hole cards, because everybody stayed in to see the raise. On the last up card Tommy got a queen, Hi a deuce, and Mr. Cooper, the boss, drew an ace to make him a pair. I was sure Hi would drop out, but he didn't. He stayed for Mr. Cooper's bet of a dime and for Tommy's raise to a quarter—even when I knew that Tommy would never buck the boss unless he had another king in the hole. I was afraid Hi might not have thought about that, so I reached a toe over and touched his boot, real easy. He moved it just enough to let me know he'd felt the touch.

After Hi drew his down card and we'd peeked at it, I thought he'd gone out of his mind. It was the nine of diamonds, leaving him only a pair of fours, and beaten in sight by every hand on the table. Mr. Cooper must have known as well as I did that

Tommy had three kings and his pair of aces topped, for he opened the betting with a nickel. But Hi was sitting between them, and slid both cartwheels into the pot without saying a word. Nobody else said a word either, but they all turned their hands down, and Hi pulled in the pot. From there on his luck changed, and he must have had twenty dollars when Mr.

Cooper said it was time to turn in.

The last thing at night Hi always walked around to see that everything was all right in the corrals, and I always went along with him, if still awake. That night we were barely out of earshot from the bunkhouse when I asked him, "Why did you pick a time to bluff when you had the very worst hand at the table?"

"Ain't no time for bluffin' like when you're beat in sight," he told me, "and there ain't no sense waitin' till you're broke. How's a man goin' to run a bluff when he's broke?"

It was certain that every cowhand in that employment office had me beat in sight, and I'd decided to tell the man behind the counter that I'd pay five dollars for any kind of a job he had, regardless of the wages. But when Hi's words flashed through my head, I changed my mind in a hurry. I slapped my ten-dollar bill up on the counter and said, "I'll shoot the whole ten for a job if you've got a good one. I don't mind riding the rough string, and can rope with the best of 'em—once I get my hand back in."

"Only got one job, and it's a pretty fair one," the man told me. Then he smiled and said, "Lookin' a bit puny; been in the hospital?"

"Yep," I said, "but I'm all right now."

"Gas?" he asked.

"No," I said, "I wasn't in the service. I was. . . ."

The man had been looking right into my eyes when he asked if I'd been gassed, but the moment I told him I hadn't been in the service his eyes drifted away and he shook his head. "Not a chance!" he told me, almost as if I'd asked him for a hand-me-out. "There's too many boys that's done their bit looking for jobs; you're in the wrong town!"

I didn't try to bluff at either of the other employment offices. I just walked up to the counters and told the agents I'd pay five dollars for any kind of a job they could send me out on right away, and that I didn't care how small the wages were. Both agents were real pleasant when I first went in, and they both thought I was a soldier just back from the war—but when I told them I wasn't, they didn't treat me so well. The one in the last office I went to shouted loud enough for everybody in the place to hear him, "I ain't got no job for a slacker today, nor no other day. Get on back where you come from!"

I hunted for another employment office until dark, then went back to the depot for my suitcase, and started out to find a room and some supper. I found a little room near the stockyards that wasn't too bad, and cost only seventy-five cents a night, but I didn't make out very well on supper. I went into half a dozen restaurants that looked as if they wouldn't be too high-priced, but none of them had any leafy green vegetables or fish, and the only kind of chicken they had was fried. I finally had to settle for three boiled eggs and a cup of coffee, but they charged me thirty-five cents, though I had neither bread nor potatoes.

I didn't really feel homesick when I went back to my room—I'd worked away from home too much for that—but I did feel sort of all alone. When I couldn't go to sleep, I got out Mother's little notebook to look up a few Bible verses, but I didn't do it. Before she had written down the chapter and verse numbers, she'd filled all the pages with things she'd wanted to say to me before I came away. At the end she wrote, "Son, you are in God's hands, so I shall not let myself worry, and I won't expect long letters, but do let us hear from you often, even though it is only a penny postal card."

I never was much good at writing letters, but regardless of what Mother said I knew she'd be worrying, so I got out the pad she had put in my suitcase and sat down to write her a little note. Then, once I got started, I couldn't seem to quit till I'd written a dozen pages. Ever since I was knee-high to a toad the thing she had insisted on most was that I tell "the truth, the whole truth, and nothing but the truth." But it didn't seem to be the right thing to do in that letter, so I just wrote whatever I thought would keep her from worrying.

After I'd written about how much I liked my diet and how warm the weather was, I told her about having landed a fine job on a big cattle ranch right near town, where they had lots of leafy green vegetables and a cook who knew all about making gluten bread, and where I could get in to see the doctor every week. Then I told her that I'd have to spend my first couple of months' wages to buy a saddle and outfit and wouldn't be able to send any money home till spring, but that I'd be getting my keep as part of my pay. In that way I wouldn't need a penny for anything except the doctor, so she should cash the Liberty bonds right away, to hold the family over until Philip had finished his apprenticeship. In the rest of the letter I just told her things I made up about how big the ranch was, and how many cattle there were on it, and how friendly everybody had been. When I'd finished, I almost believed it myself.

It was a week before I wrote home again, and I had to do some more lying, but I found it a lot harder that time, and I couldn't make myself believe a word of it for a single second. I wrote that the place where I was working was the home ranch for one of the biggest cattle outfits in the Southwest, and that the owners had other ranches scattered all around Arizona and New Mexico. Then, after I'd told how much better I was feeling and how well I was getting along on my job, I said that the boss was sending another cowhand and me to one of the ranches near Phoenix, that I didn't know exactly what my address would be, but that I'd write again when I got there.

What had really happened was that I had gone broke. I'd talked to every cowhand and every cattleman who came in to the stockyards that week. They had all been friendly when I first talked to them, and I think a couple of the cattlemen might have given me a job, but they all froze up when I told them I hadn't been in the service. I went to every employment office in Tucson, looking for a job of any kind. I found only one, and I'd have been better off if I hadn't found it. The agent charged me three dollars for a job as night dishwasher in a little hole-in-the-wall restaurant, then the boss fired me within an hour. I couldn't blame him for it because there were lots of returned Arizona soldiers, a good many of them Mexicans, who

were looking for any kind of job. One just happened to come
along at the wrong time for me.

That job, and the doctor, and gluten bread were the reasons
I went broke so fast. The morning after I wrote Mother my first
letter I had to pay thirty-five cents for three more eggs and a
cup of coffee. Three eggs alone don't go very far, and neither
does money if you have to buy them at ten cents apiece. I
decided that until I found a job I'd better try to live on the
gluten flour I'd brought from home, so I asked the cook in the
restaurant what he'd charge me to make it up into bread. Even
though I was furnishing my own flour, the best deal I could
make with him was fifty cents. But that didn't seem too bad,
because I expected I'd get five or six loaves.

Before I took the flour back to the restaurant I wrote out
Mother's recipe for making gluten bread, but the cook got
huffy and wouldn't take it. He said he didn't need anybody to
tell him how to make bread, and if I knew so much about it I
could make it myself. I'd have been fifty cents better off if I had.
I don't think he'd ever seen gluten flour before, and I don't
think he put anything but salt and water into it before he baked
it—and he must have baked it all day. When I went back that
evening he made me pay him before he'd bring the bread out
of the kitchen, and when he brought it I knew why. He'd baked
the whole five pounds of flour into two loaves that were the
same size, shape, color, and hardness as paving bricks. If I'd
been a dog with good teeth I might have been able to gnaw a
corner off one of them, but I couldn't make a dent in it with
the teeth I had. After I'd tried for about ten minutes, I threw
both loaves in an alley and bought a can of salmon for my
supper. For the rest of the week I made out on a ten-cent pound
of peanuts and a fifteen-cent can of salmon a day. I just about
had to because of a mistake I made the first time I went to the
doctor. And then too, they were the only things on my diet that
I could eat without cooking.

In the first letter I'd written to Mother I'd told her I was
going to a doctor the next morning, before I went out to my

new job on the ranch. Even though I didn't have any job, I didn't dare not to go to a doctor, because I knew Dr. Gaghan would tell Mother if he failed to get a report card every week. I put one of the cards Grace had written out for me in my pocket when I took the flour to the restaurant, then hunted up a doctor. He was a kindly old gentleman, and visited with me nearly half an hour before he made his tests on the sample I'd brought. He wanted me to tell him when I first noticed that I was losing weight, and what the specialists in the hospital said, and what Dr. Gaghan said, and what diet he'd laid out for me.

"Hmmmm. Hmmmm," he said after he'd looked at the diet pages in my notebook. "Don't know but what I'd agree with your family physician instead of the specialists, but you'll find this diet rather hard to live on in this country, particularly if you're planning to do ranch work. Most of the grub will be bully beef and beans and biscuits, or chili con carne and tortillas. On ranches that hire more than one or two hands you won't find any green vegetables, and unless the foreman has a family of youngsters he won't be milking a cow or keeping chickens. And, of course, there is no fresh fish in this country. It seems to me you'll have to depend heavily on gluten bread, nuts, and canned salmon. You can make out all right if you have plenty of fresh milk, but without it you might run into trouble. However, you'll have to lay in a supply of gluten flour here, and I'd advise you to take plenty of it along. In any other town except Phoenix they'd have to send away for it."

The doctor tested the sample I'd brought him in a little back room, and when he came out I noticed that he'd made three or four check marks on the report card. Then, as he weighed me, and took my pulse, temperature, and blood pressure, he wrote down the figures. After he'd finished he said, "Except for the sugar, it's not too bad. That will be two dollars. I'll mail the card to your physician when I go to lunch."

If I'd known I wasn't going to find a job I'd have told him I'd do my own mailing, but, of course, I didn't know it then. That's why I had to save out two dollars before I went stone broke, and go to see him the second time. That time I told him not to bother about mailing the card, that I'd take it with me and enclose it in a letter to Dr. Gaghan. So he scrawled his name at the bottom of the card and gave it to me. I didn't write any letter, and I didn't plan to, but I copied all the check marks and figures onto another card before I mailed the one the doctor gave me. I didn't bother about trying to copy the signature because no two doctors write the same anyway.

After two nights in the hotel I could see that I was living beyond my means, and that seventy-five cents a night would break me in a hurry. Besides, I wouldn't have any more use for my suitcase or the pinchbacked suit I'd worn on the train. A fellow would look pretty silly to be carrying a suitcase and no bedroll when he went to work on some ranch as a cowhand. He'd look even sillier with a pinchbacked suit and tan oxfords instead of a denim jumper and riding boots. Before I started out to look for a job that third morning I took my suit, suitcase, watch, and empty lunch basket, and went hunting for a pawnshop where the owner would do a little trading.

I had to try three or four pawnshops before I found one where I could make a decent deal. Of course, I expected to come out at the little end of the horn, but I didn't get stuck too badly. The suitcase wasn't new, I'd had the shoes six months and the suit a year, but the lunch basket had double covers and was brand new, and the watch had cost five dollars. After an hour's haggling I traded them for a pretty good blanket, a tarpaulin that looked as though it would still shed rain, a pair of boots that were just a bit scuffed and run down at the heels, a jumper and pair of jeans that had been worn only enough to fade in good shape, and a throw rope that was almost new. I could have made the deal a lot quicker if I hadn't held out for the throw rope, but I needed some practice to get my hand and eye back in, and I couldn't do it without a rope.

From the pawnshop I went back to my room, folded everything I had inside the blanket, and wrapped it in the tarp. When I had it corded up it looked like a good husky bedroll, so I took it down to the stockyards and tossed it into one corner of the scaler's office, just as if I were a cowhand in with a bunch of cattle for shipping. During the day I tried to get a job from every cattleman who came to the yards, and in my spare time I practiced with the rope. It's hard to get in any good rope practice without a horse and some cattle to work on. But I'd have made the drovers sore if I'd worked on any of the cattle in the pens, so I just sat astraddle of a fence to practice; trying to lay my loop around some pebble in an empty pen, or to make it stand close to the ground where some imaginary critter would step into it.

That night, and for the rest of the week, I slept by a feed stack just outside the pens, and I wasn't alone. There were eight or ten other fellows sleeping there, every one of them broke and looking for a cowhand job. That's where I met Lonnie, and I don't know yet whether it was good or bad.

2

Land Rolling!

LONNIE was about my age, and told me he'd been brought up on a Wyoming ranch, drafted, and honorably discharged from the service after he'd nearly died with the flu. Ever since spring he'd been drifting around the Southwest—mostly by hopping freight trains—and hunting for a job as top hand or bronc buster. I think he was too lazy to have made a top hand, and I don't know about his bronc riding, but he was friendly as the dickens and could handle a rope to beat the band; he showed me a couple of real handy tricks on turn-around fore-footing. I couldn't run past him fast enough that he couldn't snag me by either foot he wanted to. It was because of Lonnie that I wrote Mother about being sent with another cowhand to a ranch near Phoenix.

I was down to less than a dollar when Lonnie asked me how about catching the night freight and going up to Phoenix. He told me we'd be there by morning and that he knew a lot of fellows around the stockyards. He said that if we didn't go out for top hands, but would settle for jobs at thirty or forty dollars a month, it would be a cinch to get them up there. Right then I'd have been glad to get a job anywhere, doing anything, for five dollars a month and my keep, so I told him I thought it was a good idea.

It isn't easy to flip a rolling freight train for the first time, especially if you have a bedroll lashed onto your back, but I didn't have too much trouble that night in Tucson. Lonnie showed me how to do it on some empty boxcars out near the end of the freight yards, then we hid under them until the night freight pulled out. It was just beginning to pick up a little speed when we ducked out and ran along beside it. Lonnie flipped onto the step of one boxcar as it went past, and I flipped onto the next. We might have been better off if we'd been caught right then, but we weren't. It was about half an hour before the brakeman came down along the top of the train and spied us. He kicked us off at the first stop, about twenty miles out from Tucson.

That was the first of a dozen times we were kicked off freight trains before we reached Phoenix four days and nights later, and we must have walked the tracks thirty miles of the way. Lonnie could get by pretty well by mooching meals at houses in the little towns where we were kicked off. But it wouldn't have been any good for me, even if I'd have done it, because they didn't have any of the things I could eat—unless it might have been boiled eggs. By the end of the second day I'd spent my last dime for salmon and peanuts, and if Lonnie hadn't been a good forager as well as a good moocher I'd have come close to starving.

It was Thanksgiving morning and I was down to my last handful of peanuts when we had our worst luck. A brakeman about the size and disposition of a grizzly bear kicked us off right out in the middle of the desert. I think he must have seen us flip aboard just after daylight, and had waited to catch us at the very worst spot he could. If he hadn't he wouldn't have been carrying a club when he came after us. We were sitting in the end of an empty gondola car, about half asleep, when I heard a thumping above our heads. At the same moment Lonnie scrambled to his feet, grabbed his bedroll, and yelled,

"Watch it, buddy! Land rolling!" Then he dived out over the side of the car.

For a second I was kind of bewildered, then I looked up and saw the brakey coming down the ladder of a boxcar right above me. The club he was carrying looked as big as a fence post. I don't remember anything about throwing my bedroll over the side, but I did it. Then I grabbed the edge of the car and vaulted over. I didn't dare dive the way Lonnie had, but I had sense enough to throw myself far out, and not try to land on my feet. I was lucky enough to come down in a patch of rabbit brush, so I only got the wind knocked out of me and scratched up a little. The brakey must have thrown his club at the same second I went over the edge; it was lying within four feet of me when I was able to catch my breath and sit up.

It's a wonder that Lonnie and I didn't get killed, because that train was rolling at least fifty miles an hour. He couldn't have unloaded more than five seconds before I did, but he landed at least a hundred yards farther back, and my bedroll was halfway between us. When he caught up to me he cussed the tar out of me for vaulting, and said I'd have broken my back if I hadn't landed in the rabbit brush. Then he told me that if you dived straight out you'd land rolling, and if you weren't unlucky enough to hit a fence or a rock you wouldn't be hurt too badly.

It had been cold the night before, and we didn't get much sleep because we'd had to be ready to flip that freight when it came through, but by the time we got kicked off, the desert was as hot as summer. We had to walk eight or nine miles to reach the first little town; just a flag stop, with five or six adobe houses and a section hand's shack. It was past noon before we got there, and I was so dried out that my tongue stuck to the roof of my mouth. After we'd drunk about a gallon of water apiece we sat in the shade of an old tumble-down cattle pen for a while, then Lonnie went to see if he could mooch something to eat. While he was gone I finished the last of my peanuts, one by one, and watched half a dozen hens and a rooster that were scratching in the dust of the cattle pen.

Lonnie was gone nearly an hour, and when he came back he was carrying a bucket about half full of water.

"What you doing with that bucket?" I asked him as he sat down beside me.

"Brung our Thanksgivin' dinner," he said. "You know, buddy, some of these Mex women ain't so dumb. One of 'em made me pack her five buckets of water 'fore she'd give me a bowl of chile, about half of it gristle."

"Half a bucket of water won't make much of a supper," I said. "I wish it was milk. Did you find out when the next train stops here?"

"Ain't none," he told me as he fished a long piece of string and a chunk of gristle out of his pocket. "Nine miles up the line there's a water tank where all the freights stop at to fill the boiler. We'll have to hoof it."

As Lonnie talked he tied the piece of gristle—about the size of a small grasshopper—onto the end of the string, then tossed it out into the middle of the pen. The rooster saw it sailing through the air, ran toward it, and gobbled it the instant it touched the ground. It was so big that he had to crane his neck two or three times before he could swallow it. Lonnie cussed in a whisper because the rooster got the gristle instead of one of the hens, but as he mumbled he kept drawing in slowly on the string. At first the old rooster tried to hold back, but, with that piece of gristle in his craw, Lonnie had him hooked like a fish. Step by step he brought the rooster closer until he could snatch him by the neck. Then he whispered to me, "Grab that bucket o' water and duck into the brush!"

I think that was the toughest rooster I ever tried to eat. After I'd sneaked back for our bedrolls we went far into the brush, built a fire, and boiled him all afternoon. The longer we boiled him the tougher he seemed to get, but we had full stomachs when we set out for the water tank.

Lonnie saved the gristle and string, and caught us two fat hens before we reached Phoenix, but he didn't get us any jobs when we got there. He seemed to know most of the fellows hanging around the stockyards, but I think it was only because they were drifters and moochers too. None of them had a job or seemed very anxious to find one. There was only one in the bunch who looked to me as if he might be a first-class cowhand,

and he looked as though he'd just been run through a thrashing machine. He had a broken arm hanging in a sling, nearly half his face was covered with bandages, and his clothes were torn in a dozen places. Lonnie didn't know him, and he was sitting off by himself, so I went over and sat down beside him.

"Horse go through a fence with you?" I asked, just to have something to say.

"Uh-uh," he grunted, "got busted up tryin' to be a movie actor."

"In California?" I asked.

"Uh-uh," he said again. "Wickenburg."

"I don't know where that is," I told him, "but I thought they made all the moving pictures in California."

"Wickenburg's about fifty miles northwest, on the Santa Fe," he told me. "They don't make whole pi'tures out there; just horse-fall pieces that get spliced into cowboy-and-Injun filums. Reckoned I was goin' to make a big stake in a hurry, but I got busted up on my first fall. Most of the boys does. It's a wonder they ain't killed off half the cowhands in these parts."

I talked to the boy for nearly an hour, and when we were through I knew what I was going to do. It doesn't make a fellow very happy to be told that he may live only six months, but it surely cuts down the gamble on taking chances, and I'd reached the point where I had to do some gambling. I couldn't live forever on chickens that Lonnie stole with a piece of gristle, I wouldn't mooch for a living, there didn't seem to be any chance of finding a safe job, and I couldn't buy salmon and peanuts without money—or send report cards to Dr. Gaghan.

I'd learned to do trick-riding when I was a kid, and my best stunt had been a good deal like a horse fall, except that the horse didn't go down. It had to be trained to make a quick stop from a fast gallop. Then I'd be thrown out of the saddle, turn a somersault in the air, and land on my feet. I hadn't tried that stunt for nearly eight years, but I was pretty sure I could still do it. And if the worst happened, I probably wouldn't be gambling away more than five or six months—ones that didn't appear to be the best I'd ever had.

When I went back to tell Lonnie what I was going to do, he and his friends were sitting in the shade of the weigher's office. Most of them already knew about the horse-fall business, and they told me I was crazier than a hooty owl to try it. One of them had been out there, but he hadn't done any riding, and he said that knowing trick riding wouldn't help a bit; that I'd get busted up on my first or second fall anyway. I tried to get Lonnie to go along, just so I wouldn't be alone, but he wouldn't do it. He said he'd keep hunting us jobs from the drovers that came in, and if I wasn't back in a week's time he'd come out to see I got a decent burial.

I couldn't see any sense in wasting time after I'd decided what I was going to do, so I got out the copy of the last report card I'd had from the doctor in Tucson, made another copy with the weigher's fountain pen, scribbled a name nobody could read at the bottom, and put M.D. behind it. Then I mailed the card and went over to the Santa Fe freight yards.

I'd always found that when I asked a farmer if I could hunt on his land he'd let me, but that he'd tell me to get out if I tried it without asking. It seemed to me it might work the same way on a freight train, so when I got over to the Santa Fe yards I hunted up the conductor of the next freight train going toward Wickenburg. He was a little grey-haired man, with a bow in his legs that a fat hog could have run through, and he had the stub of a dead cigar clamped between his teeth. I told him right off the bat that I was flat broke, that I hadn't been in the service, and that I wanted to get out to Wickenburg to try my luck at riding horse falls for the movie company. He listened till I'd finished, then asked, "Where you from?"

"Boston," I told him.

"Long piece to come for a chance to get your neck broke, ain't it?" he asked. Then, without waiting for an answer, he nodded his head toward a boxcar with the door halfway open. "Don't smoke in there," he told me, "there's straw on the floor. You'll prob'ly need it more when I haul you back on my next run. We'll be pulling out in about an hour."

I might have worried all the way to Wickenburg if the straw in that car hadn't been so deep and soft, or if I'd had a decent night's sleep within two weeks. But I never knew when the train pulled out of Phoenix, and I wouldn't have known when it reached Wickenburg if the conductor hadn't pounded on the door of my private car. By the time I had my bed rolled and tied he was up near the engine, and when I went up to thank him he said, "Don't mention it, but don't be spreading the word neither. See that flivver over yonder with the big hombre by it? He belongs to the movie outfit. He'll haul you on out to the location. It keeps him busy hauling the whole ones out and the busted-up ones back." Then he stuck out his hand, shook with me, and said, "Good luck to you, bub."

The location was about ten miles up Hassayampa Creek, near the foot of the Bradshaw Mountains, and the road must have been laid out by a drunken cowhand on a bucking bronco. I think the Mexican fellow who drove the flivver wanted to find out whether or not I was yellow. And if he did, he went at it in just about the right way. I don't believe he ever let that flivver slow down to thirty miles an hour, and I've ridden bucking horses in roundups that stayed on the ground more of the time. I wanted to have asked the driver some questions about the riding, but I didn't dare get my teeth apart for fear I'd bite my tongue. And he was so busy fighting the steering wheel that he couldn't have answered me anyway. There was only one thing in favor of that ride: it didn't last very long before we came in sight of the location.

There was a whole tent village clustered up on the edge of a mesa, and as we pulled up to it we passed a remuda of about a hundred of the sorriest-looking old cowhorses I ever saw. The outfit must have had to scour the whole West to find them, and I don't think they'd have brought ten dollars apiece at an auction.

It was nearly sunset when we drove into the tent village, the picture shooting for the day was over, and the common help was queuing up in the grub lines. There must have been fifty or sixty cowhands, nearly as many Indians, and a whole raft of others who might have been almost anything. Strutting around the place and shouting orders were half a dozen men that I knew must be bosses or directors. Every one of them was dressed up like a drug-store cowboy, with fancy Spanish boots, brand-new ten-gallon Stetson, and a big red bandanna tied around his neck. Then I saw four or five that I knew must be cameramen, because they had their caps on backwards.

While I held on with both hands the driver skidded the flivver in a half circle and stopped in front of a tent that had a big sign above the entrance: PERSONNEL. The driver jerked his thumb toward it and said something in Spanish that I couldn't understand, but I knew what he meant, so I picked up my bedroll and went in.

A fat little man was sitting behind a big table, peering down at what looked to be a long list of names through thick-lensed, pince-nez glasses. He was all rigged up in a fancy cowboy out-fit, and looked about as much at home in it as a working cow-hand would have looked in a Little Lord Fauntleroy suit. The man didn't look up when I came into the tent, so I dropped my bedroll and said, "Good evening. I came to see about a job riding horse falls."

He still didn't look up, but penciled an X in front of a blank line at the bottom of a long printed form, pushed it toward me, and said, "Sign there, and print your name and address." He said it like a parrot that's been taught to talk but doesn't know what he's saying.

I'd thought the print in Father's Bible was small, but it was three times the size of the printing on that form, and there was enough of it to fill ten pages in a book. I read as far as "WHEREAS, the party of the second part, being of legal age and sound mind. . . ." Then I stopped. In the first place I wasn't of legal age, and the more I saw of the outfit the more I doubted that I'd been in my right mind when I came there. "I'm not going to read all this stuff," I told the little fat man, "and I'm not going to sign it till I know what it says."

There must have been a lot of other fellows who had said the same thing I did, because the little man had his answer all ready, and he said it without looking up—like a boy reciting his lesson at school. What it amounted to was that I would do whatever the bosses of the outfit told me to do, in any way they told me to do it, for anything they wanted to pay me, and that nobody could ever sue the company for any money that hadn't been paid to me when I left, or for anything that happened to me while I was there. I'd get my keep free on any day that I rode, and I'd be charged five dollars for it on any day when I didn't ride.

If I hadn't been dead broke I wouldn't have signed up, but I was hungry enough that my knees were getting a little wobbly. Then too, no matter whether I signed or not, they couldn't make me ride unless I wanted to—and unless I rode they wouldn't have much more luck in collecting a board bill from me than I'd have of collecting damages from them.

After I'd signed, the little man wrote my name down on three or four lists, then gave me a badge with a big "23" on it, and three tickets that said "GOOD FOR ONE MEAL." As he pushed them across the desk toward me he said, "You are assigned to tent fourteen, group three. Your group captain will supply meal tickets as you perform."

I didn't bother about looking for tent fourteen or group captain three, but left my bedroll right where it was and headed for the grub line. And when I got up to the serving counter I didn't bother about my diet. It seemed to me that I'd be risking a lot more in trying to ride horse falls on an empty stomach than on one that was full of beef and beans. There weren't any leafy green vegetables, and I didn't take bread or potatoes or dessert, but I filled my plate high with everything else on the counter.

As soon as I'd finished my supper I went back to the personnel office, picked up my bedroll, and went to hunt for my tent and group captain. I was lucky. I found my captain before I was halfway across the lot. He turned out to be Ted Hawkins, an old Colorado cowhand. He was a bit too old for rough riding, but he knew his business from A to Z—and he knew me, too. As soon as I'd told him that I used to do trick riding at the Littleton roundups when I was a kid he said he'd ridden there himself and had seen me ride. And he proved it by telling me which years it was. Ted was my friend right from that minute, and if it hadn't been for him I don't think I'd have made it. As soon as we'd taken my bedroll to tent fourteen we took a walk around the whole layout, and he told me most of the things I needed to know.

3

Movie Location

I'D been worried ever since I saw those city slickers shooting off orders and strutting around in their fancy cowboy outfits. I was even more worried after I'd signed the form saying I'd do whatever the bosses told me to. Riding in horse falls was bound to be dangerous at best, but if the men who were bossing the show didn't know anything about horses and riding, it could be murder—so the first question I asked Ted Hawkins was, "Who'll be my boss if I do any riding here, and how'll I know I'm going to get paid? That paper I signed said. . . ."

Ted glanced both ways and dropped his voice. "It don't make no never-mind what that contract says," he told me. "They're so far over the barrel for boys that'll tackle rough spills that they're hurtin' bad. There's talk goin' 'round that they're runnin' shy on cash. You'll be your own boss man if you can stick it out and don't get busted up too quick—and I reckon that trick-ridin' you done when you was a kid will save you a lot of grief.

"Make your dicker before every ride, and collect for it before you make another one. They'll squeal like hogs with their tails caught in the barn door, but you'll be the boy that's got ahold of the door handle. The overhead on this layout is five thousand a day, whether they shoot a foot o' film or not. It takes a lot of high-action footage to get that kind of seed back, and they can't cut the chunk unless they hold onto boys that'll take the rough tumbles. Of course, every dude with a red hanky 'round his neck will be yellin' orders at you, but don't pay 'em no heed; I'll be giving the orders at the take-off."

"They sure must have to take a slew of pictures if they're over the barrel for riders," I told him. "I saw at least sixty cowhands and thirty or forty Indians in the grub line."

"Them ain't fall riders; them's yella bellies!" Ted told me, and he spit it out as if he'd bitten into something rotten. "Leastways, the white ones is. Most o' them Injuns has guts enough, but you can't hire Injuns to ride horse falls; Gov'ment agent won't let you. Most of them white ones is extras; half-baked actors the outfit fetched along from Hollywood. Didn't you take note of their fancy chaps, and pearl-handled six-guns, and Spanish boots? All they do is ride along to make scenery. The Injuns was fetched along too. Don't dare use the local ones. They're like as not to forget it ain't a real war, and somebody'd catch an arrow in the butt."

I didn't know much about California, but I did know they had mountains and deserts out there, and that would give them about the same kind of background scenery. If most of the help was from there I couldn't see any sense in the outfit's coming way over into Arizona to take their pictures, so I asked, "Why in the world did they bring the whole works over here? Wouldn't it have been cheaper to take their pictures closer to home?"

Ted spit at a clump of cactus and growled, "Use your head, kid! Arizona's a new state and ain't got too many laws yet. California's an old one, and they've got cruelty-to-animals laws over there. The way they throw these old crowbaits there ain't one in ten don't get a busted neck or a busted leg, poor devils. But one thing I will say for the outfit; they keep a sharpshooter right handy—put 'em out of their misery in a hurry."

"A boy in Phoenix told me they threw them with wires," I said, "but he didn't know just how it worked."

"Come on out to one of the strips, and I'll show you," Ted told me. "It ain't a bad idee for you to know how it works before you take your first spill."

Ted led me out to a fairly level, gravelly place at the far end of the mesa, where there were more different kinds of cactus than I'd ever heard of, and as we went along he told me the names of all the different ones. I've forgotten the names of a good many, but I remember there being giant saguaros that stood twenty or more feet tall. In the twilight they looked like sentinels, some of them with a pair of side branches that looked like arms lifted up toward heaven in prayer. Scattered between the stunted palo verde trees, yucca plants taller than my head, mesquite, and creosote bushes, there were clumps of ocotillo cactus that looked like writhing snakes balanced on their tails. Here and there staghorn chollas—some of them grown to trees ten feet high—stretched out naked branches that looked in the twilight as if their ends were festooned with silvery lichen. When we came closer I could see that the lichen was a mass of hanging twigs, each covered with a million needle-sharp spines. Strewn in clumps and patches across the gravel there were hedgehog cholla, prickly pear, fishhook, and beavertail cactus.

As we rounded a clump of wind-gnarled palo verde trees I saw half a dozen heavy blocks of concrete lined up in a row. Bolted to the top of each block there was what looked to be a giant fishing reel, wound tightly with fine steel wire. "Them's the trippers," Ted told me as he picked up a wire with a stout little hook twisted onto the end of it. "Your horse will be wearing a shoe on his near forefoot with a ring welded to the heel. This here hook gets pinched tight into the ring, so's it can't get shook loose, and the spool's left to spin free while the cowboys chase the Injuns past the cameras. Take note o' the saw teeth on the rims of the spool, and that pair of iron hooks that's hinged atop the spool. Well, when the director spots you

right where he wants you in front of a camera he'll give a high
sign, and the trigger man will drop the hooks. With a forefoot
yanked out from under him, your cayuse will somerset in the
air, and like as not he'll land on his back. How and where you
land will depend on what kind of a horseman you are, and how
many bad spills you've lived through before you come here."

"I've lived through some pretty bad ones," I told him, "but
never where there was any such a mess of cactus as there is
around here."

"That's why I fetched you out here," he told me. "Did you
take note of which shoe the wire gets hitched to?"

"Near fore," I said.

"So?"

"So the pony'll somersault quartering to the left," I told him.

Ted slapped me on the shoulder and said, "Now you're usin'
your noggin, but there's other things you'll need to know. The
cameras will be on that side, so's to make the most out of the
fall, and they'll follow you as you fly, so's to leave out the pony
if he happens to get his neck broke. There ain't no director
that's fool enough to dump you where the cameraman will
have to make his shot through a mess o' mesquite or ocotillo,
or a staghorn cholla. But there is them that's dirty enough to
dump you into a mess of low cactus—specially if they figure
you're making your last ride anyways."

"Will the wire be loose enough that I can rein out around
that kind of spots?" I asked.

"You ain't goin' to rein out around nothin' no place," he told
me. "If you're a cowboy you'll have a six-gun in each hand,
or an old musket in the both of 'em, shooting black-powder
blanks at the Injuns. And don't forget, kid; drop them guns
quick when your pony falls away! Freeze onto one and land
with it in your hands, you'll be a goner. If you're an Injun
you'll need both hands for bow and arrow, but that don't make
no never-minds, 'cause you can't see where you're goin' noways.
You'll be turned half around, shooting arrows with rubber tips
back over the cowboys' heads. That's why the outfit will pay

double for them falls. But what I set out to tell you was this: You got to use your knees and your weight to put your cayuse where you want him. And if you don't keep him where there's clear ground on your left, specially when you're in range of a camera, you'll get messed up somethin' awful. The devil of it is that you never know what kind of a nag you'll get, or how he'll guide with knee pressure. Worst first is the way they pick the fall horses."

"Well," I said, "I haven't got much weight to swing a horse with. At double the pay, it sounds to me as if I'd be smarter to take Indian falls. I wouldn't have any saddle to get hung up in, and. . . ."

"Don't get no foolish notions in your head!" Ted told me. "Goin' into a fall backwards, and not being able to see where you're at or where you're going to land, is dangerous as dynamite. That's why you see danged few Injuns' ponies hit the ground in the movies. Mostly the riders just heave their arms up like they was hit and take a dive along the off side of the pony's neck. Then they slide on down and roll clear as the nag hightails out of camera range. There ain't an Injun on the lot that can't do that real good, and they don't get no extra pay for it."

Twilight had turned to night while we were talking there by the trip reels, but the stars had come out so bright that it hadn't grown much darker. After we'd started back toward the tent village I asked, "Is that strip you showed me the toughest one they've got?"

"Lord, no!" Ted told me. "That's the easiest one, but the one they've had to use the most. Didn't you take note how the ground was all tromped up? Have to keep the cameras up off'n it, or movin' fast enough the tracks won't show in the pictures. Let's mosey 'round the rim over here. I'll show you a set they've spent ten thousand on, and ain't shot a foot o' film on it yet. Can't find nobody 'round here that'll risk taking a fall on it. Don't know what's happened to the young bucks nowadays, less'n all the good ones is off to the war. The outfit might have to bring stunt men out here from Hollywood to take the falls on this new set, and they won't get them boys for no ten or fifteen dollars a ride."

We'd walked a hundred yards or so along the edge of the mesa when Ted stopped and said, "There she is! Ain't that a beauty! But I've took spills down a lot worse places than that when I was a cowhand, workin' for thirty a month."

I'd taken a couple myself on hillsides nearly as steep, and when I was only a youngster. But I hadn't done it on·purpose, or when a horse had a foreleg jerked out from under him so he'd somersault on top of me, or where there were boulders half the size of a chicken house. Even in the starlight I could see that the place Ted was showing me was steeper than a church roof. The ground was littered with loose stones, and all the way to the bottom the side of the mesa was studded with cactus, brush, mesquite, and boulders, with three or four saguaros that looked as solid as granite pillars. "I guess I'm yellow," I told Ted. "That looks to me like the best place on earth for a man to commit suicide."

"That's what it's meant to look like," he said, "but I'd as leave take a tumble on it as on that one we just left. Them boulders is all made out of canvas and paint; was you to fall onto one of 'em, it would crumble like a cream puff. Every jagged rock, and them bigger'n your fist, has been picked off the ground, and the worst of the stickers skun off'n the cactus. You see them staghorn trees and yuccas down yonder? Ain't a one of 'em but's been dug up and set back in loose. Bump one and it would topple over like a tenpin. Here your pony don't get throwed in a tight somerset; he'll be quick-tripped by a cross-wire and turned loose to make a longer fall."

Even at that the place looked pretty dangerous, particularly with the kind of horses I'd seen in the remuda. If ridden over the edge at the dead run, a horse with bad knees would be almost sure to fall and somersault when he landed. Or, if there were any others behind, one of them could easily stumble and come down on top of a man. After I'd thought about it for a couple of minutes I asked, "Could a man pick his horse for taking a shot at this layout?"

"I'd make you that promise," Ted answered.

"Could I be sure of being last to go over the edge?"

"I'd be bossing the job, and I ain't plumb stupid, kid! I'd be watchin' out for you. And you wouldn't have to take off on the dead run neither."

I waited another minute and asked, "What'll they pay for taking a spill down this one?"

Ted squinted an eye and looked up at the stars for a couple of seconds. "They'd go twenty-five without too much squawkin'," he told me. "Might go as high as thirty, was you to make a real showy fall."

"Think they'd go to fifty?" I asked.

Ted thought for a minute and then shook his head. "Uh-uh," he told me. "Might stretch it another five if they figured they could get a few more good falls out of you, but they wouldn't go the half-century. They'd get stunt men out from the Coast 'fore they'd crack through with fifty. Word spreads too easy; the other boys might hang out for big money on the flat strips."

"What are they getting now?" I asked.

"Ten. Mebbe fifteen where the ground's roughest. Anywheres up to twenty for an Injun fall; they don't run them on bad ground."

"Is morning soon enough to make up my mind?"

"Soon enough any time . . . if you don't mind payin' board," he said. "But was I you, I'd think a lot about tacklin' this layout. It ain't no worse than the others if a man keeps his head about him. And if he could hang on for half a dozen falls he'd make a pretty good stake."

Ted and I didn't talk about horse falls any more that evening. On the way back to our tent we talked mostly about Colorado, and the Littleton roundup, and Hi Beckman, and a few other cowhands we both had known. After we got back to the tent Ted was too busy to talk to me.

While we'd been gone, a scout whom the outfit had sent up to Wyoming to find fall riders had come in with fourteen recruits. He must have scoured the whole state to find them. There was no doubt about their being working cowhands, and I never saw a tougher-looking fourteen all in one bunch. They were all in their late twenties or early thirties, and every one of them was as stout and wild as a longhorn bull. And somewhere along the line they'd got hold of a gallon of corn squeezings. When we came into the big tent they were shooting craps in the middle of the dirt floor, whooping and yelling like a band of drunken Indians. Ted was still trying to break up the game and get them into bed when I went to sleep.

The Wyoming boys were still half-drunk the next morning, and four or five of them were uglier than grizzly bears. They seemed to be looking for trouble with anybody who didn't belong to their own gang, and a couple of fist fights were in full swing before I could get my boots and britches on. There wasn't a man in that tent who couldn't have knocked me for a loop with a single punch, so I ducked out as quick as I could and headed for the grub line. I'd been in the chuck tent fifteen or twenty minutes when the rest of Group Three came in, and among them there were half a dozen guards with night sticks in their hands. I was just getting up to leave when they came in, but Ted saw me and motioned for me to sit down again.

Most of the Wyoming boys took nothing but coffee as they passed the serving counter, then sat down at a table near the end of the line, and fired insults at the rest of our group as the boys went past to a table farther on. Ted waited until the last man was seated, then brought a cup of coffee over and sat down beside me. "You lay off this mornin', kid," he told me.

"With these fourteen, along with the twelve that was a'ready here when you come, there'll be all the riders that's needed and some to spare. The way these boys are het up there's bound to be some mighty rough goin's-on out there, and there ain't no sense of you getting mixed up in it. Them Wyoming bucks is out to make the rest of you look yella, and the way them fights went this morning they ain't goin' to have an easy time of it."

"Are you going to put them on the new set?" I asked.

"Wouldn't be no sense in that," he told me, "Not till a few busted arms and legs gets 'em cooled out a mite. Haired up the way they are now they'd hit that rim on the dead run, and 'fore noontime I'd have 'em all stove up into kindlin' wood. They're a'ready fightin' amongst themselves for the first shots at riding Injun falls, and I ain't goin' to tell 'em no different. Might as well leave the outfit get some high-action footage 'fore all that corn liquor wears off.

"Now I'll tell you what you do, kid; you shag on out to that set where we was last night. There'll be four or five crews settin' up cameras along the strip, so's't the riders won't know where to expect a spill. Pick the third camera from this end and hunker down in a clump of brush, where you'll be out of shutter sight but can see everything that's goin' on along the strip. Keep your eye peeled, and you ought to pick up some stuff that'll help you about getting hurt too bad when your turn comes. A man learns by mistakes, but in this game that's too late if the mistakes are his own."

Ted didn't give me a chance to thank him, but stood up and shouted, "Come on there, Group Three! Get that grub into you! We're due at make-up in ten minutes!"

4

Horse Falls

I FOUND a cracking good place to watch from, a tangled
bunch of creosote bush right at the edge of the strip, but I had
to wait more than an hour before I saw Ted riding out at the
head of a little band. There were eighteen or twenty riders in
it, about half Indians and half cowboys. All the Indians were
stripped down to breechclouts and moccasins, with a feather
or two stuck in their long hair. And all the cowboys were
dressed up Hollywood style, but it was easy enough to pick
out the ones that were going to take the falls; two Indians and
three cowboys. They were mounted on skinny old crowbaits,
while all the others were on real good-looking ponies.

My hiding place was more than two hundred yards from the
tripping reels, so I couldn't hear anything that was being said,
and I couldn't see too clearly. But I could see well enough to
be pretty sure that Ted was planning to take some of the fight
out of the ugliest among the Wyoming riders. The three biggest ones were rigged out as cowboys, and the two shortest
were stripped down and painted like Indians.

As others came out from the village afoot and ranged along
behind the cameras, Ted got his riders together in front of the

trip reels. From the way they were circled around, with the fall riders in the middle, I knew he must be telling each one just what he was supposed to do. But all the way through it the Wyoming boys kept yipping and howling like coyotes.

Ted wasn't the only one who was telling people what to do, and there were plenty of them to be told: cameramen, stretchermen, a doctor and a veterinary, a couple of sharp-shooters, and about forty 'leven helpers and assistants. Running around among them were the directors and bosses in their drug-store cowboy outfits—every one of them carrying a mega-phone and yelling orders. And nobody was paying any more attention than the Wyoming boys seemed to be paying to Ted.

It must have been fifteen or twenty minutes before Ted lined his riders up in front of the reels, and I saw men bring the wires out and fasten them to the fall-ponies' shoe rings. For as much as a full minute there wasn't a sound. Then somebody with a megaphone shouted, "One! Two! Three! *ROLL!*"

In the scramble away from the start it was pretty hard to see anything clearly. But as the Indians came pounding toward me with the cowboys a few lengths behind them, I did see one thing for sure. Every pony ridden by a real Indian or a Holly-wood cowboy was trained right down to a fine edge, and those ponies knew their business and that course as well as any man on the lot. With its jerk-rope hanging loose over its neck, and with its rider half turned to shoot back, every Indian's pony threaded a clean course through that gantlet of ocotillo, stag-horn, brush, and cactus. The two who were carrying riders that were going to unload knew exactly where and when. I think they gave their riders the cue, because both of them swerved aside the instant before the Indian threw his arms above his head, giving him plenty of room and clear ground when he slithered down the neck and rolled clear.

The Hollywood cowboys' horses knew their business just as well, and I could see that they were running in formation, like a drill team. But the fall horses were scared out of their wits by all the screeching and shooting. They came tearing straight

on through whatever happened to be in their way, like stampeding cattle in a night thunder-and-lightning storm. One of them that was carrying a make-believe Indian must have been blind or had his eyes shut. He veered wide, and ran so close under the branches of a staghorn tree that a festoon with a million prickers on it caught his half-turned rider in the back of the neck. That boy didn't have to wait for his pony to be tripped; he went flying as if he'd been caught up in a cyclone. I didn't see him land, but he was still on the ground, whirling around like a cat in a fit, when the show was over.

The whole run lasted barely ten seconds, and it was an hour before Ted brought the next bunch of fall riders out, but it took me the whole hour to sort out and remember all that I'd seen in those few seconds. It must be that a fellow sees a lot more than he can handle when things are happening so fast, and the only way he can remember all of them is if he has plenty of time to sort them out right after they've happened. At first I was too excited—and scared—to think. I wanted to jump up and run to help the boys who were hurt, but everybody else was running, so I figured I'd better stay where I was until the excitement was over.

After they'd carried the boys back to the village, and after I'd had time to reason out that they wouldn't have been so badly hurt if they hadn't been trying to show off, I found that I could remember almost everything that had happened during the run, and that in my mind I could see it all over again, almost as if it had been in slow motion.

Although I didn't know it at the time, I doubtlessly kept my eyes fixed on the fall riders all the way through the run, for it was they and not the real Indians and extras I could see again as I lay there in the brush with my eyes shut. The first one to go down had been the one whose pony ran him into the staghorn cholla. The second was the other boy who was playing Indian, because the Indians passed the cameras ahead of the cowboys.

I think that boy was trying so hard to hit one of the Hollywood cowboys with an arrow that he'd forgotten his pony was going to be tripped. He was riding bareback, had his legs clamped tight, and was turned more than halfway around when the pony somersaulted. He probably clamped tighter when he felt the pony going, for he didn't fly free but came down as though he'd been stuck in a saddle. He tried to straighten around on the way down, then stuck out his arms to push the ground away as he saw it coming toward him. Of course he broke them both, and a leg that was caught under the dead pony.

The first cowboy rider would have been all right if either he or his pony had been watching where they were going. He fell free and loose, and landed rolling on one shoulder, but he came down in a patch of prickly pears that was knee-high and as big as a table top. The next boy froze to his musket, landed with it under him, and broke a wrist, a collarbone, and five ribs.

Why the last fall rider wasn't killed I'll never know. He was the biggest man in the Wyoming bunch, the ugliest when he was drunk, and he tried to show off the most. He caught my eye from the moment he left the starting line, and Ted told me afterwards that he did every single thing he'd told him not to. He was supposed to have ridden at the tail end, and to have been the first cowboy tripped down, but he was never at the end. He left the line shrieking like a wildcat in a trap, and raking his pony from shoulder to flank with the spurs. I have an idea he was yellow and thought he'd throw the old pony into a crowhopping buck, so he'd never get as far as the cameras, but it didn't work that way.

That pony didn't buck a jump, and by the way he ran he must have been at least half Thoroughbred. Before he got opposite me he was leading the cowboy band, and was bearing straight down on an Indian that had just unloaded. If it hadn't been for that they wouldn't have risked tripping him with the others all behind, but they didn't have any choice. When the tripper man dropped the hook he happened to catch that big cowhand spurring back on the flanks, and with his feet driven

home tight into the stirrups. With his legs kicked back when
the pony somersaulted, he went out of the saddle like a turtle
flung by the tail. Both feet stuck fast in the stirrups, and he
came down flat on his belly, as if he'd been dropped from a
cloud.

Some mighty fast thinking by both men and horses was all
that saved that big cowhand from being pounded to a pulp.
The pony he was riding was badly hurt but not killed in the
fall. It landed with its rump between the rider's spread-eagled
legs—its heels kicking like the beaters in a thrashing machine.
When the pony somersaulted, there was barely two lengths
between him and the racing cowboy ponies. But in the fraction
of a second before they reached him, a sharpshooter had
broken his back with a 30-30 slug. Like a herd of frightened
deer going over a fence the trained ponies sailed over and left
the rider untouched. I never heard how many bones the rider
had broken in that fall, but he was still unconscious at noon,
and they'd taken him in to Wickenburg before suppertime.

I've seen some pretty good riflemen, but never one who
made as quick and dead-sure a shot in an emergency as that
sharpshooter's. As I lay waiting for the next run to be started,
it made me feel a lot safer just to have a man like that on the
lot, for one of the biggest dangers in horse falls is that the rider
may become caught in some part of the gear and be kicked to
death by his injured horse.

When Ted came riding out with the next bunch, I noticed
right away that all the Indians were real ones, but there were
a few more Hollywood cowboys, and four fall men were
mounted on old crowbaits. I couldn't be sure, but it looked to
me as if only two of them were Wyoming boys, and they were
evidently pretty well sobered up, because they weren't doing
any yipping and yelling. From the motions Ted was going
through I knew he was telling them what they should do, and
what they shouldn't do, in trying to protect themselves in both
the ride and the fall.

After Ted had talked to the fall boys for ten or fifteen minutes he took the musket from one of them, then traded mounts with him. He was barely up on the fall pony when everyone along the course began yelling, shouting, shooting off guns, and making all the noise they could. Frightened by all the noise, the pony bolted straight away, but he hadn't taken three strides before he swerved to the right and skirted the edge of an open, gravelly patch of ground. At the same time, Ted threw the musket to his shoulder, hugged his chin against the stock as though he were taking careful aim, and fired. The direction he was holding the musket kept his head turned quartering from the way the pony was running. But the pony came pounding up the course toward me, weaving in and out to keep clear ground at his left during nearly every step of the way. Ted kept on shooting, with his chin hugged tight against the stock and his head turned quartering away.

At first I thought Ted must be riding a well-trained pony, but as he came closer I could see that he was swerving it this way and that with his weight and the pressure of his knees. And he wasn't sighting down the barrel of the musket. Only his head was turned; his eye was watching the ground ten feet in front of his pony's hoofs. Just as he passed the bushes where I was hiding, he threw his arms high, let the musket fall behind him, and dived down the far side of the pony's neck. He didn't unload, but straightened up after a few strides, turned the pony, and rode back to pick up the musket. He didn't look toward my bush, but as he stepped down he asked, "Did you take note o' that?"

"Nice going!" I said, without moving.

He still didn't look my way, but as he swung back into the saddle he told me, "Stay where you're at, kid, and keep your eye peeled."

When Ted lined up his fall riders for that run I noticed that he left the two middle trip lines open. He put the two Wyoming boys way over to the right, and the other two far out to the left. Then he put the last riders among the Hollywood bunch about two or three lengths in front of them. With that much open space between themselves and the riders ahead, the fall boys had plenty of chance to watch where they were riding and to do it the way Ted had showed them. And spread out the way they were, every one of them could have made his fall with no horse behind him or within twenty feet.

They didn't do it. The instant the director yelled, "ROLL!" all four of them swerved their ponies toward the center of the strip, and spurred as if they were trying to outrun a cyclone. Not one of them was aiming his musket at the Indians, but had it swung up as if it were an ax handle. The ponies of the two riders who had started from the inside positions came together quartering, shoulder to shoulder, and went down with their riders under them in a tangle of arms, legs, kicking heels, and twanging wire. The trip man dropped his hook just as the second Wyoming boy was swinging his musket at the head of a New Mexico rider. Off balance, he had no chance to save himself, spun over with his horse, and came down with it sprawled on top of him.

The New Mexico boy tried to make a decent ride of it as soon as he was left alone. By the time he came into camera range he had his musket aimed at the Indians, was handling his pony in good shape, and made his fall within five feet of my bush. His horse was tripped just as it reached out with the lead forefoot, so it went over in a lightning-fast somersault— straight forward. The boy barely had time to heave his musket back over his head, and was shot from the saddle almost as if he'd been an arrow leaving a bow. But the horse went over so fast that the rider was only three or four feet from the ground when he flew. And he still had his arms and head thrown back, from getting rid of the musket.

Without trying to twist or turn, the rider streaked through the air for eight or ten feet, hit the ground sliding, and skidded another five or six. If he'd lit on sod, or any sort of smooth ground, he wouldn't have been hurt any more than a boy taking a belly-buster slide on a sled. But he didn't land on sod; he came down right in the middle of a gravel patch, and before he'd skidded to a stop the pebbles had ripped his clothes to ribbons and scraped most of the hair off his chest.

At first it seemed to me that the best thing I could do was to stay where I was till noon, then eat as much as my belly would hold—on my last meal ticket—and head back to town before I got killed in one of those crazy rides. Then, after the mess had been cleaned up and I was waiting for Ted to bring out the last bunch of riders for the forenoon, I began thinking about the New Mexico rider's fall—and I got an idea. The first thought that had gone through my head when I'd seen him sailing along, just a couple of feet above the ground, was that he looked like a boy who had made his run and was flopping down onto his sled. And sliding made me think of a hill, and that made me think about the new set Ted had shown me on the side of the mesa.

It's funny how one thing will lead to another when a fellow is all alone, and in no hurry, and thinking sort of loose-jointedly. The next thing I found myself thinking about was that I'd seen skiers in New England jump nearly the whole length of hills that were fully as steep and a lot longer than the one on the edge of the mesa. Of course, they'd had snow to land on, but some of those jumpers had been as much as sixty feet above the hillside on their way down, and it wasn't the softness of the snow that had kept them from being hurt when they landed. It had been because the hillside was falling away nearly as fast as they were, and because they kept right on sliding downward after they'd landed.

It seemed to me that it might work about the same way if a fellow took a horse fall down a steep hill like that. It wouldn't do any good to somersault in the air and try to land on your feet, because you wouldn't slide but would topple over like a felled tree. That wouldn't happen if you went belly-bump, the way the New Mexico rider had, but the gravel on the new set was coarser and sharper than on the patch of ground in front of my bush.

I'd have given up any idea of trying a belly-bump fall on the new set if I hadn't happened to remember the time one of our neighbor's boys nearly got killed when we were hauling gravel for a new road. He was a smart-alec kid about ten years old, and had been amusing himself by throwing pebbles at the horses while we were loading wagons in an old pit that had been dug deep into a hillside. We were about ready to wring his neck before his father told him to go home, but he didn't go. Instead, he climbed the hill and began tossing pebbles down at us from the edge of the pit.

Suddenly I heard a screech and looked up to see the boy tumbling down the face of the gravel bank. He skidded and slid about half the distance, then started a slide that buried him four feet deep at the bottom, and we got him dug out just before he smothered to death. That gravel was really rough, and we expected to find the kid torn to shreds, but there wasn't a scratch on him, so we figured the stones had rolled under him like ball bearings.

I knew the stones on the side of the mesa wouldn't roll that easily, because the grade wasn't steep enough and the ground underneath was too rough and hard, but if they'd roll at all I thought I had an idea that would make me a lot of money. I didn't wait to see the falls of the last forenoon run, but crawled out of my bush and slipped away to the edge of the mesa, keeping out of sight as much as I could. When I was sure I was alone I walked along the rim till I found a big open patch of gravel down over the edge, with no boulders or cactus on it. Then I took a run, jumped off over the edge, and landed like a baseball player stealing second base. I landed pretty hard on my hip, but the stones rolled under me, and I'd only torn my jeans a little when I skidded to a stop.

Next I tried diving off headfirst, as if I'd had a sled to come down on, but I kept my head well back and my arms up. That didn't work too well, because I stuck my chest out too far and didn't have it full enough of air. When I lit on it I knocked the wind out of myself, but I didn't skid very far, and I didn't get scraped too badly on the gravel.

Before I could try another fall I had to sit there a few minutes to get my breath back, and it gave me a chance to do a little more thinking. I hadn't seen Lonnie land when he'd dived off the freight train, but he'd told me that if you landed rolling you wouldn't get hurt, so I decided I'd try it in making a fall. That time I took a fast run to the edge, dived high, and twisted myself crossways of the hill so I'd land rolling. I did. And I'd have rolled clear to the bottom of the hill if I hadn't wound up in a tangle of greasewood bushes. But it hadn't knocked the wind out of me when I landed, and I'd only got a few scratches from the gravel as I rolled.

On the next try I didn't turn my body so far while I was in the air, but twisted a shoulder down, so I'd land on the back of it and roll diagonally. It worked all right, and after I'd tried it a few more times I found that I could steer myself pretty well in the air, so as to land and roll about where and how I wanted to. Then I brushed myself off a little and went in for lunch.

I hadn't realized that I'd spent much time in practicing, but the last run of the forenoon had been finished for an hour before I got back to the lot. A stretcherman told me it was the wildest ride he'd ever seen. All four of the fall riders were in the hospital tent with broken arms or legs, and the rest of Group Three was in the chuck tent. I cleaned myself up as well as I could before I went over, but when I'd passed the serving counter Ted motioned for me to come and sit with him. "Where the devil you been, and what you been up to?" he asked me as I sat down opposite him.

"Practicing on the edge of the mesa," I told him. "Who do I make a deal with for taking falls on the new set?"

Ted told me I'd have to make my deal with the production manager, and that he'd take me to him as soon as I'd finished my lunch, but it was more than half an hour before we left the table. First he made me tell him about my practicing; just how I'd done it and what I'd learned from it. Then he told me about the trouble he'd been having with our group that forenoon.

He said it was divided into two war parties—the Wyoming boys against everybody else—and that a man might as well waste his time in trying to talk sense to a pack of fighting coyotes. The boys didn't dare get into any more fist fights, because there were too many armed guards around and they'd get kicked off the lot, so they'd turned the fall riding into a crazy game of stump-the-leader. That was why he wanted to get started on the new set right away. He said that the way things were going, half the boys would bust themselves up before suppertime anyway, and they might as well do it on a set where the company could shoot some premium film.

The production man knew as well as we did that the other boys were steamed up enough to tackle the new set, and that they wouldn't hold out for big pay to make the falls. Even with Ted's telling him that I'd be worth more, the best deal I could make with the man was for twenty-five dollars a fall. Even at that it didn't work out too badly. Ted was right in his guess that half the boys would bust themselves up before suppertime. They did, and the next day I was able to raise my price to thirty-five.

While we were over at the make-up tent getting ready for my first ride Ted got an idea that saved me a lot of grief, and probably made me a lot of money. I was so thin that the ward-rober couldn't find anything to fit me. He was trying to make an old jacket smaller when Ted winked at me and hollered, "Wait a minute there! You can't go puttin' no pins in a fall-rider's duds, and I ain't going to have no rider out there lookin' like a dressed-up skeleton! Pad this kid up so's't he can fill man-sized cloze!" He slapped me on the back of the shoulders hard enough to rattle my teeth, and again on the chest. "Get it up high on him here, and thick," he told the man, "so's't he'll look like a man 'stead of a scarecrow! And pad out the points of them skinny shoulders!"

When we went out of there I looked like a fat bull with a starved calf's head on him, but those pads saved me an awful lot of beating when I landed from a bad fall. Even at that, I got some pretty rough bumps, because a horse was seldom tripped where I could aim myself at a decent spot to land on. And even though the biggest staghorn cholla and yucca had been dug up and reset, they knocked the wind out of me when I hit them on the fly.

I made two falls that first afternoon, four on each of the next two days, and three on the fourth day. At the end of that last day I didn't have a broken bone anywhere, but my face and hands looked like raw hamburger, every joint in me creaked as if it were rusty, and there was hardly a spot on my legs, arms, or body that wasn't black-and-blue. The next morning I was so stiff and sore I couldn't bend over to pull on my britches.

All the way through, Ted had looked out for me as carefully as if I'd been his own son. As long as the Wyoming boys lasted he never let one of them ride near me, but always put them on the other side of the strip. He saw to it that there was never a rider behind me, and always let me know about where I could expect my fall, so that I'd be as ready for it as possible. Then, at the end of every run, I collected my pay and gave it to him to keep for me. There was $435 by the end of that fourth day—more than I could have made as a cowhand in a whole year.

I was sure that with a day or two of rest I'd be able to ride some more falls, but Ted said there was no sense in crowding my luck, and that, stiffened up as I was, I'd probably break my neck the next time out. He sat on my cot and visited so long that he missed his breakfast, just talking about old friends we'd known in Colorado, and about going back as soon as spring came. Then he held the first run of the morning over for half an hour so he could see me off when I took the flivver back to Wickenburg. When we shook hands he said, "Keep your nose clean, kid, and don't flash that roll o' long green; there's them around that would knock a man off for that much dough. Come Fourth o' July, I'll see you at the Littleton roundup."

"I'll be there," I told him. And then the flivver jounced away.

It was because of my telling Ted I'd be at the Littleton roundup that I was lying flat in the ditch in the St. Joseph freight yards the night before the Fourth.

5

Friendly Phoenix

THE same Mexican who had driven me out from Wickenburg drove me back, and though I think he was trying to be a little more careful, I was off the seat about as much as I was on it, and by the time we reached town I felt as though I'd been through a dozen more horse falls. My legs were so wobbly when I got out at the depot that I walked as if I were drunk, and my bedroll seemed to weigh a ton. The only thing I could think of that I'd like to do was to crawl into a soft bed and stay there for a month. But there was no sense in staying in Wickenburg, and Lonnie had said he'd wait a week for me in Phoenix, so I went into the depot to buy a ticket.

It was only a little after nine o'clock when I went in, and I found that the next train didn't leave until four in the afternoon, and the ticket office didn't open till two. The seats in that depot were harder than the rocks on the horse-fall sets, so after ten or fifteen minutes I tried walking around a little, to see if I could loosen up the kinks in my back and legs. The first thing I saw when I went outside was a ramshackle old hotel across the street, with a sign that read, "CLEAN ROOMS $1." I was lucky enough to get one on the ground floor, so

I didn't have to climb any stairs. It wasn't too dirty, and the bed wasn't bad, but I couldn't get any rest on it. In the first place, there wasn't a spot on me that didn't hurt when I lay on it, and in the second place, the keeper for the bolt on the door was missing.

When I'd come in there had been four or five rough-looking men loafing around the lobby of the hotel, and when I'd signed up for my room the clerk had asked for my dollar in advance. I hadn't expected that when I'd gone in, a five-dollar bill was the smallest I'd had, and it was the outside bill on the roll in my pocket—with an elastic band around it. The first thing I thought of was what Ted had told me about not flashing my roll, so I fiddled around with my fingers till I could slip the band and peel off the five.

As I lay there trying to find a comfortable spot, I couldn't help thinking about the way I must have looked while I was fishing around in my pocket for that five. With my fingers as swollen and clumsy as they were, it had taken me a couple of minutes, and a man wouldn't have needed much brains to know that I was peeling a bill off a roll that was bigger than I dared to show. With no way of locking my door, and with me too stiffened up to fight back, it would be a cinch for those fellows in the lobby—or any one of them—to knock me for a loop and clean me out.

I didn't have any use for $434, and if I'd had any sense I'd have left most of it with Ted, so he could keep it for me until I saw him at the Littleton roundup. But I didn't think of that. I wasn't really able to do much thinking during those last couple of days of fall riding, and I didn't try to keep any close track of what I was earning. Right at the beginning I'd given Ted my mother's address, and had told him to send her the money if anything happened to me. Then, when nothing did, I sort of had it in the back of my head that as soon as I got to town I'd buy a money order at the post office and mail it to her in a letter. But as I lay there on the bed I realized that I couldn't do that either.

I'd already written her a big fairy tale about a job I didn't have, and about having to use my next few pay checks to pay for my outfit. If I should write within a couple of weeks' time and send her four hundred dollars, even she would have to think I'd robbed a bank or something of the kind. I couldn't write and tell her about the horse falls, because that would scare her to death. And I couldn't tell her I'd won it in a poker game, because that would make her feel worse than if I told her about the riding in the horse falls. In fact, I couldn't write to her at all until my hands healed up enough that my writing wouldn't look like hen tracks.

I don't know what I'd have done with my money if I hadn't had to go to the outhouse, for I hadn't noticed till then how ripped-up and dirty my britches were. It was partly to buy some new ones, but mostly to get away from the fellows in the hotel lobby, that I went hunting for a drygoods store. And on the way I got an idea. When I went in I told the man I wanted the longest-legged, smallest-waisted pair of Levi's he had. I was only twenty-six inches in the waist, but to get long enough legs, I had to take a pair of 32-36's. Even though I'd worn a company outfit when I was taking the falls, my shirt was nearly as messed-up as my britches from practicing, and the man couldn't understand why I wouldn't buy a new one, but I didn't think it would be good business to look too prosperous, so I just asked him if he had a place where I could change britches. When I came out with those new Levi's on I looked more like a scarecrow than when I went in. I'd had to take half a dozen tucks under my belt, and I'd had to make four folds in the bottoms of the legs before my feet would show.

From the drygoods store I went to a bank and bought eight fifty-dollar bills—the oldest and softest ones the teller could find. Then I asked him if they had a washroom I could use. They did, but I used it for only about two minutes—just long enough to unfold one leg of my Levi's, lay $420 against the bottom edge, and fold it up again. I was pretty sure I wouldn't need more than fourteen dollars for the next few days, and I was even surer that if anybody robbed me, he wouldn't steal my britches or think to look inside the folds of the cuffs. With the bills being old and soft they wouldn't rustle, and no one could feel them in there.

That seven hours I had to wait in Wickenburg seemed like a week. Even when I didn't have to worry about being robbed I couldn't rest comfortably on my bed, and it wasn't much more comfortable to hobble around the streets. I went to all three restaurants to see if any of them had stewed chicken or poached fish, but they didn't so I bought a can of salmon and a quart of milk in a grocery store and took them back to my room. Then I went to the depot and bought my ticket, just to kill time. While the agent was stamping the back of it I asked, "Is the bowlegged freight conductor who runs between here and Phoenix due in this afternoon?"

"Yep! Yep!" he told me. "That'll be Jim Magee, and he ought to pull in 'long about three o'clock. How come you to ask?"

"He did me a good turn once," I said, "and I just thought I'd like to say hello if I could find him again."

"You ain't alone," the agent told me as he took my two dollars and picked the change out of the till. "Jim, he's got a soft spot for down-an'-out cowhands—specially them that's kids and a long ways from home. He didn't get them bowlegs of his railroading. Didn't go to braking freight till . . . '98, if I recollect right . . . not till he was pretty well stove up. Time he was your age he was the bronc peelin'est cowhand in these parts. What did he, lend you a five?"

"No," I said, "just did me a good turn when I needed it."

If the agent hadn't asked me about the five I'd have hung around the depot till the freight came in, then thanked Jim Magee again for bringing me out from Phoenix. But I got the idea that the old fellow must have lent many a five to boys who hadn't been as lucky as I, and who had never been able to come back and repay him. I walked up and down the platform three or four times, just thinking about it, and the more I thought, the more I wanted to pay back the debt for one of those boys. But you couldn't walk up to a man like Jim Magee and hand him a five-dollar bill, along with some goody-goody talk about wanting to pay somebody else's debt. There was only one thing I could think of to do, so I went up to the main street, bought a box of ten-cent cigars, and was leaning against the end of the depot when Jim's freight pulled in on the siding.

I stayed where I was until the engine had been uncoupled, then started across the tracks. The old man recognized me before I was halfway to him and called out, "Hi there, bub! See you done some ridin' and come out all in one piece. Do any good?"

"Yep," I said, "I was lucky, so I won't be needing that straw car; I'm going to ride the cushions. Just came over to thank you for giving me a lift, and I brought along a few cigars I don't have any use for. That one of yours looks kind of worn down."

It looked as though the stump old Jim had clenched in his teeth was the same one he'd had when he brought me out from Phoenix. He took it out, tossed it away, and said, "Now that was right kindly of you, but you needn't to have fetched along no cigars. Most generally the boys don't bother to come back less'n they need another lift, and you a'ready thanked me once."

The cigar box wasn't wrapped, and I guess Jim had thought there'd be only two or three in it. When he took it he looked up quickly and said, "Lord A'mighty! A whole boxful! You didn't go buy 'em, did you?"

I thought it would be better to tell him a white lie, so I just said, "Side bet, and I don't smoke."

"Lord! Lord!" he said as he looked the box over. "Ten-centers! Who'd you bet with—one of them Hollywood dudes? You must'a done all right! Where you headin' for, Californy to see the sights? Most of the boys does when they make a stake."

"No," I told him, "I'm going back to Phoenix. I've got a buddy waiting for me there at the stockyards. He's going to find us jobs with one of the drovers or cattlemen that brings stock in."

Jim stood for a minute or two, looking down at the track and shaking his head slowly. "Doubt me he'll do it," he said at last. "Doubt me you'd find a job anywhere in a railroad town. Too many soldier boys coming back from the war that can't find nothin' to do. Swarming over the freights like a mess of ants. Most of the crews are kickin' 'em off."

"I know it," I told him. "My buddy and I got kicked off a dozen times between Tucson and Phoenix."

"Yep. Yep," he said. "A man's takin' a risk to haul 'em—likely to get laid off if a spotter catches him."

He looked up and grinned. "Was I bummin' the railroads, I'd never bother with no freights. Blind baggage; that's the safe place for a man to travel—and the fast one. Them mail trains will take a man further in one night than freights will in a week."

I didn't even know there were mail trains, and I had no idea as to what blind baggage might be. When I told Jim I didn't, he looked up at me sort of questioningly. "Take it you ain't been bummin' long," he said.

"No," I told him, "only to get from Tucson up here."

He turned the cigar box over in his hands and looked down at it for a couple of minutes, then he said slowly, "Well, I ain't recommendin' it to you, but if you was to get stuck bad—and broke—it might be a good thing to know." Then he explained to me that the fast mail trains picked up and dropped off mail sacks on the fly, and made stops only at large cities or division points. He said the first car behind the engine was called the blind baggage because the front door was locked tight and the train crew didn't have a key for it, so they couldn't get through to see if a bum was riding in the doorway.

"About all a man's got to do is to flip one of them blind baggages after the train gets to rolling right good," he told me, "and he's all set to the next division point anyways—maybe a couple of hundred miles down the line. Don't make no difference if the engine crew spots you flippin' on. They ain't going to stop a train to kick you off, and they ain't riskin' a layoff if they get caught hauling you."

I'd thanked him for telling me about the blind baggage, and was putting out my hand to shake with him and say good-bye, when he looked up and said, "Know what I'd do if I was a young fella in these times, and had made me a little stake, and was hunting for a cowhand job? I'd buy me one of them second-hand flivvers—a man could pick up a pretty good one for about a hundred dollars—and I'd take off into the back country. Any man with a grain of sense will hire a hand that's got spunk enough to come hunting a job quicker'n he'll take one of them that's hangin' 'round the railroad towns and the stockyards. Now you understand, bub, I ain't tellin' you what to do; I'm just telling you what I'd do was I a young fella in times the like of this."

After I'd thanked him again he stuck out his hand and said, "If you're taking the four o'clock you'd best to pick up your bedroll pretty soon. She's due in about six minutes. And if you get this way again, look me up. I reckon I'll be around quite a spell yet."

It was long after dark when I reached Phoenix, so I didn't try to find Lonnie, but took a hotel room, about a block up from the depot. Then I found a little restaurant where the owner did the cooking and his wife waited on the counter. At first they thought I'd been beaten up in a fight, but when I told them about riding in the horse falls and about my diet, they were real friendly. They didn't have much I could eat, but the man opened a can of spinach, heated it, and put on three poached eggs. He said he'd get in some cabbage and celery the next day, and would stew me a chicken. Then his wife said that if I'd bring her the flour and Mother's recipe, she'd bake me some gluten bread. They were Swedish people, and I think they believed I was Swedish too, because my hair was blond and I had a New England accent.

The room I got was a good one, in a nice clean little hotel, and only a dollar a day. It was at the back of the ground floor, had a good bolt on the door, two large windows, and the best bed I'd slept in since I left home. Maybe it was just too good, and I was too tired. I went to sleep within two minutes after I crawled in, and I must have slept in the shape of a question mark. It was well after daylight when I woke up, and though I was warm enough, my back and hips were as stiff as if I'd been rolled into a ball and frozen. I wiggled around till I could get my legs over the side of the bed and sit up, but I could barely lean over far enough to get my legs into my britches, or straighten up enough to pull them on. I had to fish for my boots with my feet, then lie down to haul them on. Anybody who saw me going over to breakfast must have thought I was the Hunchback of Notre Dame.

Those Swedish people at the little restaurant were as good to me as if I'd been their own folks. Mr. Larsen heated towels in the oven and put them on my back while I was eating. And after I'd finished, Mrs. Larsen phoned their doctor and sent me up to his office. She must have phoned him again while I was on my way. When I got there he knew all about my having ridden in the horse falls, and about the diabetes and my diet. Before he checked me over at all he made me tell him everything Dr. Gaghan and the specialists had said, and show him the diet list in my little book. Then he really did check me over. He stripped me as naked as a picked chicken, laid me out on a doctor's table, took my pulse, temperature, and blood pressure, and poked his hands into my belly as if he were kneading bread dough.

"Miraculous! Miraculous!" he said three or four times as he poked at me. "No rupture of the spleen. That liver seems nomal. Kidneys not badly enlarged. Any tenderness there? How about there?"

Every part of me was tender, but there was no sharp pain, so I kept shaking my head, and he kept poking and saying, "Miraculous." After he had me kneaded to putty he put on his stethoscope and listened to my chest and heart. He picked a spot just above my wishbone and cocked his head like a robin listening for a worm. "Hmmm," he said, "there's the damage! Considerable regurgitation."

"If that means a leaky heart," I told him, "I've had it ever since I was ten."

"Know the cause?" he asked.

"The doctor in Colorado said it was from riding too many rough horses," I said.

"Did he tell you to quit riding?"

"Only the rough ones," I said.

"Then you knew better than to go into any such escapade as this intentional falling."

"I had to do it," I told him. "I was broke and couldn't find any other job."

"Hm! It's a wonder you weren't broken in two! What's your normal heartbeat?"

"Forty-eight."

"Probably saved your life," he said. "These slow hearts will stand more abuse than fast ones, but you've done yours no good. I want you to take a full week of bed rest, or at least confinement to your room. Of course, you can go out for meals, and I want to see you each day. After I've examined your specimen I'll write a report to your doctor in the East. What's his name again, and his address?"

Of course, I couldn't let him write to Dr. Gaghan, and the only way I could keep him from it was by promising to do what he told me. I stayed in my room all day except when I went to eat, but it was one of the longest days I ever put in. He'd put some sort of plaster on my back that kept it from aching too much, but I was still bent over like a question mark, and I couldn't be comfortable either lying down or sitting up. Then too, there was nothing but local news in the paper, and the magazine I bought had only one interesting story in it.

I think I might have been a little bit homesick that day if it hadn't been for the Larsens. I didn't go to lunch till well past noontime, so I wouldn't be too much trouble to them, and when I got there Mr. Larsen had a chicken fricasseed for me, crisp celery stalks, and cabbage boiled with caraway seeds. Besides that, he'd got hold of some gluten flour, so Mrs. Larsen copied down Mother's recipe and baked bread for me that afternoon. I think it would have been better than Mother's if she hadn't put in a big handful of caraway seeds—and, of course, I didn't tell her I disliked them. Even with the seeds, my supper that night was the best I'd had in a long, long time. There was hot bread and butter, more cabbage and celery, and a whole broiled fish. I don't know what kind it was, but it was fresh and it was good.

The next morning my back was a lot better and I could straighten up pretty well, but my legs were still so stiff that the muscles pulled at every step. After the doctor had smeared salve on my face and hands, he listened to my heart for three or four minutes, nodded, and said, "A slight improvement already. A week of complete rest should repair the damage fairly well."

I'd been worried about not letting Lonnie know I was back in Phoenix, and I thought I might be able to work some of the kinks out of my legs if I went to find him, so I told the doctor, "I've got a buddy waiting for me down at the stockyards, and he'll be worried if I don't let him know I'm back in town. Would it be all right if I walked that far—very slowly?"

"Very slowly!" he told me. "This heart must have complete rest until Nature has had time to repair it. Otherwise you might be an invalid for the remainder of your life."

I grinned and said, "Well, if the specialists were right, it won't be a very long drag."

"I don't know. I don't know," he said, sort of questioningly. "That specimen I examined yesterday wasn't as bad as I expected—under the circumstances. I'm rather inclined to agree with your family physician—that is, if you behave yourself, stick rigidly to your diet, and get as much sunshine as you can on your body. Nature is a wonderful healer, and there is no better medicine than sunshine."

I waited until I had my shirt back on, then gave him one of

the report cards to fill out for Dr. Gaghan, but I didn't leave it for him to mail. When I checked it with the copy of the one I'd made out myself I found them almost exactly alike, so I knew I couldn't have done myself too much damage in the horse falls.

On my way to the stockyards I poked along slowly, stopping to look at the old guns in pawnshop windows, or at anything else that would kill a little time, and I had one of the finest pieces of luck that I ever had in my life. In one of the windows there were a dozen or so brightly painted water jars, and inside the dingy little shop an old Mexican was shaping another on a potter's wheel. The minute I saw him I knew I'd found exactly what I needed to take up my time during the week I'd have to stay in my room.

All the time I'd worked at the munitions plant I'd had a roommate who worked in the designing department. He was only a few years older than I, but before the war he'd been one of the better sculptors in New York City and had taught in one of the art schools. The reason I'd moved in with him was because he'd seen me whittling a horse's head one noon after a bunch of us had eaten our lunches in the shade of a powder shed. Ivon had been sitting five or six feet up the line from me, but when the man beside me got up he came over and took the vacant place. He watched me for maybe ten minutes, then asked, "Where did you learn that?"

"I didn't," I told him. "I've whittled horses ever since I was a little kid."

"Ever model them in clay?" he asked.

"I've tried to," I told him, "but it's no good. With clay the legs aren't strong enough to hold the bodies up."

"Don't you know how to make an armature?" he asked.

"I don't even know what one is," I said.

"If you'd like to come up to my room after supper, I'll show you," he told me.

While I was telling him I'd like to come the whistle blew,

so he scribbled down his address and room number on a card and we both hurried back to our jobs.

That evening when I went hunting for the address I found it to be one of the best apartment houses in Wilmington, with a beautiful lobby and an elevator. When I asked the elevator boy where I'd find the room number, he said, "Oh, that's the artist—top floor in the rear."

As I walked down the carpeted hall I felt about as much out of place as a catfish in a goldfish bowl. I hadn't expected to find the man living in so fancy a place, so I hadn't bothered to put on my good suit before coming. Even after I'd reached the door I had to stop a minute to decide whether to rap or to go back to my little eight-dollar-a-week room and put on my good suit. I was sure that any room in that building would be furnished like a palace, and I'd look like a ninny coming into it in my old working clothes. I'd just made up my mind to go back and change when the door opened and Ivon stood there in a dirty linen smock, holding a letter in his hand.

"Oh," he said, "there you are! Go on in while I drop this letter down the chute. Should have sent it away last night."

I couldn't have been more surprised if I'd stepped through a doorway and found myself on the moon. The floor, about fifteen feet square, was covered with sheathing paper, splashed with plaster, and pockmarked with bits of stepped-on clay. Instead of the fancy furniture I had expected, the room was bare except for a big worktable in the center, a cluttered tool bench at one side, an easel, and a couple of plaster-spattered chairs. Standing here and there were a dozen or so pedestals, some with plaster heads or busts on them, and some that were covered over with pieces of damp cloth. On a shelf under the worktable were plaster hands, arms showing the overlapping and twisting muscles as though the skin had been peeled away, a broken foot, and three or four bas-reliefs.

I was still standing just inside the doorway, looking around, when Ivon said from behind me, "This is my shop; I live in the other room. Come, toss your hat into the bedroom, and we'll see what we can do about an armature."

As Ivon spoke we walked part way down along the wall, and he opened the door to a bedroom that was as spick-and-span as the shop was messy. There was a thick carpet on the floor, pictures on the walls, and all the furniture was dark, satiny mahogany. "How good a shot are you?" he asked as he pointed toward a post on the nearest twin bed. "I don't go in from the shop without changing my shoes. Fortunately, I have another door from the hallway."

I sailed my hat for the top of the bedpost, and I happened to have good luck. It lit like a horseshoe over a peg, and spun around a couple of times without falling off.

"Good eye!" Ivon said. "No wonder you can whittle a horse. Can you make them look like any special one?"

"If people know the horse himself I don't have to tell them which one I've whittled," I told him.

"Tie him up somewhere and use him for a model?" he asked.

"No, I never tried that," I said. "If I've known him well I can remember what he looks like, and I guess I just kind of see him in my head."

"Good! Good!" he said. "Now let's get at that armature. How big a horse do you want to make?"

That evening Ivon showed me how to twist the wires and make an armature for a horse a foot high. I never knew anyone, except my own father, who was so patient. He didn't try to do it for me; just showed me how and let me do it by myself. And with all the horses I'd whittled, he told me something I'd never noticed—that the average horse is square; his body the same length as his height at the withers, with his forelegs, neck, and head each about half of that length.

Before we started he took a piece of charcoal, knelt, and with a few quick strokes he sketched a rearing stallion on the floor. "The armature is simply the skeleton," he told me as he drew a heavy black line that looped through the head, along the arch of the neck, curve of the back, and length of the tail. "There's the main stem," he said. "Now we'll attach lighter wires to it and shape them into the bones for the shoulders, hips, and legs." As he spoke he drew in the lines to show me exactly how the wires would be bent and shaped, so as to be hidden inside the clay. And how those for the tail and hind legs would extend down through a wooden base to hold the framework firm and solid. Then along the back he sketched in hanging wires, with heavy crosses at their lower ends. "Those are wooden bats," he said, "to support the weight of the body instead of ribs." The whole thing hadn't taken more than five minutes, but when he'd finished I knew everything I'd need to know about armatures.

The second evening Ivon showed me how to moisten the clay, work it pliable in my hands, lay it on the armature with the face of my thumb, and scrape it into the shapes I wanted with his tools. The third evening he watched me as I finished the head and neck of my horse, making suggestions to help me here and there. Then, when I was putting the damp cloth on it to keep it from drying out until I could come again, he asked, "Why don't you move in here with me? That would save you a long walk these evenings, and you could be quite a help to me with some tricky castings I'd like to make this winter."

"I'd like to," I told him, "but I couldn't afford the rent."

He asked me how much rent I was paying for my room, and when I told him he said it would cost me the same there. My eight dollars a week couldn't have been a quarter of what that apartment cost in wartime, but it was the nearest to a home I'd ever had away from home, and Ivon taught me all that I had the ability to learn. By the end of the war I'd made hundreds of horses, and eight or ten portrait busts of friends we had at the plant. They didn't have the lifelike look that Ivon's did, but anyone could tell whose portraits they were.

My hands were itching for the feel of the clay again as I stood there on the sidewalk in Phoenix, watching the old Mexican build up the sides of his jar with his wet hands. I waited until the jar was finished, then went in and asked him what he'd charge me for a bucket of clay. He started off with a dollar, but I worked it down to sixty cents for the clay and an old bucket to carry it in. Then I told him I'd come back and get it within an hour.

Lonnie wasn't at the stockyards when I got there, but I recognized a couple of the boys who were hanging around. One of them thought he might have hopped a freight back to Tucson, and the other thought he'd gone west—maybe to look for me at Wickenburg, or to go on through to California for the winter. I told them where he could find me if he came back, then hunted around the yards for pieces of baling wire and sticks I could use for making armatures.

I don't suppose that bucket of clay weighed more than twenty-five pounds, but with my back and legs and arms as lame as they were, it felt as though it weighed a ton before I got back to my hotel room. After I'd made another trip out for a pair of pliers, I spread the tarpaulin from my bedroll on the floor and spent the rest of the morning twisting up an armature for a little horse, dampening my clay, and working it over to get out any particles of sand or grit.

My fingers were too rough to do a good job of smoothing the clay, but I whittled myself little tools that worked real well, and that afternoon got away from me as though it had been only a half hour long. When I went over for my supper I took the Larsens the horse I'd made—an old mare we used to have when I was a boy—and anyone might have thought I'd brought them a present worth a hundred dollars. Of course, it was worthless in clay, because it would crack and warp out of shape as soon as it dried, so I told them I'd take it back to my room and cast it in plaster of Paris.

The rest of that week was fun. I made a horse for the doctor and another for the hotelkeeper, and my plaster casts came out better than I expected. In Arizona the plaster dried a lot faster than in Delaware, and the matrix chipped off cleaner. In the middle of the week I sent Mother a money order for fifty dollars, with a long letter telling her that my boss had furnished me with an outfit, so I hadn't had to buy one, and that he'd given me a raise in pay. Then I told her a long story about his sending me around to the back country to inspect his cattle herds, and I said I didn't know just where I'd be but that I'd write often.

The Larsens must have spent hours in finding things I could eat and cooking them for me. Even with the few things on my diet, every meal was different, every one was enough for two men, and after I'd taken them the horse they wouldn't let me pay them a penny. Each day I went to the doctor the first thing after breakfast, and each time he said my heart sounded a little better. Each day my back ached less, the stiffness drained out of my arms and legs, the black-and-blue spots faded, and the scabs began peeling off the scratches on my face and hands.

I could have been happy to stay right there in Phoenix all winter, just fussing with the clay and going over to Larsen's for my meals, but of course I couldn't afford to do it. I'd told Mother I had a good job and could send her fifty dollars a month, my room was costing a dollar a day, I'd already told the Larsens they couldn't feed me any longer for one little plaster horse, and I had no idea how big my doctor's bill might be. I was already down to $364, and if I didn't find some kind of job pretty soon I'd go broke again.

6

Outfitting

EVEN though I knew that Lonnie was sort of a lazy bum,
I wished he'd show up again. I didn't know how to drive a
flivver, and he'd told me he knew all about them. Besides that,
he was a happy-go-lucky boy and good company, and I didn't
exactly like the idea of starting out into the back country alone,
particularly with a flivver. If it broke down I wouldn't know
how to fix it, and it seemed to me that a fellow would be in a
pretty bad way if he were stuck like that, alone and out in the
middle of a desert.

I waited until the doctor said he'd release me the next day,
then I took another walk down to the stockyards. Lonnie was
there, sitting in the shade of the weigher's shack and talking
with some cowhands I'd never seen before. He seemed as glad
to see me as if I'd been his long-lost brother. I'd just come
around the corner of the shack when he jumped up and came
running to meet me. "Jeepers Creepers, buddy!" he shouted,
"I figured you'd lit out for home with all that dough you made
up to Wickenburg! When you didn't show up for three-four
days I moseyed on up there to find you, and a guy named Ted
told me you'd done right good—only got skun up a little."

I knew from what Lonnie said that he'd been to the movie lot, and I knew from the looks of him that he hadn't done any riding, but I asked, "Did you try your hand at the falls?"

"Uh-uh!" he told me. "I watched a couple of them runs, but that ain't my kind of ridin'! Don't mind getting spilled off a bronc, but I ain't about to let nobody tip one over on top of me. 'Course, if I'd been a trick rider the likes of you, I'd have tried it, but I ain't never took up that end of the business. How much dough did you make?"

I didn't think there was any sense in telling him, so I just said, "Not as much as I wanted to, but maybe enough to buy a secondhand outfit and a cheap flivver." Then I told him what Jim Magee had said about driving out through the back country to find jobs, and asked if he'd like to go along. It didn't take him two seconds to decide that he would. The first thing we did was to take his bedroll from the stockyards to my hotel room, and on the way I told him how I'd planned things out —but I didn't tell him that I planned to leave four fifty-dollar bills in the cuff of my britches.

"The way I figure it," I said, "is that we can go as much as $130 for a flivver, an outfit, and grub and room rent until we get started. I expect the doctor to charge me about twenty, and that would leave us with fourteen bucks for grub and gas on the road till we find jobs. Do you think that will do it?"

"Jeepers!" Lonnie shouted. "You bet your sweet life it'll do it, buddy! Man alive, that's a fortune! This town's full of broke-down old flivvers we could buy for forty to fifty bucks, and there ain't one of 'em so bad I can't make it good as new with four or five dollars' worth of spare parts—secondhanded stuff we can pick up at a junk yard. That would leave us eighty or ninety for outfits, and this time of year you can pick up a dang good outfit in a hockshop—saddle, blanket, chaps, and the works—for forty to forty-five bones. Jeepers, buddy, we're in the chips! You musta took the jackpot at Wickenburg!"

"No," I told him, "only a piece of it. Not enough to buy more than one outfit till I'm sure you're right about the price of flivvers. Remember, it's going to cost money to live till we're ready to hit the road."

"Look, buddy," he asked, "do I get an outfit if I can find a flivver for fifty bucks and fix it for ten, all in one day?"

"You bet your life!" I said. "As good a one as I get for myself."

We spent the rest of that day and evening looking in the secondhand lots and junk yards, and going to see every old jalopy that was advertised in the paper. But the only thing we could find for fifty dollars was an old Maxwell that wouldn't run and looked as if it had been caught in a tornado. At breakfast next morning I told Lonnie to keep on hunting while I made my last trip to the doctor, got a card filled out, and paid my bill, then I'd meet him at our room at ten o'clock.

When I told the doctor I was leaving for the back country in a day or two he went over me from head to heels. Then he talked to me for more than an hour—telling me he was still inclined to agree with my family physician, but that I mustn't ride any bucking horses under any circumstances, must get all the sunshine I could on my body, and must stick rigidly to my diet. He made me promise that I wouldn't leave Phoenix without at least fifty pounds of fresh cabbage, fifty pounds of gluten flour, a case of canned salmon, two dozen eggs, and ten pounds of peanuts. Then he charged me only ten dollars for all my visits. I think it was because I'd made him the little plaster horse.

Lonnie was waiting for me when I got back to the hotel, and so excited that he began talking before I had the door half open. "Listen, buddy," he shouted, "I found a crackerjack of a bargain—1914 Ford tourin' car—one of them that's got the brass radiator. The bloke wanted a hundred bucks for it, but he'da took seventy-five, and there ain't scarcely nothin' wrong with it 'cepting a couple o' loose connecting-rod bearings. The tires is almost next to new, and with two bucks' worth of Babbitt bearings I could have that engine fixed up so's't she'd climb Pikes Peak on high. 'Twouldn't take no more'n a couple or three hours."

"Even at that," I said, "seventy-five dollars sounds like a lot of money for an old flivver. Couldn't we fix that Max . . . ?"

"Wait a minute there, buddy!" Lonnie broke in. "The trans-mission—the gears you shift with—they're all shot to the devil on that Maxwell, and that's what you got to watch out for when you go to buyin' an old jalopy. It would cost leastways twenty bucks for a secondhanded transmission, and it would take me four or five days to take the busted one out and put the other one in. And what would we have when I got done? Nothin', that's what! The tires on it ain't no good, Maxwells is always bustin' down and they drink up gas like a cow drinks water. Fords'll run all day on a gallon o' gas and a spoonful of oil. You *can't* wear 'em out, and if anything busts you can always fix it with a piece of balin' wire. Jeepers, buddy, I'd trust that old flivver out in the desert a lot quicker'n I'd trust a Rolls Royce. You come take a look at it and I'll betcha my life you'll see the light."

The flivver was in a combination garage and blacksmith shop, way out at the edge of town, and when we got there it looked worse to me than the Maxwell had. It must have been a desert car all its life, and through a hundred sandstorms. A coat of yellow paint had been daubed on thick over the original black, and a coat of red smeared on top of that—with a broom, I think—then it had been sandblasted until it was speckled from radiator to tailpipe, with all three colors showing through. The top was turned back, but I could see that the covering was stripped to tatters, and there were holes in the seats big enough for a rabbit to hide in. In hunting for some excuse for not buy-ing it I asked Lonnie, "How about the gearshift on this one? Are you sure it's all right?"

"Gearshift!" he hollered. "Fords don't have no gearshift! They're shiftless. Work off'n bands around a transmission drum."

"Well, this one looks shiftless to me," I said. "This corner sags down like an old nag standing on three legs!"

"That don't amount to nothin'," he told me, "just a couple of busted leaves in the spring. You can get all of them you want

for a dime apiece in any junk yard, and it don't take no time at all to put 'em in."

"Well, it still looks shiftless to me," I said. "I'll bet it's been driven a hundred thousand miles."

"No it ain't! Not a bit of it!" the owner of the garage told me. "This little car ain't been drove over five thousand miles. Just took it in on a trade with old man Henderson, up Cavecreek way. Trouble is he didn't have no place to keep it—left it stand out in the weather, so the paint got chawed up a mite by the wind. Some good-for-nothin' hired hand drove it over rough country, hunting strays. Busted a leaf or two in the springs, and left it run low on oil. 'Twouldn't take next to nothing to put it into apple-pie shape. Time you boys put a fresh coat o' paint on it a man couldn't scarcely tell it from new. Them wore places on the seats would patch up slick as silk with a few strips of oilcloth and a little glue—I'd throw that in as part of the deal."

The flivver still looked like a tired old nag that was on its last legs, so I shook my head and told Lonnie, "Shiftless is sure the right name for it. It's even ding-toed. Look how the front wheels turn inward."

Before Lonnie could answer, the garageman called out, "Bent radius rod, that's all. Couple o' swipes with a maul would straighten it right out. I told you that fool hired hand drove it over a bit of rough country."

I'd heard people talk before when they'd been trying to sell something that wasn't any good, so I didn't pay any attention to the man but said to Lonnie, "There's no sense in buying this one. It would take you a week to fix it up and wait for the paint to dry, and we can't afford to hang around Phoenix that long. Besides, you'd have to buy tools for doing a job this big."

Again the garageman beat Lonnie to the punch. "Not a bit of it! Not a bit of it!" he told me. "You boys could fix it up right here, and I'd leave you use my tools. Wouldn't cost you a penny. I'd even lend you a hand on it, so's't you could have it ready to roll by tomorrow mornin'."

"That's kind of you," I said, "and maybe we'll come back to

see it again, but . . ."

I hadn't noticed Lonnie until he cut in, "Look buddy, let's you and me take a little walk."

When I glanced around he looked as sad as a little boy who's been told he can't have a puppy he's fallen in love with, so I said, "Okay but I'm not going to buy it, Lonnie."

As soon as we were outside Lonnie asked, "Look, buddy, didn't you ever take note how the best cuttin' horses usually looks the laziest and most no-account?"

"Sure I have," I told him, "but what's that got to do with buying a flivver?"

"Plenty!" he said. "Plenty! To a man that knows flivvers like I do, there's just as much feel to 'em as there is to a horse. They're either all good or no good, and a man that knows 'em don't need nobody to tell him which. I knowed that speckled one was plumb good the minute I laid eyes on her."

"I'm not saying it isn't," I told him, "but for a hundred dollars I think we ought to be able to find a better one. That's a lot of money, and I'm not going to spend it till we've looked around some more and . . ."

"Listen, buddy," Lonnie pleaded, "I can easy talk the bloke down to seventy-five, and you heard him say I could use his tools, and that he'd lend me a hand. With the both of us workin' on that engine we'd have it purrin' like a pussy 'fore suppertime, and the looks of the body don't make no difference to us now. What we'll need in the back country is a car with an engine we can trust. There's no sense stopping to do the paint job till we're on our way. I can do that and patch up them holes in the seats any time along the road. When I get through with her she'll look and run like she just come out of the fact'ry. How 'bout it, buddy? I'm tellin' you, we couldn't do no better if we was to waste a month's time huntin'."

There did seem to be some sense in what Lonnie said, and it would cost money for every extra day we spent in Phoenix, so I told him, "All right, Lonnie, I'll tell you what I'll do. If you can buy that one for seventy-five dollars, and if you can have it all fixed up and ready to roll by tomorrow noon, I'll go along with the deal, but not for one penny more. Is that fair enough?"

Lonnie was hurrying back into the garage before I had the last words out of my mouth. "Fair enough! Fair enough!" he sang out. "I'll guarantee you'll never live to regret it, buddy. Now you watch your old uncle drive a sharp deal."

I think the look on Lonnie's face ruined his deal the minute he stepped back into that garage. He haggled for more than an hour with the owner, and the lowest they ever got was eighty-five dollars. When I was sure that was the best deal he could make I said, "Come on, Lonnie. We've wasted enough time here."

As I said it I turned and walked out of the place, but I hadn't gone fifty feet before Lonnie caught up with me. "Listen, buddy," he said as he trailed along at my elbow, "I had him right on the edge of a deal when you busted it up. And besides, what's a ten-spot to a guy like you anyways? The work I'll get out of the bloke will be worth double that. You know these mechanics charge a buck and a half an hour for their time."

"Sure I know it," I said, "and he'd probably run us up a bill of twenty or more before we ever got out of there."

"Uh-uh! Not a penny! That's a part of the deal," Lonnie told me. "He ain't goin' to charge us a nickel for nothin'—just the dough we pay him for the flivver, and he'll furnish all the spare parts we need."

I kept right on walking, and said, "No deal! I wouldn't trust that man any farther than I could reach him with a throw rope. He's lied to you forty times and in forty different ways during the last hour. I'd walk before I'd pay him eighty-five dollars for that old pile of junk."

Lonnie caught hold of my arm and looked up at me like a puppy that's begging for a cookie. "Listen, buddy," he said, "leave me buy it and I'll pay you back the extra ten-spot outa my first pay check when we get a job. I'll do better'n that. I'll go halvers on the flivver . . . . and on the gas and oil . . . . and on the grub bill. Look, buddy, I didn't never mean for you to buy me no outfit and give it to me. Tell you what: I'll just keep a fiver for myself each payday till you're all paid back—clean as a whistle."

I didn't expect Lonnie to pay me back, but he seemed to have fallen in love with that old rattletrap Ford, and I didn't have the heart to tell him he couldn't have it. I just passed him my roll and said, "That's fair enough, and since you're making the deal it'll look better for you to do the paying, but have the bill of sale made out in my name. I'll make a new one, putting Shiftless into partnership, when you pay me back the first five dollars."

Lonnie grabbed the bills and ran, and he was already peeling the eighty-five off our little roll by the time I got back to the garage. I don't know which looked the happiest, he or the garage owner.

It was noon by the time the bill of sale was made out, and the motor vehicle office was right near Larsen's restaurant, so I told Lonnie we'd better go and have the flivver registered, buy a license, and eat our lunch right away. "Uh-uh!" he told me, "I ain't hungry. I et a big breakfast, and it'll hold me over till suppertime. You go on down while I and Joe fix up them connecting-rod bearin's. We'll have to hump right along to get 'em finished 'fore closing time."

When Joe, the garage owner, went to his truck for his lunch pail, Lonnie slipped me what was left of our roll, and whispered, "Say, buddy, while you're down that way why don't you mosey 'round to the hockshops and see what you can find for outfits? Look, you don't need to get me as good a one as you get for yourself. Just so's it's got good stirrups and a horn to snub a rope onto, that's all I'll need. And there's no sense you botherin' about chaps for me. My legs don't skin up easy, and there's no tellin' we'll be workin' brush country anyways. Understand, buddy, I ain't tryin' to rush you none. Just figured it would be a shame—us having to hold up and hunt outfits tomorrow, after we're all set and ready to roll. It don't make no never-minds if you ain't back before dark, 'cause you couldn't do no good here noways. It takes a real mechanic to work on automobiles. Kind of like a watch. A man's got to know what he's about before he goes to fussin' with 'em."

I had better luck than I expected on the license. Because a quarter of December was past and the 1919 plates had gone on sale, the clerk told me I'd only need to buy one for the new year. Even at that, I began finding out there were more costs to automobiles than just the buying price and gasoline, but I didn't begrudge the expense. I was more proud to be the registered owner of an automobile than of the automobile itself. Before I went to hunt for outfits I took the ownership ticket to Mr. Larsen, so there would be no chance of my losing it.

Mr. Larsen didn't come right out and tell me we'd been stuck when I told him about the Ford and what we'd paid for it. But he asked me dozens of questions I didn't know anything about—were there any shorts in the magneto, were the cylinder walls scored, and was I sure the crankshaft hadn't been worn egg-shaped? When I said I'd never even heard of a magneto he hunched his shoulders and spread his hands, as much as to say, "Well, you've been caught for a sucker, but it's too late to do anything about it now." Then he said that if we were going to leave early next morning I'd better let him order the groceries the doctor had told me to take with us. I told him I'd appreciate his ordering the stuff, but I forgot to ask how much it would cost.

To me an automobile was only a collection of dead iron parts, but a saddle was a living thing—almost a part of a cowhand himself. Each one is different in some way from any other, particularly after it has been used a year or two, and a man with a saddle that is wrong for him can be as out of luck as if he were trying to work cattle bareback. If it's right, his behind will cuddle into the hollow of the cantle securely and, no matter how hard a bull hits the end of a line or a pony pitches, he'll be topside when the fun is over. Then too, a saddle talks. On night herd it whispers at every step of the pony, just to let a cowhand know he's not alone.

I was thinking all these things as I left the restaurant and headed for the back streets where the pawnshops were—and the more I thought the faster I found myself walking. That's what saved me from getting cheated on our outfits. It made me remember how Lonnie had clutched my roll and run back to the garage to buy Shiftless. Common sense told me that we could have bought that old heap for half the price if he hadn't shown from the very start how much he wanted it. I made up my mind that I'd see every saddle in every pawnshop in Phoenix before I bought one. And the more I liked any one of them the less I'd show it.

The first shop I went into had at least thirty saddles displayed in a long row, and the pawnbroker led me straight to one at the center of the line. I was hooked as quickly as Lonnie had been hooked by Shiftless. There in front of me was exactly the saddle I wanted—the only saddle I wanted. It was an Oregon half-breed, with the back ring hung straight down beside the cantle, so the saddle could be used with or without a flank cinch. The whole outfit yelled "custom-made." The cantle was low and sloping, the fork just wide enough for my thin shanks to cling to, and the short seat curved upward enough in meeting it to make a neat pocket. It would have cramped a heavy rider, but was exactly the right size for my skinny behind to fit into. Over the well-shaped, but not too high horn hung a split-ear bridle, with a light spade bit and braided rawhide reins.

I think I could have moved on from any other saddle in the place without a word from the little shopkeeper, but when I passed up the half-breed he grabbed me by the sleeve and pulled me back. He wanted me to feel the tooling, twisted a stirrup leather to show me how pliable it was, and started giving me a long story about having paid two hundred dollars for the saddle. When I pulled away he caught my sleeve again and told me that because it was the off season he'd sacrifice both saddle and bridle for seventy-five dollars.

"You're making your sacrifice at the wrong altar and in the

wrong town," I told him. "That's an old Oregon half-breed, probably older than I am, and it was custom-made for a midget. You couldn't find an Arizona cowhand who would give you five dollars for it, but I'll give you ten if you want to get rid of it."

"Sixty!" he shouted, like an auctioneer who senses a rising bid. Then, "Fifty!" as he tried to pull me back. I only shook my head and walked out of the shop.

From there I went to every pawnshop in Phoenix, and did a little haggling in every one, just to get in some practice and to find out exactly how much they'd come down before letting me walk out. I found that thirty percent was just about the limit. If an outfit was priced at a hundred dollars, I could have bought it for about seventy, and if it was priced at fifty, I could have it for thirty-five.

I waited until about an hour before closing time, then headed back for the shop where I'd seen the Oregon half-breed. The little shopkeeper pounced on me like a hungry cat on a fat mouse. He grabbed my sleeve and dragged me straight down the row to the half-breed saddle, and that time he tried to start the haggling off at fifty dollars. There was only one thing I could do. I shook my head without more than glancing at the saddle, then pulled away and went to look at a real good double-rigged job farther up the row. He started off with sixty dollars on that one, but I turned my mouth down and said, "Thirty. With bridle, blanket, and chaps."

For a minute or two I thought the little man was having a stroke of apoplexy. He shouted at me in such broken English I couldn't understand a word, and scurried around the shop like an insane pack rat. First he pawed over a stack of saddle blankets till he found one that was fairly good. He slapped it down on top of the half-breed saddle, glared up at me, and yelled, "Fifty!"

I only shook my head and kept on examining the double-rigger. It was a better saddle than I had thought at first—not more than a year old, and exactly the right kind of saddle for a fellow built like Lonnie. I made up my mind I'd buy it for him, even if I had to go as much as fifty or fifty-five dollars for it—that is, with the rest of the outfit. If I hadn't really liked that saddle, I might have had trouble keeping my eyes turned away from the half-breed, and could have ruined my deal. But instead of paying any attention to the shopkeeper, I went over and began sorting through the pile of saddle blankets.

At first I think he had the idea I didn't like the blanket he'd put on the half-breed and was hunting for a better one. He stood, rubbing his hands together and grinning, while I pawed nearly to the bottom of the stack and pulled out a real fine

Navajo. Then he went wild again when I carried it to the double-rigger, tossed it on, and said, "Thirty-two fifty."

He rushed toward me, snatched up the Navajo blanket, ran to exchange it for the poorer one he'd put on the half-breed, whirled around, and yelled, "Fifty!"

When I turned my mouth down he snatched a fairly good pair of cowhide chaps from a peg, tossed them on top of the Navajo, and again yelled, "Fifty!"

I didn't even bother to turn my mouth down that time, but hunted around until I'd found a better pair of chaps, laid them across the double-rigger, and said, "Thirty-five."

I did the same when the little man added a slicker to the heap on the Oregon saddle. And as he added a throw rope and spurs, I did too, but I always hunted until I'd found something a little better than what he'd added. Each time he tossed something on the half-breed he yelled, "Fifty!" And each time I tossed something better on the double-rigger I went up fifty cents or a dollar on my offer.

I knew it must be way past his regular closing time when the shopkeeper gave up trying to sell me the Oregon saddle— and I knew that I'd just about run out my string. His shoulders drooped, he came up where I was beside the double-rigger, examined everything I'd put on it, and said, "Sixty-five. Final!"

I was sure it was awfully close to it, and that I'd have to make my move right then, or he'd throw up his hands and walk away. "Well," I said, "I'll tell you what I'll do. I'll give you eighty-five dollars for both outfits together, but I won't buy one without the other."

Half an hour later we made our deal—at $87.25. It was more money than I'd intended to spend, but I wasn't a bit sorry. We'd have outfits that were a lot better than the average, and a good rancher will usually hire a cowhand quicker if he has a good outfit than if he has a poor one. With jobs as scarce as they were, it seemed to me that the few extra dollars were well invested.

7

Shiftless

I FOUND a bum who was glad to make a quarter by helping me carry our new outfits to the hotel, but when we got there Lonnie hadn't come in, and it was nearly seven o'clock. I laid each outfit separately on the bed, with the saddles on the folded blankets, but I put the Navajo under Lonnie's saddle instead of mine. Then I left the lamp lit when I went to the restaurant to see if he'd been there to eat. He hadn't, so I went on out to the garage. A couple of lanterns were sitting on the floor by Shiftless's front wheels, and both Joe and Lonnie were underneath. There were greasy nuts, bolts, and odd parts lying all around them, and they were so busy arguing that they didn't hear me come in. I stooped down just as Joe shouted, "There ain't no need of haulin' the engine, I tell you! Them main bearings ain't so bad but I can fix 'em right up where they're at. Shim 'em up a mite and pour in some hot Babbitt, they'll be as good as new."

I didn't want Lonnie to find me there and think I was snooping so I asked, "What is it, all shot to the dickens, Lonnie?"

He rolled his face toward me, and his eyes looked as though he were peeking through holes in a black rag. "No, buddy," he said. "Honest, it ain't bad. It's only the bearin's. A bolt come loose in the oil pan, and some fool run it after the oil had all leaked out."

Joe seemed to think Lonnie needed a little help. He reached up above his face, grabbed hold of something, and jiggled it. It sounded like a handful of stones being shaken in a bucket. "Ain't scarcely no play in 'em at all," he shouted. "Like I was tellin' Lonnie, all them main bearin's need is a shot o' hot lead. Come morning, so's't I can see to get at 'em, I'll . . ."

I didn't have the slightest idea what Joe had hold of, but I did remember a few of the questions Mr. Larsen had asked me, so I broke in, "What's that you've got hold of, the crankshaft?"

"Yep. Yep," he called back. "Ain't scarcely no play at all in it."

"Is it worn egg-shaped?" I asked.

"Not enough to 'mount to nothin'!" he shouted. "You won't notice it none after I get some hot Babbitt poured 'round them . . ."

I didn't want to go any further till I'd talked to Mr. Larsen some more, so I broke in, "Come on Lonnie. It's about time for the restaurant to close. If we're going to get any supper you'd better start cleaning up."

All the way downtown Lonnie kept telling me there was nothing wrong with the flivver that he couldn't fix the next day, and the more he talked the more I realized how badly we'd been stuck.

The restaurant was already closed when we got there, but Mr. Larsen unlocked the door and let us in. Then, while Mrs. Larsen was in the kitchen cooking our supper, he and Lonnie talked about Shiftless. As far as I was concerned they might as well have been talking Choctaw. It was all about camshafts, and piston rings, and carburetors, and differentials, and a lot of other things I'd never heard of. After a while I got tired of it and went out to talk to Mrs. Larsen till supper was ready.

Lonnie didn't say three words while we were eating, and when we'd finished Mr. Larsen beckoned for me to come to the kitchen. He whispered to me that Lonnie knew we'd been stuck, but wouldn't listen to reason when he'd suggested that we take our loss and sell the car back to the garageman.

"I'm not surprised at that," I told him. "For some crazy reason he seems to have fallen in love with that old rattletrap."

Mr. Larsen hunched his shoulders and spread his hands. Then he smiled and said, "Maybe you're not too bad off. He knows more about engines than I'd expected, and if he loves that old flivver he'll nurse it. I've advised him to tear the motor right down to the block and replace every worn part. It's risky business to drive into the back country with a bum engine."

"Did he say he'd do it?" I asked.

Mr. Larsen spread his hands and said, "Just froze up and wouldn't talk."

I think Lonnie was afraid of what Mr. Larsen might have told me. All the way to our room he walked along with his head down, and I couldn't get two words out of him. I unlocked the door, then held it back for him to go in. He took two steps, then stopped as if someone had been in there pointing a gun at him. For fully a minute he stood looking at the outfits as if he couldn't believe what he saw. He didn't move until I said, "The one on the far side is yours. This one of mine wouldn't be big enough for you to get your fat butt into."

Lonnie made it to the bed in a single leap, dropped to his knees, and rubbed his hands over the smooth leather, across the Navajo blanket, and along one leg of the chaps. When he looked up at me his eyes were swimming. Then he looked back at the saddle and said, "Honest-a-God, buddy! Honest-a-God! You'll never be sorry you done it. I'll never leave you down. I'll give you every dime out o' my pay checks till . . ."

I never would have guessed that Lonnie could bawl about anything, but he seemed on the verge of it, so I said, "You wait here a few minutes. I'm going over to the livery stable and get some saddle soap. I don't have an idea these old hulls have been soaped up since they lit in that hockshop."

It was midnight before I could get Lonnie to stop working

on his saddle, and he wouldn't have stopped then if I hadn't reminded him that he had a big job ahead of him next day.

By the time I'd known Lonnie two days I'd come to the conclusion that the hardest job he ever did was to wake up in the morning. Most cowhands are wide awake the moment they open their eyes, and unless they've been on night herd they usually open them at the first crack of dawn. But not Lonnie. He could have slept with a stampeding herd all around him. And no matter if he turned in at sundown he'd sleep through till noon unless someone shook the tar out of him. Even after I'd get him on his feet he'd still be more than half asleep, and it would often take him as much as an hour to get out of low gear.

When, the morning after we got our outfits, he shook me long before daylight, I thought the hotel must be afire. I flung the covers back and started to jump out of bed, but Lonnie whispered, "Take it easy, buddy. There ain't no sense of you rollin' out for another couple of hours. It ain't much after five, but if I'm goin' to get Shiftless fixed up and ready by nightfall I'd best to be gettin' at her."

That was the first time Lonnie ever called the old flivver Shiftless, and for a couple of seconds I didn't know what he was talking about. Then, when the cobwebs cleared away, I said, "You're out of your head, Lonnie. Joe won't have his garage open at this time in the morning. And besides, there's no sense in going out there till you've had your breakfast. The restaurant doesn't open till six."

"I don't want no breakfast," he told me. "I'll go on out to the garage so's to be there when Joe opens up. And look, buddy, when you go over to breakfast don't let that Swede talk no foolish notions into your head. He don't know nothin' 'bout automobiles—leastways, not about flivvers that's been wore a bit and has to be fixed up some."

"Oh, I thought he did," I said. "He told me we weren't too bad off with Shiftless, and that you knew a lot more about autos than he'd expected."

For a minute Lonnie stood there beside the bed with his

mouth hanging open, then his face lighted up gradually—just as a mountaintop does when the morning sun first touches it. "Jeepers!" he said. "Maybe that old Swede knows more than I reckoned on. You know, come to think of it, I believe I could go for a bite o' breakfast. We could finish soapin' up our outfits while we're waiting for the joint to open."

Lonnie and I were waiting when Mr. and Mrs. Larsen came to open the restaurant, and we were there till nearly time for Joe to open his garage at eight o'clock. Of course, we weren't the only customers, but Mr. Larsen told us to come back to the kitchen, and he talked to Lonnie as he fried eggs and sausages. And every now and then, when his face was turned my way, he'd let one eyelid drop. There wasn't a cotter pin, nut, bolt, or gear in a Ford that he didn't know about, and he must have mentioned every one of them and told Lonnie to check it. But the thing he kept harping on was that we shouldn't try to hurry too much, and that every moving part that was worn should be replaced. When we left Lonnie wasn't calling him the Swede any more, but Helgar.

"Know what we're goin' to do the first thing, buddy?" Lonnie asked as we left the restaurant. "We're goin' to pull that daggone engine, that's what we're goin' to do! Like Helgar says, how's a man to know them crankshaft bearin's ain't egg-shaped less'n he gets 'em out where he can put a pair o' calipers on 'em?"

Joe was mad as the dickens when Lonnie told him we were going to pull the engine out of Shiftless. He shouted and yelled, and told us we were a pair of fools. "I ain't goin' to waste my time on no such nonsense!" he hollered at me. "All that little car needs is a shot o' hot lead here and there—just enough to tighten up them loose bearin's—and it would run like a rabbit. Sure I said I'd lend a hand and furnish the spare parts, and I would for any reasonable sort of a job. But if you go to haulin' that engine all to pieces I'll have to charge you for 'em."

It took Lonnie and me all day to get the engine out and taken to pieces, and I didn't need to be a mechanic to know why Joe didn't want us to do it. The cylinder walls were worn a quarter inch bigger around than the pistons, and were scored so badly they looked as if a wildcat had scratched them. Every bearing was melted out, the valve stems were burned half in two, the combustion chambers were plugged with rock-hard carbon, and there wasn't a shaft anywhere that wasn't worn lopsided. But by quitting time we had nuts, bolts, and entrails scattered all over the floor, and a list six inches long of parts we'd need for making the repairs.

The next forenoon we found a 1914 Ford in a junk yard, and it was exactly what we needed. When it was almost new it had been hit by a train and smashed to smithereens, but the only trouble with the engine was that the cylinder block had been cracked and the magneto ruined. After a little haggling we bought whatever parts we wanted to take out of it for ten dollars. By borrowing a lantern from Mr. Larsen and tools from Joe, we'd stripped out everything worth taking by midnight— and I'd learned quite a bit about the inside of a Ford engine. Before we started, Mr. Larsen had told us not to take bushings, bearings, valves, rings, and gaskets, because we'd always have trouble if we tried to reuse them, and it was cheaper to buy new. But they weren't very cheap at that.

In the four days it took us to put that engine back together the money leaked out of my pocket as if it had been water. The first list of parts we bought at the auto supply store cost more than twenty-three dollars, and I had to pay Joe about half that much, in quarters and half dollars, for little things we'd forgotten to put on the list. Even at thirty-five cents apiece, our meals had amounted to nearly fifteen dollars, the groceries I'd promised the doctor we'd take along had cost $14.10, and the hotel had gone up half a dollar a day on my rent when Lonnie moved in.

Mr. Larsen knew I was worried, but he kept telling me we'd only make trouble for ourselves by cutting corners or hurrying, so we scraped every bearing to a tight fit, ground the valves till they shone like glass, and made sure that everything fitted snugly before we put it back together. With each new piece we put into place the crankshaft turned harder until, finally, it wouldn't turn at all, but Lonnie said not to worry about it, that it would work all right when the engine was filled with oil.

It was almost closing time on Friday night when we got the engine back into Shiftless, a gallon of oil in the crankcase, and the tank filled with gasoline. Lonnie was too excited to keep quiet. While I was paying Joe for the gas and oil he climbed in behind the steering wheel and shouted, "Twist her tail, buddy! Wind her up tight! And don't get scairt when she starts up with a roar; I'll cool her right down with the throttle."

I engaged the crank handle and jerked up on it with all my might, but the engine wouldn't turn an inch. "You know what, buddy?" Lonnie called, "we might of got a couple of them bearin's a smidgen too tight. Well, that don't make no never-minds. They'll loosen right up, time the engine's been turned over a few times. Oh, Joe! How 'bout givin' us a little pull with your truck?"

"Well," Joe said with a broad grin, "I reckon that could be took care of after we get settled up. The way I figure it, you boys owe me fifty dollars for the work I done that first day, along with the use of my garage and tools. You can have the car when I get the fifty."

I had to hold Lonnie to keep him from going after Joe with his fists, but I knew that fighting would only get him arrested, so I told him, "There's only one way to do business with a crook, Lonnie, and that's through a lawyer. Let's go see Mr. Larsen."

Joe laughed as though he'd never heard anything so funny. "That's the ticket!" he told me. "Go crack your whip and listen to the noise it makes!"

Our whip didn't make much noise. Mr. Larsen phoned a lawyer, but when he was through talking he told us, "There isn't much he can do beyond trying to get the bill cut down, and he can't do that till morning. If he took the case to court it would cost you a lot of time and money, and you'd probably lose anyway."

I didn't sleep worth a dime that night. As near as I could figure, Shiftless had already cost me over a hundred and fifty dollars—counting in meals and room rent while we were fixing her up—and another fifty would leave me in a bad way. I'd had to take one fifty-dollar bill out of the cuff of my britches when I bought our outfits, another before we were through buying parts, and there was only $13.90 of it left. After Lonnie went to sleep I took out the third fifty and put it in my pocket, but I made up my mind that I'd sell our outfits, or Shiftless, or anything else we had before I'd spend the last one. After writing Mother the big yarns I had about my fine job and sending her fifty dollars every month, I couldn't write and tell her a bunch of different lies. I'd just keep right on with the story I'd begun, and I'd send her fifty dollars a month just as long as I could get hold of it without stealing—but if we didn't get out of Phoenix pretty quick, it looked as though that time wasn't far ahead.

The next morning each hour dragged like a week, because there was nothing we could do but sit around Larsen's restaurant and wait for a phone call from the lawyer. I'd have forgotten all about the doctor if Mr. Larsen hadn't reminded me that it was a week since I'd been to see him, and that I'd better get a report sent off before we left town. I did, and it cost two dollars.

It was after ten o'clock when the call came. Mr. Larsen answered the phone and said the lawyer wanted to talk to me. His voice sounded as if he were an old gentleman, and a kindly one. He said he had been out to talk to Joe, and though there was no doubt advantage was being taken of us, the best he had been able to do was to get the bill reduced to thirty-five dollars, but that included getting the engine started and running. When I asked him what we owed him he said there would be no charge, that he had done it as a favor to Mr. Larsen.

When we got out to the garage Joe had Shiftless chained to the back of his truck, and was as pleasant as if we'd never had a bit of trouble. "With all them new bearin's and bushin's and piston rings, she's likely to pull a mite stiff till the oil gets worked in good around 'em," he told Lonnie. "Might take two-three turns around the block 'fore she gets limbered up and runnin' good, but that's all right with me. I won't make you no charge for my time, nor for the gas it takes neither. Just hold her in neutral till I get you out on a straightaway and to rollin' good, then leave her into high gradual, and fish around a mite with the spark. If she don't take right holt and go to firing in high, kick her into low. That'll fetch her 'round in a hurry."

I climbed in beside Lonnie, and he was as excited as a little boy at a carnival when Joe pulled us out of the garage. We started at a crawl, and every couple of feet Lonnie turned the wheel a little to one side or the other, but I couldn't see that it made any difference. Shiftless seemed to have her own ideas about where she wanted to go, and wandered a little from side to side, like a cow following a crooked path through a pasture. And the more Joe picked up speed, the more Shiftless wandered.

When Lonnie let the clutch pedal up Shiftless sort of hunkered for a fraction of a second—like a horse getting set for a buck jump. Then I thought she was going to sunfish instead. Her hind end slewed around, and from under the floorboards there was a shriek that sounded as if we'd run over a hog. Shiftless bucked and switched her tail for a few lengths, then began bouncing, sort of like a little girl skipping down a sidewalk. After a hundred yards or so the skipping smoothed out, and I could tell that the engine was turning over, but no matter how much Lonnie jiggled the spark and gas levers Shiftless never fired a shot.

After Joe had pulled us around the block a couple of times, he stopped his truck, came back, took the engine hood off, and fiddled with the ignition wires a minute or two. Then he looked up at me and said, "Now wouldn't that frost your eyeballs? This magneto has went deader'n a dodo. But that won't make no difference to you. It'll build right up again soon's you've drove it a few miles. All you need is a hot-shot battery to get it started off with, and I've got an old one I'd leave you have for fifty cents."

The hot-shot battery was all we needed to get the engine started. As soon as Joe wired it up, he pulled us again, and Lonnie had barely let the clutch pedal up before the engine backfired a couple of times and started with a roar. Old Shiftless acted as happy as I felt, and put on a shimmy dance that nearly rattled my teeth loose. The minute the engine started Joe stopped his truck and came back again. He didn't pay any attention to Lonnie, but above the roaring, rattling, and backfiring, he shouted to me, "There she is—runnin' like a top. Thirty-five fifty and she's yours."

Lonnie couldn't get the chain unhitched fast enough to suit him, and by the time I'd paid Joe he was back behind the wheel. He didn't wait for Joe to pull his truck out of the way, but backed Shiftless a few yards, reversed, and went around the old truck as if he'd been heading for a fire. As far as I could tell, the engine didn't have any knocks in it, but it would have been hard to hear a blacksmith's hammering above the rattle of the doors and fenders. Joe had folded the engine hood when he took it off, and had tossed it onto the back seat. The sides were slapping together like cymbals in a jazz band, and every few seconds the exhaust would backfire as though a sheriff's posse were after us.

Lonnie's face was beaming, and above the noise he yelled, "Got to expect a little backfirin' till she gets warmed up! Listen to that engine, buddy! Ain't she sweet! I'll just take her a turn down the road till I get used to the feel of her."

Warming up didn't do much for the backfiring. By the time Lonnie had driven a quarter of a mile a wisp of steam was shooting out of the radiator cap, and by the time he'd gone a half mile anybody might have thought we were driving Old Faithful geyser, but Shiftless was backfiring as much as ever. Lonnie slowed to ten miles an hour, and we went down the street to Larsen's, sounding as if we were celebrating the Fourth of July.

I don't know how we'd have got out of Phoenix without the

Larsens, and I hate to think of what might have happened to us afterwards. As soon as we drew up in front of the restaurant Mr. Larsen came out to meet us. He didn't say anything about the geyser that was shooting up from Shiftless's radiator, or the firecrackers that were shooting out of her exhaust pipe. He leaned over the engine, put an ear down toward it, and told Lonnie he'd done a fine job on the bearings. "Bound to heat up until they get worn in a bit," he said. "Want to borrow my hose to set a trickle of water running through the radiator?" As he said it he reached down and moved the spark rod back to the retarded position. The backfiring stopped, and the exhaust sounded like the feet of a galloping pony.

"Nice job! Nice job," Mr. Larsen said as he listened to it. "Hitting on all four." While he listened he turned the adjustment screws on the carburetor a trifle, and the sound of the exhaust changed to the steady four-beat rhythm of a trot. "This needle point is in good shape," he told Lonnie. "Honed it, didn't you?"

I'd never heard Lonnie say "sir" to anyone, and I had to be careful not to grin when he said, "Yes, sir, Mr. Larsen, I honed it right to a fine point like you told me, and I leveled them distributor points with a platinum file. If you'd tell me where your hose is at I'd go get it."

When Lonnie had started away for the hose Mr. Larsen winked at me and said, "You'll be all right. He'll take care of it, and he learns quick. He hasn't wanted you to know it, but he's been pestering me with questions all week. Don't let him advance the spark more than half an inch when you crank it. The timing gears are set a bit forward, and it might kick your head off. You'll get a spark knock on the hills, but don't let that worry you. It won't hurt anything. Decided yet where you're going to head for?"

"Lonnie's been talking about going east toward Globe," I told him.

"That's all right," he said, "but go much farther east and you'll run into Indian Reservation. You wouldn't do any good there, and if you turn north toward Flagstaff you'll run into mountain country. Thought about following the Gila? The river has some pretty good ranches along it, and the weather's warmer down that way if you want to get lots of sun on you."

"Does the railroad follow the Gila?" I asked.

"Most of the way," he said, "and there are towns all along it, so you would have no trouble finding a doctor and sending in your report every week. Here comes Lonnie. I'd let him idle the engine and run water through the radiator an hour before I started out if I were you, and I'd take along some extra. A tight Ford is apt to boil away a lot of water in the desert."

It was well after noon before we got away from the Larsens, and anyone might have thought we were their own sons. Mr. Larsen went all over the engine with Lonnie, answering questions and showing him how to adjust the carburetor and the condenser points and the distributor. Then he helped him fix a rack on one of the running boards, and load it with our groceries and extra gas and water. While Mr. Larsen worked with Lonnie I did what I could to help Mrs. Larsen with the few customers they had. I waited on the counter while she did the cooking and dished up the orders, but in between she was scurrying around like a squirrel getting ready for winter, packing an orange crate with things for us to take along.

She filled one side of the crate solid with food—four big loaves of gluten bread, nearly half a baked ham that she said was for Lonnie, a quart jar of stewed chicken for me, coffee, condensed milk, onions, potatoes, carrots, and half a dozen bunches of celery. In the other side of the crate she had packed a frying pan, coffee pot, dishpan, butcher knife, a couple of cups, plates, knives, forks, and spoons of different sizes. Then she gave me a black iron pot—about ten inches across and five inches high—with a heavy iron lid that had an inch-high rim. Except for a pint jar in the center, the pot was packed tight with dish towels.

"That's your sour dough," Mrs. Larsen told me as she showed me the jar. "You won't find many ranch cooks who can make you gluten bread that's fit to eat, but there's no reason you can't make it for yourself. That recipe of your mother's is fine —only that it needs a few caraway seeds to make the bread tasty—and you'll have to use sour dough in place of store yeast, because you can't count on finding yeast at a ranch cookhouse."

Every time I'd come back with dirty dishes Mrs. Larsen would catch me and tell me things I'd need to know—how I'd have to keep the sour dough jar not too warm and not too cool, and how to add a bit of grated raw potato, flour, and warm water each time I used any, so as to keep the starter alive and fermenting. Then she explained how to mix my dough in the dishpan and bake it in the Dutch-oven pot—clearing a place for it at the center of a burned-down campfire, filling the lid with live coals, then heaping others around the sides, and covering the whole thing with sod or hot ashes. She said we could roast chickens in it the same way, or use it for making stews.

When we pulled away from the restaurant the Larsens were standing on the sidewalk, waving to us, and they hadn't let me pay them a penny for anything.

We stopped only a few minutes at the hotel—just long enough for me to pay what was due on our room, and to carry out our bedrolls and outfits. I was going to throw away the bucket of clay I'd been playing with the week I was laid up, and the sticks and wires I'd used for armatures, but there wasn't any place I could throw them easily, so I just set them in the back end of Shiftless along with the rest of our stuff.

8

Back Country

IT was midafternoon on my twentieth birthday when we pulled away from the hotel in Phoenix, and I think Lonnie was the proudest man in Arizona. Shiftless's engine started up with a roar when he pulled the throttle open, and she bucked a little when he let the pedal back and threw her into high, but once we were rolling she perked along as steady as a trotting horse. We were making about fifteen miles an hour as we headed for the outskirts to pick up the eastbound highway, and Lonnie was watching the road and twisting the wheel back and forth as if we'd been making fifty-five.

"What did I tell you, buddy?" he called out above the rattle of the fenders and the squeaking of the springs. "Didn't I tell you I'd fix her up good as new? Listen to the sound of that motor, would you! Tickin' like a five-dollar watch! But I ain't goin' to press her none—not while her guts are brand new. Don't aim to go no further'n Superior tonight. From there we'll get out into the back country and find us a coupla good jobs."

"We'd better," I told him. "I've only got twenty-four twenty left in my pocket." There wasn't any sense in telling him about the fifty in the cuff of my Levi's.

"Jeepers!" Lonnie shouted. "You must have did better than you told me in the horse falls, buddy! I reckoned you'd be dang near dead broke by now—what with all the little extry parts we had to buy and all—but shucks, with twenty-four twenty and all the grub we've got, we're set for the winter, even if we don't find no jobs. Old Shiftless, she won't cost us nothin' from now on—only two-bits for gas now and again. Betcha she'll make twenty-five miles or more on a gallon."

"She'd better, if we don't get jobs pretty soon," I told him. "Don't forget, I have to go to a doctor every week, and they seem to have a standard price of two dollars."

Lonnie took one hand off the wheel long enough to reach over and slap me on the shoulder. "Look, buddy," he told me, "you don't have to worry none about the dough. Like I told you, I'll toss my pay checks into the pot—the whole works, 'ceptin' for a buck or two for makin's and the likes of that—till I've paid you back every dime you've spent up to now. Way I look at it, I got more need for an automobile than what you have, so I'll just buy you out and take Shiftless off'n your hands. That way I could furnish the car and you could furnish the gas, and it would be a fifty-fifty deal. 'Course we'd split whatever little it'll cost us for grub when we ain't workin' steady."

"There's no need of that," I told him. "If you pay half that's plenty, and when we're done with it you can have it. I'm going back to Colorado in the spring, and I wouldn't have any use for an automobile there, even if I knew how to drive one."

"It's a deal, buddy!" Lonnie shouted, "It's a deal!" He drove on for a quarter of a mile or so, then without taking his eyes off the road he asked, "Say, buddy, how much do I have to kick in 'fore we put the papers in partnership?"

"Five bucks," I said. "Wasn't that what I told you when we bought her?"

"Uh-huh, I know," he said, "but I wasn't sure you'd remember. You understand, buddy, I ain't talkin' about buying in halvers for five bucks. It's just . . . Well . . . It's just that I'd be mighty proud to have my name wrote down on the records as half owner of an automobile—a good one, the likes of what Shiftless is now we got her fixed up."

"That's all right," I said. "I'll go and have your name registered along with mine whenever you pay the first five."

We were already out of town, and Lonnie was sort of herding Shiftless along a gravel road. Sometimes she'd wander over to the right side, and sometimes over to the left, and Lonnie would spin the wheel just in time to keep her from wandering off onto the desert. He got so excited he didn't stop her in time when I told him I'd have his name registered with mine. He threw an arm around my neck, hauled my head onto his shoulder, and told me, "You're a buddy! That's what you are! And look, buddy, I'll never leave you down—not while there's an inch o' skin left on these hands."

"That won't be long," I yelled, "unless you watch where you're going."

The instant Shiftless had caught Lonnie off guard she'd headed for the desert, and in pulling away from him my arm happened to hit the throttle lever and push it wide open. Shiftless let out a roar, plunged down over a low bank at the side of the road, and took off, bouncing and swaying, toward a big bunch of greasewood and cactus. Lonnie had all he could do to fight the wheel and keep us out of the cactus, and before he could get a hand free to pull the throttle back up we were a hundred yards from the road—right in the middle of a lake of loose sand six or seven inches deep. It had happened so fast that Lonnie never thought about his feet until he'd pulled the throttle up. Then he hit the brake pedal so hard he nearly drove it through the floor boards. For a second I thought I was in the horse falls again, and that Shiftless was going to somersault, but she didn't. She just slewed around to one side and stopped dead—engine and all.

Lonnie started to yell at me, then caught himself. "Don't never touch the throttle when I'm drivin'," he told me in sort of a shaky voice. "If I hadn't caught aholt of the wheel right when I did, we could of been in bad trouble."

"Well, don't grab me around the neck again when you're driving," I told him. "And it looks to me as if we're already in bad trouble."

"No, we ain't," he said, "but we're lucky that nothing got busted. Go give the crank a spin 'fore we settle too deep into this daggone sand."

The crank wouldn't spin. All I could do was to engage it near the bottom of the turn and jerk it up. But nothing happened. After I'd jerked it a dozen times or more, Lonnie climbed out and opened the hood. "Flooded!" he told me. "There's gas leakin' out the top of the carburetor. Maybe I shouldn't ought to have goosed her. Turn her over a few more times and it'll dreen away."

The engine was so tight that I nearly had to lift Shiftless off her front wheels every time I yanked the crank handle up, and it took fifteen or twenty more yanks before the engine backfired and started. When I climbed back in beside Lonnie I was so winded I couldn't say a word. He retarded the spark and fiddled around with the throttle till the engine stopped backfiring, then let the in-gear lever down and stepped on the low-speed pedal. We didn't move, but I could feel Shiftless's hind end swaying a bit, as if she were a horse switching at flies.

Lonnie held the low pedal down hard and opened the throttle little by little, but nothing happened except that Shiftless seemed to be hunkering down on her haunches. Lonnie put her back into neutral, and we both got out to see what the trouble was. Shiftless had dug her hind wheels in clear to the hubcaps and looked as if she were getting ready to sit down. "Well," Lonnie said, "we got to dig her out, that's all. Wish't we'd remembered to bring along a shovel. What have we got to dig with?"

"You can use the dishpan," I told him, "and I'll use the iron pot. Will we have to dig all the way to the edge of this sand pit?"

"Naw," he said, "just a coupla feet in front of each tire—

just enough so's't the hind wheels can get a holt on the ground."

We scooped out a trough between the wheels, and for six or seven feet ahead of the front ones, then Lonnie climbed in and gave her the gun. Shiftless slithered and switch-tailed till she came to the end of the troughs, then bucked on for a few feet and dug her heels in again.

We tried the scooping four or five times more, but it always worked the same way. Then Lonnie decided it would be better if we cut brush and made a corduroy road for the wheels to run on. It did work better, but it was slow going because Lonnie had to stop every two lengths while I moved the road ahead. It was after sunset before we got Shiftless out of the deep sand, and by that time she was boiling so hard she looked like a locomotive blowing off steam. But we were on our way. We'd made nearly six miles out of Phoenix, so I thought it was best for us to make camp right where we were.

It's amazing how hungry scooping sand will make people, and camping out always seems to sort of whet their appetites. That night Lonnie fried himself a couple of big slices of ham, two potatoes, and three eggs. And I warmed up the whole quart of stewed chicken Mrs. Larsen had put up for me. I didn't plan to eat more than half of it for supper, and to save the rest for breakfast, but Lonnie and I got talking as we ate, and before I realized it I was scraping the last of the gravy out of the pot. It certainly made gluten bread taste a lot better than just eating it dry.

The next day being Sunday Lonnie didn't think we should start out too early, and it was nearly ten o'clock before I could get him awake enough to roll out of his blankets. By that time we were both hungrier than bears, so Lonnie fixed himself the same breakfast that he'd had for supper. Of course, I couldn't eat ham or potatoes, so I just boiled myself three eggs and finished up the first loaf of gluten bread.

Shiftless was a little balky about starting, but not bad, and by noon we were on the road for Superior again. I think we'd have made the whole sixty-five miles before dark if it hadn't been for Shiftless's boiling. She started in before we'd covered more than three miles, and from there on the day was sort of off-again, on-again. Even though it was the middle of December the desert was as hot as summer. Every two miles we'd have to stop, drain out some of the boiling water, add fresh from the can we'd brought along, and wait for Shiftless to cool down. And every time we had to start her again the hot-shot battery was a little weaker, and it took more yanking on the crank handle before we'd get a spark strong enough to explode the gas. Worse still, the hotter Shiftless got, the harder I had to jerk the crank to turn the engine over, and the more she smoked when we had her going.

It was nearly dark when we pulled into Mesa, only about twenty miles from Phoenix, and anyone might have thought we were driving a freight engine instead of an automobile. The cloud of blue smoke pouring out of the exhaust pipe was just about equal to the cloud of white steam pouring out of the radiator. We'd long since stopped bothering to put the cap on when we refilled, we were entirely out of water, and the new parts had swelled enough from the heat that Lonnie was having to drive with the low-speed pedal held down. We'd just made it as far as the garage when Shiftless coughed a time or two and stopped. Even then she smelled like a red-hot stove.

"Out of oil and water?" the garageman asked as he came out to see what we wanted.

Lonnie tried to tell him we had plenty of oil and were only out of water because all the engine parts were new, but the man wouldn't believe him—and he was right. When he opened the petcock at the bottom of the engine only a few drops of thick black oil dribbled out. In that twenty miles we'd only burned two gallons of gasoline, but we'd burned nearly three quarts of oil, and it was twenty cents a quart. The garageman showed us where it had seeped up around the base of the spark plugs, and he said we were pumping it up the scored cylinder walls like water out of a well. The only thing we could do was to wait a couple of hours for Shiftless to cool down, buy

a couple of gallons of extra oil to take along, then camp as soon
as we were out of town.

While I was cooking supper Lonnie told me he thought it
would be better for Shiftless if we turned north and got away
from the deserts until her new parts had worn in a little more.
He said the best cattle ranches in the state were north of Globe,
and that if we held to the northeast it would bring us right
in among the biggest of them. Anything sounded good to me
that might lead to jobs before we went broke, but I told him
there would be no more lying around camp until noon, that
I wanted to be on the road by daylight, so as to cover as many
miles as we could in the cool of the morning.

I had to bully Lonnie a little, but we'd had breakfast and
were on the road at the crack of dawn. For the first twenty
miles we drove almost straight east, and Shiftless behaved
fairly well. Then, soon after she started boiling, we came to a
Y where the roads forked—one to the northeast toward the
mountains, and the other southeast across the desert. Lonnie
hadn't been more than half awake since I rolled him out that
morning, but he perked right up as soon as he'd swung Shiftless onto the road toward the northeast. "Don't you worry no
more about Shiftless boilin', buddy," he told me. "Soon as ever
we get into them mountains she'll cool right down, and with all
them new parts she's got in her she'll pull like a team o' mules."

She did—like the most headstrong and balky team that ever
lived—and within ten miles that road turned out to be one that
had been built only for mules. As soon as we got into the mountains it twisted like a snake in agony, both sideways and up and
down. On the downgrades Shiftless would take off like a mule
headed for the barn, weaving from side to side and picking up
speed at every length. The only way Lonnie could hold her
back enough to keep her on the road was by pulling up the
hand brake and bracing himself against the foot-brake pedal.
If the upgrades weren't too steep, we could grind them out
at low speed, then stop at the top of the hill while Shiftless
blew off enough steam that I could get close to the radiator

and refill it.

By afternoon we'd worked out a system for the steeper hills. Lonnie would stop on the downgrade, a hundred yards or so before we reached the bottom of a gulch. Then I'd get out and run ahead till I was about halfway up the next hill. After I'd had time to catch my breath he'd turn Shiftless loose, come racing down to the bottom with her pitching and weaving, then give her the gun for the climb. By the time he reached me he'd have slowed to three or four miles an hour—with his foot braced against the low pedal and the throttle wide open. Then, with me pushing from the back, we could make it to the top before we came to a dead stop.

By late afternoon it was noticeable that our new engine parts were beginning to get worn in a little. Shiftless began pulling better on every hill, and she didn't boil so badly when we reached the top.

Darkness was just beginning to settle when we came to a canyon that looked impossible to me. The road leading down into it twisted like a corkscrew, and on the far side it seemed to rise at a forty-five degree angle until it curved out of sight around a mountain shoulder. Worse still, we'd worn out our hand brake, were out of water, and the only person we'd seen since morning was a woman in a little hamlet eight or ten miles back. "Let's camp right here and turn back in the morning," I told Lonnie. "If we'd ever make it to the bottom we'd never get up the far side, and if we should have an accident nobody would find us for a month of Sundays."

Lonnie didn't like the idea at all. "Jeepers Creepers, buddy," he told me, "there ain't no sense turnin' back now! Them big cattle ranches I told you 'bout is just the other side of these hills. We're almost to 'em. Look, buddy! The way old Shiftless pulled that last hill she'll go up that little one yonder on the fly. If you're scairt why don't you get out and walk? I can put her through there as easy as pie."

I was scared, but I didn't like to admit it, so I said, "All right, but you stop halfway down. Then I'll go ahead to give you a push up the far side. You'll never make it without."

Lonnie didn't stop halfway down. Shiftless acted as if she'd taken the bit in her teeth and was headed for home. With one foot on the brake pedal and the other on the reverse, Lonnie could no more hold her back than he could have held Niagara Falls. How he ever managed to hold her in the roadway is a miracle. From the time we plunged over the brink until we reached the bottom of the canyon there was never a second when her hind wheels followed the front ones. She switch-tailed from side to side, flinging rocks down into the canyon at our left and sideswiping the cut bank at our right. I don't believe there was ever a moment when she had all four wheels on the ground.

All I could do was to hang on, but Lonnie rode Shiftless out as if she'd been a bucking bronco. Just as we reached the bottom of the canyon he yanked the throttle wide open and sent her tearing up the far side. For the first hundred yards or so she raced upward as though she still had the bit in her teeth, then as we rounded the first curve, high on the cliff side, the engine began knocking and she slowed her pace. Without touching the wide-open throttle Lonnie jammed the low-speed pedal to the floor boards. For a fraction of a second Shiftless surged ahead, then stopped as though she'd seen something that frightened her, and began rolling backwards, gaining speed at every turn of the wheels.

Lonnie braced his back against the seat and threw his full weight onto the low-speed pedal, but Shiftless's only answer was an angry roar from her motor. Desperately Lonnie grabbed for the useless hand brake and stamped the foot brake to the floor, but Shiftless paid no more attention to him than if he'd been a fly on her windshield. She seemed to have decided it was time she took matters into her own hands—and maybe it was just as well that she did.

Lonnie was so busy fighting the useless control pedals that he never once turned his head to see where we were going. I did. And for a few seconds I thought it would depend on the lives we'd led. The road we were careening down backwards was no more than a pair of rough wheel ruts, curving around the shoulder of a canyon wall. On the outside of the curve there was a sheer drop-off of thirty feet or more. On the inside the cliff rose straight up, with a rubble of broken stone at its base.

As if Shiftless were human and could see where she was going, she followed the wheel ruts around the curve for a hundred feet or more, bouncing and pitching wildly. Then, at the only spot where the rubble heap was wide enough to have held her, she leaped out of the ruts, backed onto it, and came to a neck-cracking stop—her engine still roaring defiantly.

For a few seconds both Lonnie and I were too numb to think or move. Then he reached for the ignition switch, as if in a dream, and said, "Jeepers Creepers, buddy, we musta sheared off the half-moon key."

The whole thing had happened so fast that neither of us had time to become frightened—only numbed. But when Lonnie spoke, it broke the tension and our nerves let go. For two or three minutes we just sat there, shaking as if we had chills and fever. As soon as I could speak without my voice quavering I asked, "What's the half-moon key?"

"The key that wedges the drive shaft into the main driving gear," he told me. "Shear it off—when your hand brake's petered out the likes of ours—and you ain't got no more control over a Ford than over a bicycle that's throwed its chain, 'cause the foot brake is on the shaft."

"Well, I guess we're licked," I told him. "It would cost more than old Shiftless is worth to have her hauled to a garage from way out here."

"Aw, Jeepers, buddy," Lonnie wailed, "you're all the time runnin' Shiftless down. It wasn't no fault of hers. She only done it 'cause we fixed the engine up too good—made it too stout for that little bitty key. It won't cost next to nothin' to fix her up good as new again. Them keys only costs a nickel apiece. Tell you what we'll do, buddy; you make camp and I'll hike on back and get one."

It was already growing dark, so I told Lonnie there was no

use in starting out for the key till morning. Then we got out and looked Shiftless over to see how much damage she'd done herself when she backed up onto the rubble heap. It didn't amount to much of anything. The gasoline tank was battered in but not broken through, one fender was crumpled, the tail-light was smashed, and there were three or four big dents in the body, but the axle and wheels were undamaged.

The only place to make camp was right there in the roadway, but we weren't much worried about the traffic, so we built our fire between the wheel ruts, ate our supper, and spread our bedrolls. I'd pushed Shiftless up so many hills that I was bushed; I couldn't wash the dishes because all the water we had was in the radiator, and it had turned cold at sundown, so we rolled in between the blankets as soon as we'd eaten. As always, Lonnie was in first, for he never bothered to take off anything but his hat, boots, and britches. He was already snoring by the time I'd crawled into my roll and pulled the tarpaulin up over me.

The next thing I knew I was awakened, half frozen and sure I'd heard some strange sound. The night was coal-black and bitter cold, but I threw the tarp back and sat up to listen. From the direction of the rubble heap where Shiftless was perched I heard the intermittent sound of rocks being grated against each other. There could be no doubt that something was prowling around on the rubble—something big and heavy. Suddenly there was the ring of tin against stone. That sound could have been made only by our dishpan. I was sure that some large wild animal, probably a bear, had smelled our food supply and was into it—and if we lost that we were really licked. I didn't have nerve enough to launch an attack in the blackness, so I felt quietly around until I'd found a rock the size of a baseball, yelled, "*Get out of there!*" and heaved it.

Lonnie's howl and the sound of broken glass came back before the last word was out of my mouth.

"Jeepers Creepers, buddy! What got into you?" he shouted from the blackness. "You've went and busted the windshield, and you dang near brained me!"

"What in the world are you doing out there?" I shouted back.

"Dreenin' the radiator," he hollered as if I were a mile away. "What else would I be doin'? Leave old Shiftless freeze up solid on a night the likes of this and she'd be ruint. It would bust the engine block, and then where'd we be at?"

It seemed to me that might be the best thing that could happen to me. It would be as easy to walk and carry my outfit as to push Shiftless up every hill—and a lot cheaper—but it would only have hurt Lonnie's feelings to tell him so, and he already felt bad enough about my having broken the windshield. I just pulled the tarp up over me, and was asleep before he came back to bed.

The next morning was freezing cold, but I rousted Lonnie out as soon as I had the fire built and breakfast on to cook. By half an hour after sunup he'd shown me what I'd have to do while he was gone, and had started back to get a half-moon key—a dollar in his pocket, a loaf of gluten bread under one arm, and two cans of salmon under the other.

I didn't expect to see Lonnie again for a couple of days. It was nearly forty miles back to Mesa, and since leaving there we hadn't passed any place where he might get a half-moon key. The job he'd left me was a big one, but there was no need to hurry on it. He'd said I'd have to jack Shiftless up, block her on stones, take the rear axle off, and the differential housing apart. That was the only way we could get the broken key out and put the new one in.

I didn't have to jack Shiftless up, just wedge big rocks under her frame, right where she was perched, then work others out from under her hind wheels until they were hanging free. But the taking apart was tough. The only tools we had were the set wrench that had come with her, an old monkey wrench that slipped open if I put much strain on it, a battered old carpenter's hammer, and a pair of pliers. Every bolt was rusted solidly into place, and no one of them took me less than an hour before I was able to fight it loose. It was nearly sundown, and I was still fighting the last bolt, when I heard a clattering of stones on the far side of the canyon. Again I thought it must be a bear, grabbed the hammer in one hand, the monkey wrench in the other, and wriggled out from under Shiftless.

It wasn't a bear. It was Lonnie. He was riding a horse, without saddle or bridle, down the steep roadway at a pounding trot. As he crossed the bottom of the canyon and started upward, still at a trot, he shouted, "I got it, buddy! I got it! Had to go clean in to Mesa!"

"Where did you get that horse?" I shouted back, "and how did you make it so fast?"

"Borrowed him! Borrowed three-four of 'em," Lonnie told me as he rode up and slid to the ground. "Jeepers, wish't I'd thought to take along my saddle! My behind's dang near wore to hamburger."

I could only take Lonnie's word for his own condition, but it was easy to see that the horse was nearly worn to hamburger. He stood with his head hanging to the ground and his sides heaving. Lonnie wouldn't go into much detail, but admitted he'd swiped a horse at the first ranch he came to, and had traded off whenever he had a chance. When I told him he was going to get us into bad trouble, he only laughed and told me, "Shucks, buddy, I ain't stole nothin'. Them nags all headed for home again as quick as ever they could catch their breath."

As if the horse he'd ridden into camp had understood him, he turned and plodded off down the road.

It took us only a couple of hours the next morning to put old Shiftless back together, but it took us two more days to cover the thirty miles to Roosevelt. Each hill was steeper than the one before it, Shiftless boiled from morning till night, the hot-shot battery went completely dead, and the only way we could get the engine started in the mornings was by camping at the top of a hill, so we could get coasting fast before we threw it into gear.

Before we reached Roosevelt we'd eaten everything we had

except cabbage, canned salmon, and gluten flour, and we'd have run out of gas and oil if a rancher hadn't sold us some. That's the most we got out of any cattleman we went to see. The rest of them just shook their heads and told us to come back and see them in the spring. We decided that the best thing we could do was to turn southeast and get down to Globe, where I could see a doctor and we could pick up some more grub.

It took us three more days to get as far as Globe. We followed every wagon track that led off the road, so as to be sure we wouldn't miss a ranch where we might find jobs, but all the good it did was that Lonnie managed to mooch a few free meals. I spent most of one night trying to make gluten bread, but I guess I'd let my sour dough get too cold some night when we'd been in the mountains. It was just milky slop when I poured it into the flour, and it turned out to be as dead as our hot-shot battery. The bread baked all right in the Dutch oven, but it came out like the stuff the cook in Tucson made for me. The only way I could eat it was by holding a chunk in my mouth until it softened up enough to chew, or by soaking it in the juice left at the bottom of a can of salmon. I tried boiling some of it with cabbage, but it went all to mush and spoiled the taste of the cabbage.

9

Christmas Eve

THE doctor at Globe charged me two dollars and a half, and when I asked him why it was so much he said the extra fifty cents was for filling out the card. Everything was higher in Globe than it had been in Phoenix. They were charging forty-five cents for meals in the restaurants, gasoline was eighteen cents a gallon, and oil two bits a quart.

When I'd bought a whole case of salmon, fifty pounds of cabbage, and ten pounds of peanuts in Phoenix, I'd thought I had enough grub to last me for a month. But with the two of us eating out of it during most of the eight days we were up in the Salt River country we were down to less than half a case of salmon and, of course, most of the gluten flour. Then too, we'd decided to take Mr. Larsen's advice about following the Gila River eastward. To do that we'd have at least two days of driving through the San Carlos Indian Reservation where there'd be no chance of finding jobs. There was nothing to do except to lay in a supply of groceries at Globe, regardless of how high the prices were. While Lonnie was at the restaurant and I was waiting for the doctor to examine my specimen, I made out a list of the things we'd get. And I was careful to put on it plenty of cheap things Lonnie could eat—a side of bacon, ten pounds of dry beans, potatoes, and white flour for pancakes, and I remembered to put down dry yeast and baking powder. Even by getting the cheapest things I could think of, one orange crate of groceries cost over six dollars.

It was getting along toward dark by the time we'd bought the groceries. There were only two days left till Christmas. I got to thinking about it while we were stowing the stuff along Shiftless's running board, and for a few minutes I thought it would be nice if I just went over to the dime store and picked up a few little things I could send the folks back home—nothing expensive, but just any little things to let them know I remembered them at Christmas. Then I had to change my mind. In the first place it would look pretty chintzy for me to be sending dime store presents—after all the stuff I'd written Mother about having a fine job and plenty of money. Then too, the postage would probably cost as much as the presents, and they wouldn't get there anyway till long after Christmas, and Shiftless's gas tank was nearly empty, and I was already down to $12.60.

But I couldn't just let Christmas go by without doing anything for anybody, so I gave Lonnie three dollars and told him to go and get the gas tank filled and two quarts of oil put in the crankcase, and to buy another hot-shot battery and see that we had plenty of air in the tires. Then I told him I had to go see a fellow about a dog, and I'd meet him on that same corner in twenty minutes.

As soon as Lonnie was out of sight I beat it for a clothing store where I'd seen some pretty cheap prices in the window. The stuff they had was even cheaper than the prices, but I got Lonnie a fairly decent pair of jeans and a blue shirt for $1.89. While we'd been fixing Shiftless he'd got so much grease on the ones he had that he looked more like a coal miner than a cowhand, and I was afraid that might hurt our chances of getting jobs—so I was really doing more for myself than I was for Lonnie. When he came past the corner where I was waiting,

I tossed the bundle on the back seat and jumped on the running board so he wouldn't have to come to a full stop. We only drove two or three miles out of Globe, then made camp for the night before crossing the line into the Indian reservation.

That night we went on a cooking spree. We built two campfires, and while Lonnie boiled beans and bacon in the dishpan I baked him a batch of biscuits in the Dutch oven, mixed up what I thought was enough gluten dough to make a good-sized loaf, covered it with a dish towel, and set it near the fire to rise. Lonnie was going to have filled the dishpan half full of beans, but I knew better than that, because I'd done some baching and found out how much they'd swell. My trouble was that I'd never tried to make any raised bread—except the batch with the dead sour dough.

I'd learned to bake biscuits when I was water boy and cook's helper on the Y-B ranch, but I never had better luck than I did with that first batch I baked in the Dutch oven. I'd been too tight to buy any butter with our groceries, but fried some bacon so Lonnie could dip them in the hot fat. I watched him dip two or three biscuits and stow them away, then decided that I might as well die of diabetes as starvation, so I dipped one myself. It was awfully good, and before we stopped we'd eaten every last biscuit. While we were doing it my bread dough went wild. When I first thought to look, it was the size of a basketball, and I didn't know what I should do to stop it from swelling any more, so I got out Mother's recipe and read it over again. It said, "Let rise, knead, let rise again, and bake in moderately hot oven."

I couldn't knead the bread in the dishpan—Lonnie had it full of beans—and the only boards we had were those in the orange crates, but they were rough and covered with splinters. The only smooth thing I could find was the engine hood, so I washed it off, sprinkled on a little flour as soon as it was dry, and kneaded the bread there. It worked to beat the band. So did the bread. As soon as I set it back by the fire for its second rising it started growing. I let it go till it was nearly the size of a basketball again, then greased the inside of the Dutch oven, put the dough in, and crowded it down enough so I could get the lid on.

Everything seemed to be going all right till I filled the lid with hot coals. It lifted a bit and began to teeter, so I scooped up handfuls of sand and put it on top of the coals to hold the lid down. That seemed to do the trick all right, so I heaped up more coals around the sides of the pot and covered the whole works over with sand. Anyone might have thought it was a live dog I had buried in the pile of sand. It squeaked and groaned and wiggled, and looked as if the dog were trying to stick his head out. Of course, we knew the dough was still rising, but there was nothing we could do about it, so we just sat there till after midnight—waiting for the bread to get baked all the way through, and talking about Christmas coming in a couple of days, and about its going to be easy to find jobs as soon as we got down to the Gila valley.

I've wished ever since that I could remember just how I made that gluten bread. Of course, it got a necklace of sand where the top pushed up out of the pot, but that whittled off easy enough, and it was the best gluten bread I ever tasted. I'm sure the bacon grease I used for shortening didn't have anything to do with it, or kneading it on the engine hood, or covering the coals with sand instead of sod, because I tried all those things a dozen times afterwards, but the bread never came out so good again.

The next morning I had Lonnie up and wide awake by seven o'clock, and I let him have only pancakes, three strips of bacon, and coffee for his breakfast. I told him I didn't want to be tight but it would have to be that way till we found jobs, that I was going to eat only one egg at a meal and make out the rest on gluten bread and peanuts—with a little cabbage for supper.

From where we camped that night it was about sixty miles across San Carlos Indian Reservation, and we'd planned to make the whole distance in a single day, because there'd be no ranches where we could stop to look for jobs. For the first three or four miles it looked as though we were going to make it. Then Shiftless went into a fit of shimmying. She'd always wandered more or less, but it had always been in sort of long sweeping curves, and Lonnie had become so used to the feel of her that he could usually keep the curves from being very wide. But as soon as we got onto the Indian reservation that morning she began wiggling her front wheels the way a polliwog wiggles his tail. If Lonnie tried to go more than five miles an hour she'd shake herself like a wet dog.

At first Lonnie thought he might have put too much air in the tires, so he let a little out, but that didn't help a bit. Then, because we had to drive so slow, the fan wouldn't suck air through the radiator, so Shiftless boiled like a teakettle on a forge. At our first three or four stops we drained out part of the boiling water and added fresh from the can we always filled whenever we reached a town or river. The only trouble was that we had to put in five times as much as we drained out. The rest had blown off in steam. And we'd already found out in Globe that we'd have a twenty-five-mile waterless drive before we reached the Gila River. It took us till midnight to make the twenty-five, and we'd used up every drop of water we had long before we got there.

The next day the boiling didn't bother us so much, because we were following the river and could get plenty of water to cool Shiftless down, but she wouldn't quit her shimmying. Even at that we thought we'd be able to make Fort Thomas for Christmas Eve, but we didn't do it. It was just turning dark when we left the reservation and passed the little flag station at Geronimo. Halfway between there and Fort Thomas one of our front tires whistled like wind around the eaves of a barn. By the time we were stopped, it was flatter than a dropped egg. Between the shimmying and the rough gravel of the road, the rubber of both front tires had been filed away till the canvas lining showed through.

I thought we were finished. Even with the change Lonnie

had brought back after he bought the gas I had less than eight dollars in my pocket, and I was sure a new tire would cost more than that. Lonnie got down on his hands and knees, lit matches, and felt all along the tread of the tire. "We ain't bad off!" he shouted after a minute or two. "We ain't bad off at all, buddy! It just blowed out a little hole no bigger'n a lead pencil. Jeepers Creepers! I wish't I'd remembered to bring along a vulcanizin' set and a boot! I could fix this old baby up so's't she'd run another thousand miles."

"How much would one cost?" I asked him.

"Well . . ." he said. "A good one would cost three, four bucks. But I could patch this little old hole up with a five-cent rubber plug and a ten-cent tube of rubber cement. And I could make a good enough boot by stickin' in a piece of old shoe sole. How far do you reckon it is from here to Fort Thomas?"

"According to the map it ought to be three or four miles," I told him.

"Gi'me two bits and go to gettin' supper ready," he told me. "I'll hoof it into town and be back by the time you get the grub cooked."

We drove Shiftless off the road, I gave Lonnie the quarter, and he was starting off down the road toward Fort Thomas when I remembered it was Christmas Eve. I wasn't a bit sure he'd be able to fix the tire when he got back, and it seemed to me that we'd probably have to spend Christmas Day right where we were. Then we'd have to decide which we'd sell first, our outfits or Shiftless. That was what made me call Lonnie back. I knew how much he'd hate to part with either, and if we were going broke anyway, we might as well go in style. When he got back to me I passed him two dollars and said, "Tomorrow's Christmas. You spend all of that for our dinner—a good fat chicken we can roast, and all the trimmings.'"

"Jeepers Creepers!" he shouted, grabbed the two dollars, and started away down the road at a trot.

I found some good dry greasewood for the fire, put a head

of cabbage on to boil, and a pot of water for coffee. There wasn't any sense in warming up what was left of Lonnie's beans and bacon until he came back, and I could bake him some biscuits while he was fixing the tire, so there was nothing for me to do but sit and wait for him. But just waiting was no good because I couldn't stop thinking, and there wasn't much comfort in thinking right then. Just to have something to kill time with I got the clay bucket and box of sticks and wires out of Shiftless. Then I sat down beside the fire and began twisting up a little armature for a horse.

As we'd come through the reservation I'd seen an old Indian pony standing out on the desert; three-legged, with his head hung nearly to the ground. I felt about the way that old pony looked, and before I realized what I was doing I found myself bending an armature for a horse standing just as he had been. The light from the greasewood fire was good, and I dug deep into the bucket to find some clay that wasn't dried out too much. It had just the right feel about it, and when I began working it onto the armature it slipped under my thumb like wet silk. I fished around in the box till I'd found most of the little tools I'd whittled in Phoenix, and began scraping and shaping the clay the way I wanted it. I didn't try to make a nice smooth job of it, but let the tools pull on the clay a bit, so as to make it rough like that old pony's hair. And I put a big hay-belly on him, and sprung knees, and a bone spavin below one hock.

I was so busy with the old pony that I didn't hear Lonnie when he came back. I didn't know he'd been gone more than a few minutes when, from right above my shoulder, he said, "Jeepers Creepers, buddy! That's the Injun pony we seen on that little hill this afternoon! Why didn't you tell me you could do that stuff?"

"What's the sense?" I said. "It wouldn't help us to find a job . . . nor to find tires for Shiftless. I only do it when I've got time to kill. I've whittled them out of wood since I was a little kid. How did you make out?"

"Well, I've did worse," he chuckled, and dropped two big fat hens down beside me. "And I got sweet potatas, and celery, and onions, and a pie. I had to snitch the vegetables off'n a sidewalk stand. The pie was four bits—it's mince."

"And by the looks of these hens you snitched them too," I said.

"Look, buddy, I had to," he told me. "I wasn't goin' to leave Christmas go by without getting you nothin'." As he spoke he fished into his hip pocket, brought out a real nice jackknife, and passed it toward me. "It ain't much," he said, "but it might do for whittlin' horses."

I knew that knife had cost at least a dollar, so before I reached for it I asked, "Did you swipe that too?"

"Buddy," he said, "you ought to know me better'n that. I wouldn't steal stuff! Not out of a store or nothin'. But chickens, that's different. A man's got to eat."

That time I put my arm around Lonnie's neck and told him he was my buddy, and I didn't say another word about his having swiped most of our Christmas dinner. While I was warming up his beans and putting the coffee on to boil he sat holding the little clay Indian pony, looking at it, and turning it over in his hands. "Could you make one of these here with a rider on it?" he asked.

"Sure," I told him, "but it wouldn't be much good. As soon as the clay dried, it would warp out of shape and crack. Without a rider I can cast one in plaster so it will last forever . . . or until it gets dropped, but it would be too tough a job to cast one with a rider. The hat brim and the reins wouldn't come out of the mold clean, and the least little bump would break them."

Lonnie was still looking at the little horse when I dished up his beans and poured the coffee. "How long does it take to cast one in plaster?" he asked.

"Oh, a couple of days in dry country like this," I said. "One to dry the mold and one to dry the casting. Why?"

"Nothin'," he said. "I was just thinkin'. Will this here one last over Christmas?"

"Sure," I told him, "if I keep a damp rag around it. It'll last as long as the clay's kept moist."

"Well, hadn't you best to wrap it up then 'fore we have our supper? You could use one of them dish towels. There's one of 'em ain't too dirty."

Before he'd touch a bite Lonnie got out the cleaner of our two dish towels, wet it at the water can, wrung it out, and wrapped the little clay horse as carefully as if it had been a sick bird. After he'd stowed it away in the grub box I tossed him the package with his shirt and overalls in it, and said, "There's something Santa Claus left while you were gone to town."

It's funny how happy you can be over just little things, and how quickly you can forget all about your troubles. Neither Lonnie nor I could sing worth a whoop, but we both knew a few of the old Christmas songs, mostly hymns we'd heard at Sunday School. With the moon hanging over the mountains beyond the river, and a coyote barking somewhere up the valley, we sat by our little fire and sang till we were sure it was past midnight. Then we shook hands, told each other "Merry Christmas," and turned in as if we didn't have a worry in the world.

10

Rice Pudd'n

CHRISTMAS morning I let Lonnie sleep late while I heated a dishpanful of water and washed my underwear, spare shirt, and jeans. I couldn't do much about Lonnie's washing. He was sleeping in his dirty shirt, and his old overalls were so full of grease that I couldn't have got them clean without boiling them in lye water. After I had my washing done and hung out on a creosote bush I washed our dishes and silverware, and scoured the frying pan and Dutch oven with sand. With Shiftless shimmying the way she was, we kicked up as much dust as a cavalry regiment, and most of it seemed to have settled in the orange crate we used as a pantry. And from cooking over greasewood campfires the frying pan, Dutch oven, and dishpan had grown a black shell as thick and hard as a turtle's.

After the dishes were done I started cleaning the hens Lonnie had swiped, but the job would have been easier if he'd just wrung their necks and brought them with their clothes on. In that way I could have rubbed clay into the feathers, smeared on a coat half an inch thick, and roasted them in the coals from a campfire. Then when we were ready to eat them all I'd have to do would be to whack them against a rock. The hard-baked shells would break like an old flourpot, taking the feathers off as clean as a whistle and leaving the meat hot and juicy. But I guess Lonnie had thought he could fool me about having swiped them. He'd yanked off about three-quarters of the feathers—just in handfuls—had torn the skin in half a dozen places, and had got sand ground into the torn parts.

Lonnie never would tell me where he swiped the hens, but it must have been off somebody's roost, and it must have been plenty dark in that hen house. He'd picked two fat ones all right, but it had been years since they'd been pullets. There were dry scales along their breastbones, and they were poochy —like geese—in the rear. That kind of a hen will roast fine in clay, if you give it three or four hours in a good deep bed of coals, but if you try to roast it in an ordinary oven it will usually come out tougher than bullhide. I was afraid ours would come out even worse if I tried to roast them in the Dutch oven, so I decided to cut them up, roll the pieces in white flour, brown them in grease, and stew them into a pot of fricassee.

I could hear Lonnie snoring when I picked off the last pin-feathers and washed the sand out of the torn places, but I'd barely picked up the butcher knife to cut the old hens into pieces when he wailed, "Aw, buddy, it's Christmas Day. You ain't about to make stew out of them chickens, are you? I spent near onto an hour huntin' fat ones like you told me, so's't we could roast 'em."

"Sure I'm going to roast 'em," I called back. "I was just getting ready to take their insides out. But if you want them stuffed you'd better shake out of that bedroll and fix our flat tire. I can't make stuffing without stale white bread and sage."

I don't believe Lonnie ever woke up or got up any faster in all the time I knew him. By the time I had the hens cleaned, he'd jacked up the wheel and was going at the flat tire like a coyote trying to dig a gopher out from under a rock. "Come gi'me a hand, buddy!" he hollered. "Don't reckon this here tire's been off in a month o' Sundays. It's froze to the rim like as if it was ceemented. Here, take this piece of broke spring and pry that side loose while I get the tire iron and screwdriver in over here."

It took us nearly half an hour to pry the tire off the rim, and when Lonnie took the inner tube out it looked like a patchwork quilt. There were already two rubber plugs in it, and six or seven glued-on patches. "Jeepers!" Lonnie said as he turned it around and looked it over. "It's a wonder we didn't have a blowout on one of them mountain roads—and, brother, that would of been all! . . . what with Shiftless bein' a mite loose in the steerin' gear and wheel bushings. Hmf! I'd about as leave have a paper sack in there as this thing—'twould hold air better. Well, you go on with your housekeepin', and I'll get this hole plugged up, one way or 'nother."

I'd daubed a good thick covering of clay on the biggest sweet potato so it would bake in the coals, had peeled the onions, and was cleaning the celery when Lonnie came over to the fire and asked to borrow my new knife. As soon as I passed it to him he reached down and began cutting one leg of his overalls off at the knee.

"What in the world are you doing that for?" I asked him.

"Got to make a boot for that tire," he told me. "Where it blowed out it's wore down to paper-thin, and I won't be wearin' these dirty britches no more noways. Anyhow, not to town, and on Christmas Day. A man's got to get dressed up once in a while."

I helped Lonnie while he folded the piece he'd cut off his overalls and stuck it over the broken place inside the tire. Then we put the mended tube back in, pried the tire onto the rim, and pumped, and pumped, and pumped. The old air pump hadn't been used for so long that the leather valve washers were all dried out, and the only way we could get it to take hold at all was by unscrewing the top and pouring in water every few minutes. I think we got about as much water as air into the tire, and when we had it about halfway up Lonnie told me, "Leave it go. That's enough to get me into town, and I'll fill it up at a garage. They don't charge you nothin' for air. You just tell 'em you'll come back later and buy some gas."

He peeked up at the sun and shouted, "Jeepers Creepers!
It's near onto noon. Mind fillin' the radiator while I change my
cloze?"

I'd filled the radiator and wiped the thickest of the dust
off Shiftless by the time Lonnie came back, and he really looked
like a gentleman. He had on his new shirt and overalls—with
the cuffs turned up the way I wore mine, but nearly six inches
above his ankles. He'd shaved, combed his hair, polished his
old boots as well as he could with bacon grease, and dusted off
his hat. "Reckon I'll need about four bits," he told me as he
peeked at his reflection in the windshield. "Spent myself clean
broke last night . . . what with that mince pie and all."

I gave him a half-dollar and said, "That ought to do it all
right. All we need is a loaf of stale white bread and a dime's
worth of sage."

I'd cranked Shiftless and Lonnie had warmed her up till
she began hitting on all four, then he leaned out over the door
and asked, "Look, buddy, if I was to get some rice and raisins,
do you reckon you could whack up a rice pudd'n? My maw
always used to make it on Christmas, and it was larrupin'
good."

"Rice custard?" I asked him.

"I don't know," he said, "but there was yellow all in amongst
the rice . . . and lots o' raisins."

"Then you'll have to get a quart of milk and a nutmeg," I
told him. "We've got plenty of eggs. Both those hens were
laying, and they were full of yolks."

Lonnie gave Shiftless a shot of gas, kicked the pedal into
low, and started off with a roar. By the time he'd gone a hundred feet he had old Shiftless up to fifteen miles an hour, and
she was going down the road like a drunk running for a train.
Every time the front wheel came around to the place where
Lonnie had put in the piece of overall leg it hopped and made
a sound like a flapping sole on a worn-out shoe.

I didn't expect Lonnie to be gone more than an hour at the

most, but it was nearly two before he came back, and when he came he was as excited as a little boy at his first carnival. "We're all set, buddy! We're all set!" he yelled as he turned Shiftless off the road and came dodging toward camp through the creosote bushes. "I was pretty dang sure of it when I seen that little horse last night!"

When Lonnie turned off the road I'd expected our patched tire to blow at any second, and I was watching that wheel when he pulled around the last clump of brush between us, but the old tire wasn't on it. Instead, there was a pretty fair looking one—not new, but without any of the canvas lining showing.

Lonnie jumped out over the door as Shiftless switched her tail and came to a stop. He threw his arm around my neck and hollered loud enough to nearly break my eardrums, "We're set, buddy! We're set, I tell you! Look what I got for that little old horse you made—and two gallons of gas to boot. Boy, howdy! If you can make enough of 'em I can trade 'em for all the gas and grub we'll need! Even tires! If that little critter had of been made out of somethin' hard, 'stead of mud, I could of got a brand new tire for him."

"That's fine," I told him. "I'll bet I can make them as fast as you can trade them off, but did you get the other stuff you went after?"

"All but the milk," he said, "and that's a cinch. There was only one store open, and they didn't have no milk, but I seen some cows on the way back—three, four of 'em with fall calves. All we got to do is catch one of 'em and milk her. Calves the size of them don't suck till late in the afternoon. If we was to go right now we'd likely get a gallon or two. Wish't I had a horse—a live one—I'd catch one of them old heifers and bring her on into camp, so's't we could milk her whenever we wanted. Ain't you supposed to be drinkin' milk regular anyhow?"

Lonnie's idea sounded like a good one, especially since he said there were no houses between our camp and Fort Thomas. We shook out our throw ropes, took a few practice tosses at creosote bushes, put the dishpan on the back seat, and started

off down the road. Lonnie said the cattle were on a desert
pasture where there was plenty of fairly tall brush, so we didn't
think we'd have a bit of trouble in catching a cow. We'd each
pick one with a good full bag, sneak up on her from behind
a bush, and toss a loop over her head.

It didn't work that way. Those cows were as wild as antelope,
nearly as fast, and they must have had eyes and ears like eagles.
We could see them from the road when we got to within a
quarter mile, and they didn't pay a bit of attention to Shiftless's
clatter. But when we'd pulled off the road, hidden Shiftless
behind a clump of mesquite, and were sneaking up on them
afoot, they began drifting away. They didn't do any running
at first, but just drifted on whenever we'd get within fifty yards
of them. Then, when we tried to close in faster, they ran—all
except a big white-face bull that seemed to be on the prod.
He kept between us and the cows, and he covered their retreat
in grand style. If we tried to gain an inch, he'd whirl around,
paw dirt up over his back, and dare us to come on, halfway
between a bellow and a growl.

From behind a bush Lonnie made signals with his arms to
show me that we should circle wide around, but that didn't
work either. The old bull caught on as quickly as I did. Instead
of just turning and pawing, he began charging back and forth,
toward one of us and then the other, shaking his head and bawling. And the cows kept drifting farther back into the brush.
At last Lonnie motioned for me to come over where he was.
"There ain't no sense in this," he told me. "If we keep on this
way we'll drive 'em clean into Mexico 'fore we ever catch one.
Tell you what we'll do. It's open enough in here that I can drive
Shiftless easy, and you can stand on the runnin' board and
catch one of them old heifers as I go past her. You could snub
her on one of them irons the top's supposed to bolt onto, and
if the bull gets proddy we'll lead her on back to camp before
we milk her. He'd never leave the herd to folla that far."

Lonnie was right about being able to drive Shiftless through
the brush, and by not being too careful about missing the

smaller clumps he didn't have much trouble in catching up to the cows, but I had all kinds of trouble in trying to stand on the running board and swing a rope. On horseback you don't have to worry about balance when you go high-tailing after a cow in brush country. The pony will follow right behind, dodging whichever way she does, and he leans as he turns, so the rider can go along with him. But Shiftless didn't work that way —or Lonnie either. He couldn't turn one tenth as fast as the slowest of those old cows, and Shiftless leaned the wrong way when she did turn. The horse falls were nothing compared to the spills I took off the running board before we discovered how to do it.

We had to take Lonnie's rope, make a harness for me, and lash it to a door hinge. In that way I had both hands free, and I didn't get tossed every time we made a sharp turn. But it still didn't work, because Lonnie couldn't turn sharp enough. The only thing that saved us was that one old cow—the one with the smallest calf—decided to desert the herd. She took off in a straight line for Mexico, and Lonnie took off after her. Of course, he had to do a little weaving to get through the brush, but it wasn't bad, and when the cow got a little winded he pulled almost alongside of her. I didn't have a bit of trouble in tossing my loop over her head, and Lonnie stayed close enough that I had her snubbed tight to the top-iron before she hit the end of the rope.

Anyone would think a cow that had been run full tilt for a mile would be ready to give up and act reasonable, but that was the most unreasonable cow I ever had anything to do with. Five or six times she hit the end of that rope so hard she threw herself, and each time she nearly jerked Shiftless off her wheels. Then when one of us would try to follow up the rope toward her, so we could twist her down for milking, she'd charge. After we'd barely escaped from a dozen charges Lonnie shook out his rope and hind-legged her, but she was stout as an elephant. Even with Lonnie weighing a hundred and fifty she could drag a leg behind her and pull him around like a poodle on a string, and she kept shrieking like a train engine on a cold night.

If we could have stayed with it and worn her down a little more, I think we might have been able to throw her and hogtie her for milking, but we gave out before she did. We had to sit in the shade of a bush for awhile, to catch our breath and figure out what to do next. It was Lonnie who figured out the scheme that worked. Moving real slowly so as not to excite the cow, we unhitched the head rope, ran it through the spokes of the near front wheel, under the engine, and snubbed it to a spoke in the far wheel. Then we did the same with the heel rope, but used the rear wheels. In that way the cow couldn't charge the one doing the snubbing, and since she couldn't see him, she didn't worry too much about Shiftless. I did the hazing-in as quietly as I could, and each time the cow sidled nearer to Shiftless, Lonnie took in on the snubbing ropes, first one end and then the other.

It wasn't more than twenty minutes before we had that cow winched up against the side of Shiftless so tight that she couldn't wiggle. With the heel rope on her outside leg, she couldn't kick with the inside one, and her head was plastered tight against the front wheel. The only thing she could have done was to flop over onto me while I was milking her, but Lonnie took care of that by climbing on the back seat and hauling on her tail.

All the time we'd been trying to make the old cow listen to reason her calf had been standing back at the edge of the bushes, bawling us out for trying to swipe his dinner, but he must have done all right before we got there. I stripped right down to the last drop and didn't get over three pints, but it sloshed around so much in the dishpan that I couldn't have handled much more anyway.

That old cow acted as if her whole fight had been only to protect her honor. As soon as I'd finished milking her she stood as quietly as if she'd been barn-raised. And she didn't fight at all when we slipped the ropes off. She trotted away into the

brush, then stopped just before she was out of sight and looked back over her shoulder, as if she were telling us, "I'll let my husband know about this." I don't know whether or not she let him know, but he didn't give us any trouble when we drove back to the road. I couldn't watch where we were going very well, because I had to hold the dishpan high to keep the milk from slopping.

It didn't seem as if we'd spent very much time in getting that three pints of milk, but the sun was halfway down toward the mountains when we got back to camp. And, of course, the fire had gone out. While Lonnie built a new one—with lots of greasewood roots, so we'd have plenty of big coals for the roasting—I made the stuffing for the hens. It wasn't as good as Mother used to make, but it wasn't too bad either. I broke the stale bread into little chunks, moistened it with milk, tossed in a couple of egg yolks from one of the hens, sliced in plenty of onion and celery, and sprinkled it good and heavy with salt, pepper, and sage. I was pretty sure those hens were going to be awfully tough if I tried to roast them dry, so I jammed the biggest one into the Dutch oven, put in a little water, covered it tight, and hung it over the new fire where it could steam till the roasting coals were ready.

I'd made custard pies when I was baching with my grand-father, so I knew how to make the custard part, but I'd never tried to make a rice custard pudding. I knew Mother baked hers in the oven, but I didn't know whether she put the rice in raw, or boiled it first. It really didn't make much difference, because I was going to have to boil our rice anyway, since we had only one Dutch oven. And the only thing I had to boil it in was the dishpan, so we poured the milk into the quart jar Mrs. Larsen had put my stewed chicken in. There was just a little more than enough to fill it, and we drank that.

After I'd washed the pan I dumped in the pound of rice Lonnie had brought from town, explained to him that the raisins would be added later, and poured in enough water to cover the rice. Then Lonnie found some good-sized rocks, and we propped the pan up over the fire. Everything went fine at first, and we sat watching the grains of rice bubble up to the top as the water began to boil, but it drank that water as if it had been a herd of cattle. I had to keep adding more and more to keep it from sticking on the bottom of the pan and burning. We tried setting it off the fire to slow it down, but that didn't do any good. And it swelled even faster after we put the raisins in. By the time it was cooked soft we had nearly a dishpan full, and it was sort of sticky. "That's all right," I told Lonnie. "Of course, I can't eat it, and you won't want this much pudding, but you can always eat the rest of it for breakfasts, like mush."

Lonnie didn't like the idea of eating rice for mush, and he didn't think we had too much for pudding, but I was kind of licked for a way to make the custard—with the dishpan full of rice and the Dutch oven full of hen. We finally worked it out by pouring part of our milk into the coffee cups. Then I added what were left of the eggs out of the hens—some of them were as little as peas—poured in more or less sugar, and grated in some nutmeg by using a rough stone for a grater. The jar worked fine for mixing. All we had to do was to screw on the top and shake it. Then, of course, we had to keep pouring back and forth between the cups and the jar till we had the mixture all alike. Lonnie poured it over the rice while I stirred it in and grated more nutmeg on top. Even though we couldn't bake it, I think it would have been pretty good rice pudding if I'd stirred it a little harder and broken the sticky lumps up more than I did. The custard cooked fine, just set up close to the fire, and the nutmeg on top made it look almost as though it had been baked in an oven.

We let the first hen sort of steam and stew along until we'd finished the pudding, then drained off what broth there was, drank it, and covered the Dutch oven over with coals for roasting. It was dark before that old biddy was cooked enough that the breast meat would break when I stuck a fork into it and twisted. But she was almost tender by the time Lonnie's sweet potato was done. We put what was left of the onions and celery right into the pot with her, and even if it was a little late when we had our Christmas dinner it was a durned good one. Lonnie wouldn't say the rice pudding was as good as his mother's, but he ate nearly a quart of it, so it couldn't have been too bad.

I didn't dare leave the second hen lying around raw, even though the nights were chilly, so we cooked her while we were eating and resoaping our saddles before we turned in. It gave us a lot of time to talk about what we were going to do after we got steady jobs, and we sang some of the old songs over again three or four times. Lonnie didn't know but a few of them—"Silent Night," "Jingle Bells," and ones like that. But even if we were nearly broke and out of jobs, it wasn't a bad Christmas.

11

Little Clay Horse

STARTING the morning after Christmas we hunted jobs just as hard as we could. We followed every pair of wheel tracks that turned off the road anywhere between Fort Thomas and Safford, on both sides of the Gila River. But we found only one job—not too bad a one—but Lonnie wouldn't take it. The rancher passed me up like cold soup, but he let Lonnie show him that he was good with a rope, and offered him thirty a month—more when roundup time came. Lonnie tried to take us both in on the deal, but when the rancher shook his head he backed away. "Naw," he said, "it's the both of us or none. My buddy here, he can't drive our automobile, and I wouldn't want to leave him stranded. We'll mosey along, but maybe we'll drop back and see you later."

I tried to tell Lonnie that I could learn to drive Shiftless without much trouble, and that I thought he'd better take the job. I said I'd try to find one near by, and that if I didn't we'd keep in touch with each other during the winter. Then we could find jobs together when roundup time came. When Lonnie shook his head I thought it might be because he was afraid I wouldn't leave him his saddle and outfit, so I said,

"You don't need to worry about the outfit, Lonnie. If you want to, you can send me a little out of your pay checks, but it's yours anyway. It has been right from the beginning."

Lonnie shook his head again, climbed in behind the wheel, and said, "Twist her tail, buddy, and let's get a move on. We're wastin' time here."

The day Lonnie turned that job down we had to drive to Safford, so I could go to a doctor and get a report card to mail. While I was waiting for the doctor to examine the specimen I wrote a short letter to Mother, telling her our boss was sending my partner and me over into New Mexico for some cattle, and that he was going to meet us in El Paso, Texas, so she could write me there. Then, when the doctor was too busy to notice, I took the last fifty-dollar bill out of the cuff of my Levi's and put it in the letter. I didn't dare not to, for fear I might be tempted to break it. Then too, if the doctor charged me two dollars I'd have only $1.85 left in my pocket, and I couldn't feel right about telling Lonnie we were dead broke while I still had the fifty.

During the first few days of January we worked our way back along the south side of the river, going to see every rancher between the highway and the mountains. The only thing that saved us from getting right down to our last penny was that I made a little clay horse every evening, and that Lonnie had pretty fair luck trading them in the towns for a few gallons of gas or some grub. But it was Shiftless that brought us our best luck. Her shimmying got so bad that we couldn't drive her over five miles an hour, and we'd put her over so many rough roads in the back country that we'd worn out her transmission bands.

The brake went first, but Lonnie was able to stop by using the reverse pedal. Then the driving band started slipping so badly that he had to ride the low pedal all the time. As we were pulling into a little town one evening it gave out entirely, so there was nothing we could do but stop and camp.

There wasn't any sense in trying to make clay horses enough

to pay for new bands and bushings for the front wheels—or for the grub we'd need while we were making the repairs. Lonnie had already traded two horses in that town, one to the only store and one to the only garage. The market was already flooded, but that night I made a horse's head. It was about six inches high, with an arched neck and curly mane. I worked

on it till way after midnight, and did the very best job I could. The next morning I told Lonnie to sleep in while I cleaned up our dishes and made my last gluten flour into bread. At ten o'clock he was still sleeping, and I had the bread all covered over in the coals to bake, so I took the horse's head and went into town.

I didn't go to the store or the garage, but to the bank. It was a little one, not much bigger than a bedroom. A girl about my age was in a cage at the front; beyond her I could see the bald head of a man who was writing at a desk, and behind him was the iron door of a vault. I was barely inside the door when the girl in the cage called, "Good morning." Then she noticed the little clay head, and sort of squealed, "Oh, you must be the artist who sculped that cute little horse at the store."

With what I had in mind I couldn't tell her that I wasn't an artist; only a cowhand out of a job. So I went to the window, passed the little model in to her, and said, "It's an American Saddlebred horse. I saw him at a horse show in Boston."

The girl was a pretty one, and her eyes sparkled as she turned the head in her hands, oo-ing and ah-ing over it. I was so busy watching her that I didn't notice the bald-headed man until he bent over her shoulder, looked at the model, then up at me, and asked, "You do that yourself?"

On the way in from camp I'd rehearsed what I was going to say to that banker, but with the girl having said what she did when I came in, and with our being so hard up right then, it didn't come out the way I'd planned. "Yes, sir," I told him. "I'm the cowboy artist . . . just passing through this way. Had to come west for my health. This is just a little toy I knocked out last night by the campfire."

Then to make things sound sort of offhand I said to the girl, "You may have him if you'd like to. I just make them as a pastime. My regular line is portrait sculpture . . . you know, making likenesses of people's faces."

Quicker than a wink the banker asked, "What do you charge?"

"Well, that depends," I told him. "If I make several in a town—just out of clay like this—I charge ten dollars apiece. But if it's an exclusive commission . . . if I agree to make only one in the town . . . for the leading citizen, or the banker, or someone like that, then I charge twenty-five . . . in advance . . . but when I make a deal of that kind I cast them in plaster . . . so they look like marble, you know. If they're only clay they warp out of shape as soon as they dry."

The old gentleman peered at me over the top of his glasses and said, "You don't say!"

I knew right then I had him hooked, but I was scared. Anyone could have seen that he'd been a range man before he became a banker. His face was craggy and weatherbeaten, there were deep sun wrinkles flaring out from the corners of his eyes, deep clefts in his cheeks, and if he had false teeth he wasn't wearing them. When I'd lived with Ivon I'd modeled several busts of young fellows we worked with, and some of them had come out fairly good, but I'd never tackled anything so tough as a face like that banker's. My mouth was so dry my tongue clucked when I said, "Yes, sir. They'll warp till you'd hardly recognize them if they're left in clay."

"Hm," he said, "you ought to have come along forty years ago. I might have gone for that marble deal, but I'm not just what a man might call an artist's model any more."

I thought I saw my way out; the juice ran back into my mouth, and I said, "Oh, that doesn't make any difference. All I'd need would be an old picture or a tintype. If you've got something like that it would be easy enough to use it as a model . . . I could make you look any age you wanted me to."

"Hm," he said again. "Hm, there might be an old tintype or two around the house at that. Tell you what you do; you visit with Mabel here a few minutes, and I'll go take a look."

I did visit with Mabel, and it was the best part of my selling job. After I'd told her I'd cast the horse's head in plaster for her, I mentioned that I was pretty busy and didn't know just how long I could stay in that part of the country. But I said that if she wanted to call some of the other bankers in the nearby towns, I'd be glad to stay around till I'd finished their busts. She wanted to start telephoning right away, but I told her she'd better wait till we saw how her boss liked the one I was going to do of him.

The tintype that banker brought back must have been fifty years old. It was so badly faded that I couldn't have copied it, even if I'd had the ability. About all I could make out was that he'd had a heavy head of hair and a good big mustache, both parted in the middle and twisted into spit curls at the sides of his face.

"Don't know as you can make much out of it," he told me as he held the tintype up by the window, "but that's the way I used to look. Let's see . . . That was at the time of my first marriage."

I took the tintype, turned it back and forth a little so the light would strike it in different ways, and peered at it closely. "Believe I could do a pretty good job with this one," I told him. "Some of them are faded a lot worse than this. I'll tell you what we'll do: I'll take this along with me, and you pay just ten dollars down. Then, if you like the clay model when I bring it in tomorrow, you can pay the balance, and I'll make up the marblelike casting. If you don't like the model we'll just call the deal closed. Is that fair enough?"

He thought it was and gave me the ten.

If I hadn't been the cowboy artist, I'd have run all the way back to camp with that ten dollars, but it wouldn't have seemed very dignified so I walked as slowly as I could make myself.

12

We're in the Dough

LONNIE was still in his bedroll and snoring, but I shook him till he was wide awake, showed him the ten, and told him, "We're in business, partner, but we won't stay there long unless you roll out and get going. If this thing works the way I hope it will, we'll need Shiftless—and we'll need her in tiptop shape. You get into town and buy whatever you need to fix her with—up to seven-fifty. We'll have to save the rest back for grub, at least until after tomorrow."

"Jeepers Creepers!" Lonnie hollered, threw the blankets back, and made a grab for his britches. As he hauled them on he hollered again, "Boy, howdy! We're in the dough!" Then he dropped his voice and said, "Look, buddy, for seven-fifty I can get enough stuff to make her good as new again . . . maybe for seven. How 'bout me gettin' some bacon and eggs while I'm in to the store? Honest, buddy, I'm gettin' to where I can't hardly go gluten bread and salmon no more."

Lonnie didn't even think to ask me what kind of business we were in, but went hurrying off toward town as soon as I told him it would be all right to get a dozen eggs and a pound of bacon. As soon as he was gone I took my loaf of bread out of the Dutch oven, then sat down in Shiftless's shadow to make a life-sized armature for a man's head and neck. When I had it finished I worked up all the clay left in the bucket till it was soft and pliable. I was putting it onto the armature and thumping it into general shape with the heels of my hands when Lonnie came back. He stopped by the smoldering fire to lay the bacon and eggs down, then came over and stood watching me for a couple of minutes. "That ain't no horse," he said at last. "What you doing that for? Thought you said we was in business."

"If this comes out any good we might be," I told him.

He stood and watched me a few minutes more, then asked in a puzzled voice, "Well, what the devil is it, buddy? One of them jars like the old Mexican in Phoenix makes? What do you, scoop the inside out after you get the outside made?"

"No," I said, "it's going to be a man's head, and if the banker in town thinks it looks the way he did when he was young and handsome, we might be in business."

"Jeepers Creepers!" Lonnie shouted. "Why didn't you tell me you could do that kind of stuff, buddy—not just horses?"

"I don't know if I can—without a live model to take measurements from," I told him, "but I'm going to try. It won't cost anything but my time, and that hasn't been very valuable for the past month."

Ever since I'd sent the last fifty to Mother I'd been telling Lonnie just where we stood on cash, but the only time money meant anything to him was when we didn't have any. Right until that minute he hadn't even wondered where the ten came from. Then when it began to dawn on him he whispered, "Creepers, buddy, that old buzzard didn't give you a tenner 'fore he ever seen it, did he?"

"Mmm, hmm," I told him, "but you'd better cook your breakfast and get started on fixing Shiftless. If this comes out any good we'll have to get in to Safford for plaster, and it's too far to walk."

Lonnie was so sure we'd struck it rich that he fried himself four eggs and half a pound of bacon for breakfast. Then he changed into his greasy old jeans with the missing leg and went to work on Shiftless. From then till twilight he was too busy to come and see what I was doing, and I was too busy to think about stopping to eat.

I never did take the old tintype out of my pocket. As I'd talked to the banker I'd been studying his face, and it crossed my mind that when he was a young man he must have looked a good deal like William S. Hart—except for his mustache and the way he combed his hair. That was all I wanted to remember. I'd always liked Western movies, and Ivon and I had gone to see every William S. Hart picture that was shown in Wilmington. All I had to do to see that face again was to close my eyes, and as I worked on the clay I kept closing them every few minutes.

When it began to get dark enough that the light wouldn't reflect back off the damp clay I called Lonnie. He came around Shiftless, looked over my shoulder for half a minute, and said in a shocked voice, "That ain't the old buzzard at the bank, buddy! That there's Bill Hart."

I jumped up, grabbed him, and swung him around in a couple of dance steps. "If you think that's Bill Hart we're in business," I told him. "No need to hold back on the grub now. Want to beat it into town and buy yourself a steak and me a chicken? But don't you dare swipe the chicken. We've still got business to do in this town."

That evening after we'd had our feast I made Bill Hart over a little while Lonnie watched me. I took his cowboy hat off, put a good big lump of clay on his head, and worked it into a mass of wavy hair—parted in the middle, and with spit curls above the temples. Then I rolled pigtails of clay between my palms, laid one on each side of the upper lip for a mustache, pressed them into shape, curled the ends, and marked in the hair with a broken stick. When I was finished, the bust didn't look a bit like the old banker—and it didn't look much like Bill Hart either—but I hoped it would look the way the banker wanted it to.

It did. I don't know whether or not it would have if Mabel hadn't told him how handsome he must have been as a young man. He didn't seem to mind her telling him, and he said it was a "spittin' image" of what he had looked like at the time of his first marriage.

I didn't even have to mention the fifteen dollars; he had Mabel give it to me out of the till, and his only worry seemed to be that I might not get the clay cast into "marble" before it warped out of shape. For several minutes he walked back and forth in front of the cage, trying to make up his mind where the marble bust should be set. There really wasn't a spot in the little room where a plaster bust wouldn't look as out of place as the angel Gabriel—wings and all. The only thing I could think of was to hang it on the wall above the door, so I said, "If you'd like me to I could cast it with a metal hook at the back of the base. Then you could hang it on the wall right above the door. Don't you think it would have an impressive look up here, Mabel?"

Of course, the thing I was thinking about was that no direct light could hit it up there, and it would be kind of hard for anyone standing close under it and looking up to tell how little it looked like the old gentleman. Mabel was sure it would look impressive, and the banker was even more sure of it. "Now you're talking!" he told me. "Never would have thought of that myself, but I'm no artist—just an old wore-out cowman, like all the rest of 'em in the banking business hereabouts. It's what you might call a haven for men that last till they're too old to work and too ornery for the women folks to have around a house. There's not a one of us, up or down the line, but's long past seventy. Have a cigar, son. Come on in and sit a little spell. Always did want to talk to one of you artist fellows. Guess a man's either born with it or without it."

As he talked he led the way back to his desk, and I said I'd save the cigar to enjoy after I'd had my dinner. There was no sense in telling him I didn't smoke and that it would make me sicker than a locoed pony. When we were seated, the old

gentleman leaned back in his swivel chair, looked out the barred window toward the mountains, and said, "Yes sirree, a man's got to be born with it, just like he's got to be born with the feel for cattle . . . or a horse. Take me, I couldn't draw a straight line. All I know about art is that I like it . . . if it's good, you understand. A range of mountains like the Pinalenos yonder, or a sunrise in spring . . . when the sky and the land's blood red. Seen one of our red dawns yet? Been up to the Canyon?"

After I'd told him that I hadn't but intended to, he went on asking me other questions, about when I'd first taken up art as a livelihood, and what great artists I'd studied under, and if I'd been to Paris. I didn't tell him any straight-out lies, but I had to stretch the exact truth out of shape a little. I couldn't tell him I'd taken up art as a means of livelihood about half an hour ago, and I thought he might feel as if he'd made a better bargain if I let him think I'd studied in foreign countries, so I mentioned Ivon three or four times, and the shape of the mosques in Moscow. Really, I wasn't listening to him too closely. I was listening to Mabel. She'd been talking on the telephone ever since the banker and I went back to his desk, and she was more than bubbling over about the beautiful bust I'd made, and how I'd done it all from a faded old tintype so it looked real enough to talk, and that I was going to be in the neighborhood for only a few days, and that my price was ridiculously low— only twenty-five dollars for an exclusive marble bust.

Mabel's talking made me proud, scared, and embarrassed all at the same time, and I got out of there as soon as I could find any excuse for breaking away. When I went past her cage she asked anxiously if I'd be able to stay in eastern Arizona long enough to make five or six more busts. She said she'd taken the liberty of promising two other bankers I'd do theirs before I left, and she knew that three or four others would feel left out if they couldn't have them. I didn't want to seem over-anxious so I said I'd agree right then to do the two she'd promised, and I'd talk to my partner about stopping long enough to finish the others. I was almost to the door before I remembered she hadn't told me which bankers she'd promised. Then I told her it would take two or three days before the casting was ready, so I'd make the two clay models in the meantime.

That afternoon while we were putting the wheel bushings in Shiftless and tightening up her front end, I told Lonnie as much as I thought I should about the bust business, but I didn't tell him that ten dollars wasn't the full price. I knew he'd want to spend most of it in trying to make a new automobile out of Shiftless, and I thought I had more than enough in her already. Except for her boiling, she did well enough after we'd finished with her. Her front wheels didn't wobble, the new bands didn't slip, and we made twenty miles an hour when we drove to Safford for the casting materials I needed. The only real trouble was that she still wandered back and forth across the road like a cow on her way to pasture—and she rattled and shook as if she had St. Vitus's dance.

I knew well enough there would be no artist's supply store in Safford, but I was lucky enough to find everything I really had to have for making the castings. Of course, there was no casting-grade plaster of Paris to be had, but I found a sack of fired gypsum at a lumber and building materials yard. I found Castile soap at the trading store, and an old broken parlor heater in a junk yard. All I wanted from the old stove was the isinglass behind a row of openings in the front, but I had to buy the whole stove to get it. It cost two dollars, and Lonnie thought we could use it for cooking, but it would have been a terrible nuisance to haul around, so I just slipped out the strips of isinglass and left it where it was. At the hardware and implement store I found a set of enamel pans that fitted inside each other, a couple of enamel buckets, a wooden mallet, a whetstone, and a few chipping chisels. And I had the man put them in a good clean burlap sack.

If Lonnie had been much of a thinker he'd have known I'd got hold of some extra money somewhere, but thinking wasn't his strongest point. While I was picking out the things I needed in the hardware store, he was busy rummaging around the auto supply and paint counters. Then when I was ready to pay my bill he came up with both hands and his arms full of stuff he'd picked up—a side view mirror, a fancy radiator cap, two quarts of paint, a dozen or so small tools, and a whole bundle of emery cloth. I tried to head him off easy so I wouldn't have to tell him right in front of the clerk that we didn't have the price, but Lonnie wouldn't head off.

I had to take him aside and whisper to him that he could buy the stuff later if we had good luck, but that we couldn't afford it yet. He looked up at me like a little boy who has just been told that Santa Claus really doesn't come from the North Pole. "Well, buddy," he whispered, "you told me last night we was in business . . . if that was Bill Hart."

"We might be if we're lucky . . . and if I can fool enough people," I told him, "but we're not yet. I don't know if this gypsum I got will work for casting. If it won't, or if these people find out that I'm not really an artist, we could be sunk."

Lonnie stood for a minute with his head down, but peeking up under his eyebrows at the enamelware the clerk was stowing into the gunny sack. "Look, buddy," he whispered, "we ain't goin' to eat so much we'll need all them pots and pans to cook it in . . . and old Shiftless don't boil away enough water we'll need more'n one bucket to lug it in."

"Those are things I need for making the castings," I told him. "Without them we wouldn't have a chance of getting into business."

Lonnie thought that over for a couple of minutes while he stood looking at the floor as if he were looking down on a grave. Then he peeked up quickly, grinned, and whispered, "Charge it, buddy! Tell 'em to call your banker and check on your credit . . . you know, the old buzzard you made the face of."

It took me ten or fifteen minutes to convince Lonnie that he couldn't have all the stuff he wanted for Shiftless, but I had to compromise. I let him keep half the emery cloth and one quart of paint, but we were nearly broke again when we rolled out of town.

Even in January the sun was too hot in southeastern Arizona, and the wind too dry, to do much work with wet plaster in the open during daylight. Then too, I wasn't sure enough of myself that I wanted to run the risk of people coming out from town to watch me work, so we didn't go back to our old camping place near the village. We hunted along the river near Pima till we found a gulch we could get Shiftless into and out of easily. It wasn't far off the road, but completely hidden. The walls were high enough so there would be shade in some part of the little canyon all day long, and a sunny ledge where I could lay castings out to dry. And down in there it was sheltered enough that the wind couldn't get at us to blow dust on my work.

It was nearly dusk when we pulled into the little canyon, but before I'd gathered enough wood for our campfire Lonnie was at work on Shiftless, scrubbing layers of old speckled paint off her engine hood with a piece of emery cloth. He kept right at it till I had supper ready, then he called, "Hey, buddy, come look what I've did! Boy, howdy! Shines like a cat's eyes in the dark!"

When I went over I could see where Lonnie had scrubbed a spot about a foot square until the bright metal was exposed. "That's fine!" I told him, and reached out a hand to feel how smooth it was.

He caught my hand and held it away. "Mustn't touch it, buddy," he cautioned me. "After messin' with the grub you might get it greasy so's't the new paint wouldn't take good. Automobile paintin' is tricky business. A man's got to know his stuff and be right careful or it won't come out professional . . . like it was brand new out of the fact'ry. But you just wait, buddy. Time I get through with this old baby she'll look. . . . Say, buddy, you sure we picked a good place to camp? The river bein' right alongside and all, it might get damp o' nights, so's't she'd rust where I got her cleaned off."

"Oh, I don't think you'll have any trouble," I told him. "You

could cover the cleaned part over with a saddle blanket or a
tarp."

He shook his head. "Not no saddle blanket," he told me.
"Too liable to be grease on it . . . from the pony's back, you
know."

"Use a tarp then," I said, "but you'd better come along now
and eat your supper. It's getting cold."

Lonnie wouldn't come until he'd covered Shiftless's engine
hood with the tarpaulin from his bedroll, and he tucked it in
carefully at the sides, as if he'd been putting a baby to bed.
All during supper he kept telling me the things he was going to
do to make Shiftless brand new, but he said he didn't dare work
on her any more that night for fear the damp air might rust
her. He kept right on telling me about it while I washed the
dishes and got things ready for making my first plaster mold.
I was a little nervous about it, and Lonnie's continual talking
made me sort of edgy. "Never mind about Shiftless for now,"
I told him. "If we're going to have any money to fix her up with,
you'd better keep enough greasewood on that fire to give me a
little light here."

I'd helped Ivon enough with casts, and made enough of
them by myself, that I shouldn't have been nervous, but I
couldn't help it. My hands shook as if I had palsy while I cut
sections of isinglass for making a dam. For some reason my
hands will shake to beat the band when I'm getting ready to
do something I'm a little bit afraid of—and I was plenty scared
about tackling that first casting—but they usually stop the
minute I get started on it. They did that night. The pieces of
isinglass had to be cut into the clay, so as to make a little fence
running from the base of the neck up through the center of the
chin, the mouth, nose, forehead, and on back through the
parting of the hair. And if my hand shook a particle as I pressed
them into place I'd turn a rough edge on the clay and spoil
the casting. I held my breath as I cut each piece into the clay,
and I think Lonnie held his, too. "Jeepers Creepers," he whispered after I'd stood in two or three sections. "You ain't goin'

to cut him in two now you got him made, are you, buddy?"

"No," I told him, "this is just a dam to separate the two sides of the casting, so they won't stick together and I can pull them off."

"Jeepers," he whispered again and again as the wall grew up through the face and back over the head, but the sound of his voice there beside me helped to keep my fingers steady.

Lonnie watched like a squirrel as I mixed a pail of soft plaster, scooped up a little on my cupped fingers, took aim, and flipped it over one clay eye. "Jeeper Creepers!" he shouted as the plaster plopped into the eye depression and spattered out onto the cheek. "I seen guys I'd like to do that to myself. Can I sling some of it on, buddy? Just a little teeny bit?"

"Sure," I told him, "but sling it here on the cheek. There's a knack to throwing it into the eyes and ears and mouth, or you don't fill all the wrinkles and corners."

Lonnie picked up nearly a cupful of plaster and heaved it against the cheek as if it had been an overripe tomato. Then he giggled as if someone had been tickling his feet. "Leave me sling a little more, buddy," he pleaded. "Just one more shot at the old buzzard 'fore you get him all covered up."

That gypsum worked nearly as well as plaster of Paris, and in the cool damp air of evening there by the river it didn't set up so quickly but what I could make a good strong mold, with strips of burlap in between the layers to strengthen it. But I was as careful with it as I knew how to be. I didn't try to hurry, and when a batch of plaster began to stiffen, even a little, I threw it out and made a fresh batch. Neither of us had a watch, but from the position of the stars I knew it was long past midnight before I had both the banker and Mabel's little horse head safely in their molds and stood on the ledge to dry.

13

Cowboy Artists of the Southwest

Next morning the molds had hardened enough to take direct sunlight, but there was nothing more I could do with them until they'd dried nearly as hard as stone. I let Lonnie sleep until I'd shaved and cooked breakfast. And I fried him four eggs, half a pound of bacon, and a whole plateful of hashed brown potatoes. I was fairly sure we were going to make a go of our business, and there seemed no reason for being stingy about the grub.

When I had everything ready I woke Lonnie. He rolled over, rubbed his eyes, and said, "Aw, buddy, why didn't you rouse me when you rolled out? I could of had Shiftless half . . ." And he was sound asleep again. I was feeling pretty happy that morning and thought I'd have a little fun with him, so I shook him again. He only mumbled and hunched the blanket higher around his shoulders. "You don't need to get up yet," I told him. "I just didn't want you to wake up later on and miss me. I've got to go see a banker about a bust, but I won't have any trouble with Shiftless. I think I know how to drive her."

Lonnie jumped to his feet, grabbed me by one arm, and told me, "Uh-uh, buddy! You'd kill yourself! You can't never tell when old Shiftless might take a notion to go off the road . . . the steerin' wheel bein' loose the way it is and all. I'll drive you right on over there soon's I get my britches on."

"Oh, there's no need of that," I told him. "Somebody ought to stay in camp to keep an eye on those castings, and I wouldn't have a bit of trouble with . . ."

There was no use in going any further with the joke. Lonnie had hauled on his boots and greasy old jeans, and was hurrying off toward the river. I watched him scoop up three or four handfuls of cold water, splash them on his face, and come hurrying back to the fire. He started shoveling bacon, eggs, and potatoes into his mouth as if he were feeding a thrashing machine, drops of water still dripping off the four-day stubble on his chin.

"When did you shave last?" I asked him.

He swiped a hand across this chin and said, "Jeepers Creepers, they sure grow fast in this hot country, don't they?"

"Sure do," I said, "but when did you shave last? You know, if we're going to be the cowboy artists of the Southwest we're going to have to keep spruced up a little."

Lonnie stopped with a forkful of potatoes halfway to his mouth, seemed to be puzzling something out for a half minute, and said, "Creepers!" under his breath. Then he looked up at me and said earnestly, "Honest-a-God, buddy, you won't never have to be shamed of me. I'll keep slicked right up to the handle, but you know yourself, buddy, with Shiftless bein' broke down and all these last couple o' days . . ."

"That's all right," I told him. "I know how busy you've been, and I wouldn't be ashamed of you anyway. You're my buddy, you know. Better get that grub into you; we'll have to be rolling pretty soon."

I don't think Lonnie was listening to me. He sat looking down at his plate for maybe a minute. "Jeepers!" he whispered at last. "Cowboy artists!" Then he looked up quickly, grinned, and said, "Say, buddy, that sounds all right, don't it? Cowboy artists, that's us! Reckon I'd have time to shave and change

my duds 'fore we go to town?"

There was no need of our starting right away, so I told Lonnie to go ahead and get cleaned up if he wanted to. He wasn't gone more than fifteen minutes, and when he came back his face was as smooth and shiny as an apple, his hair was combed, and he was wearing the new shirt and jeans I'd given him for Christmas. All the way to town he kept babbling about our being artists, and how neat he was going to keep himself.

The banker I went to see that morning was about the same age as the first one, but he was built like an Angus bull: short, broad-shouldered, and heavy in the barrel. His face was deeply weather-beaten, and there wasn't even a fringe of hair on his head. I was afraid I wouldn't be able to sell the idea of letting me make his bust from a picture, but he was all ready with one. I hadn't talked to him two minutes before he reached in his pocket and dug out a faded old daguerreotype.

"Civil War picture. I was lieutenant of volunteers," he said as he held it up to the light and squinted at it. "Had this likeness made when I was on furlough in Richmond. Faded a mite, but Mabel tells me you can do wonders with 'em, faded or no."

As he spoke he handed me the daguerreotype, and I nearly fell off the chair. It was taken in uniform, his hat was pulled down on his forehead, and his whole face was covered with a scraggly beard. I could no more have made those whiskers look real than Lonnie could.

In the next thirty seconds I did some of the fastest thinking I'd ever done in my life. The only thing I could get hold of was that the old gentleman had been a lieutenant in the Civil War and was proud of it. "Hmmmmm," I hummed, acting as if I were studying the picture. "A bust of you should have a little different treatment than for most men. It would be a shame not to get in those shoulders." Then I happened to remember that I didn't have enough clay to make them, or know where to get hold of any more, so I added, "Not the whole shoulders, you understand—just enough to show their depth . . . and the collar . . . and a couple of buttons of the uniform . . . making the base sort of in a V shape, you know."

"How much extra would that be?" he asked quickly.

"Oh, not much; five dollars would do it," I told him.

"Fair enough!" he said. "That's the way I'll take it. Don't forget the crossed swords there on the collar."

I wasn't a bit worried about the crossed swords, but those whiskers were giving me fits, and I was afraid he might be as proud of them as of the swords. "Hmmmmmm," I hummed again, to give myself a little more time to think of some way out. "Hmmmmmmmm, you know I could trim this beard for you in making the bust . . . a Vandyke, or something like that?"

"Never wore a Vandyke," he told me. "Always let 'em grow natural."

I had to find some other tack, and fast, so I asked—sort of offhand—"Always wore a beard, I suppose?"

He sniggered till his shoulders shook, then haw-hawed. When he could catch his breath again he said, "Not always. There used to be times when the graybacks would get so thick I'd have to shave 'em off. Some of those army camps used to be mighty thick with vermin."

I tried to laugh as loud as he had, but it wasn't from happiness. "Of course," I said, "I can make it any way you'd like, but I was just thinking. Hmmmmmm, if I remember right, I haven't made a bust with a beard in several years. They seem to have gone a bit out of style, and most men tell me to leave them off."

"Well, now," he said, "that hadn't come to mind, but now you mention it I don't know but it might be a good idea."

He sat thinking and I sat fidgeting for a minute; then he asked, "How you going to know what my face looked like under the whiskers? Can't shave 'em off from a picture, and I don't believe I've got one without 'em . . . not of those years."

My fidgets faded away in two seconds; I chuckled a gurgle or two, and said, "Oh, that doesn't make a particle of difference. You know, we artists go a great deal on the structure of a man's bone, the expression around his eyes, the width of his forehead, and the character they show so plainly. No matter how old a man may be when I talk to him, I can get a pretty close likeness of him at any age. Of course, not photographically perfect, but close enough that no one could tell the difference by remembering back."

"Well, now," he said, "I can understand that. Take me, I can look at a week-old calf and tell you what kind of a bull he's going to make . . . almost to a T."

As he spoke, he reached into his pocket, pulled out a roll the size of his fist, and peeled me off three tens. "Thirty, that right?" he asked as he held them out to me.

I told him it was—and got out of there as fast as I could. At the door I remembered, looked back, and said, "Of course, you wouldn't want me to make it with your hat on. You'll have to tell me what your hair was like and how you wore it."

"Lots of it," he called back. "Brown, and parted on the left. A little on the curly side."

As soon as we got back to camp I went right to work on the second clay model. That time there was no excuse for looking at the picture, except to see the shape of the uniform neck and where to put the crossed swords. I'd known a young wrestler who had the same shaped head, bull neck, and type of features as the banker. In shaping up the clay I used my memory of him as my model, but made it a little more gentlemanly looking than the wrestler had been. Then I put on a couple of handfuls of hair, bushed it a bit above the ears, and worked a marcel into it. I hadn't thought to ask the banker if he wanted a mustache, but the upper lip came out fine, so I left the mustache off.

After I'd washed the supper dishes that evening I heaped plenty of greasewood on the fire. As soon as it was burning brightly I brought the hardened molds for the first banker's bust and Mabel's little horse head, then sat down to work on them. While I'd been shaping the clay model that afternoon Lonnie had drowsed in Shiftless's shadow, and hadn't seemed very interested. But when I began working on the molds he became as eager as if I were opening Christmas packages. He watched without saying a word while I sat cross-legged by the fire with the mold for the banker's bust in my lap—trimming away the excess plaster that had hardened along the sides of the isinglass dam, and drawing out the sections with a pair of pliers. Then he moved closer as I carefully pried one of the mold halves away from the other, jiggled it a bit, and pulled it away from the clay core. It didn't come away clean, and I didn't expect it to. Most of the clay eye, part of the hair, and, of course, the ear, pulled away with the mold.

"Jeepers!" Lonnie whispered in an awed voice, "you've ruint him, buddy."

I wasn't at all worried about the clay that had pulled away, but I was worried as to whether or not the builders' gypsum I'd used for plaster had made a good true casting. I turned the half so light from the fire would strike against the inside surface. It was smooth wherever it had pulled away clean, and the ridges that marked the forehead and flared out from the corner of the eye showed that the plaster had settled tightly into every cleft and wrinkle.

"No, I didn't ruin him," I told Lonnie. "I've got him caught so tight he can never get away." I held the casting half around so he could see inside, and said, "That's him, right in there. All I've got to do is to clean out every particle of clay and give him a bath with real soapy water, so the casting won't stick to the mold. Then, after I've bound the two empty sides back together, I'll pour in soft plaster and roll it around till it makes a firm shell on the inside. When it hardens, it will come out looking exactly the way the clay did when we flung the plaster on it last night."

"Jeepers!" Lonnie said. "If the inside one hardens, how you goin' to get it out?"

"That's easy," I told him. "I won't need the mold any more, so I'll crack it off with a chisel and throw it away."

I was so busy in getting the second half of the mold off the model that I didn't notice Lonnie until I heard a scraping sound behind me. When I looked around he was sitting cross-legged on the other side of the fire. He had the first mold-half in his lap, and was digging into it with the mixing spoon as if he were scooping beans out of a pot.

I don't remember, but I must have yelled at him. He looked across the fire at me with a half-sore, half-hurt expression on his face, and told me, "Don't get your insides all riled up, buddy! I'm only diggin' out some of the mud for you. Didn't you say we was the cowboy artists?"

It took a lot of explaining before I could make Lonnie understand that cleaning and soaping the inside of the molds was one of the trickiest parts of the business, and that the slightest scratch made on the surface would show up on the finished casting. The only way I could pacify him was by promising that he could pour the plaster when I made the castings—and that I'd let him throw plaster at the clay models of the "old buzzards."

Fortunately, Lonnie had made his first gouge into the top of the mold, and had scraped away only half the parting place in the hair. It could easily be carved back in when I trimmed up the finished casting. After I'd stopped him he lost interest in the cleaning, and sat by the fire more asleep than awake, but he wouldn't go to bed.

It was past midnight before I had both molds cleaned, soaped, and bound tightly back together. Then I let Lonnie pour in the creamy casting plaster, a little at a time, while I rolled and turned the molds until I was sure I had a good even casting, not less than half an inch thick. After the poured castings had been set on the ledge to harden Lonnie asked me, "Say, buddy, ain't the stuff I poured in there all that's goin' to get saved?"

"That's right," I told him. "That's what is going to make the finished product."

Lonnie seemed to be thinking deeply as he spread his bedroll, hauled off his battered boots, wriggled out of his jeans, and crawled in between the blankets. I undressed a little more than he did, so it took me longer, but I was already in my bed when he said, "Look, buddy, I was just thinkin'. . . . If what I put in them molds comes out art, then ain't I an artist? . . . sort of . . . as a man might say?"

"Sure you're an artist!" I told him. "You're my partner, and we're the Cowboy Artists of the Southwest."

"Jeepers!" Lonnie whispered, and within two minutes he was snoring.

Even though I'd told Lonnie we were partners, I hadn't meant that we were fifty-fifty partners, and I was sure that if whatever money I might make with my amateurish busts were put into a general pot it wouldn't last long. As soon as Lonnie was snoring good and loud I reached for my Levi's, rolled one cuff down, laid in two of the tens the last banker had paid me, and rolled the cuff up again.

No man ever took to a new profession more seriously—or with greater pride—than Lonnie. The next morning I didn't even have to call him to get him up. "Mornin', buddy!" he called to me as he headed for the river with his razor and a dishtowel. "What'll the Cowboy Artists o' the Southwest get started off on this mornin'?"

"Well, we'll have to call on that banker I saw yesterday," I told him. "I want him to see the clay before I . . . we cast it. I'm not too sure he's going to like it. You get slicked up while I cook breakfast, then we'll go and find out."

I had breakfast ready by the time Lonnie had shaved, and as he picked up his plate he told me, "If you don't mind, buddy, don't throw out no more bacon rind. It comes in handy for a man to keep his boots clean and neat. Wisht we had a good stiff little brush. Way the wind blows dust around these parts my hat's gettin' to look somethin' awful."

Lonnie's hat had looked awful ever since I'd known him. Where he grabbed it by the crown there was a hole big enough for a quarter to slip through, and oil from his hair had stained it in a jagged band to more than an inch above the brim.

"We'll do better than a stiff brush," I told him. "If we get as many jobs around here as Mabel thinks we're going to, we'll get brand new outfits—hats, boots, and all—before we cross the line into New Mexico."

"Jeepers Creepers!" he shouted, and went at his breakfast as if he were starving, then stopped with a forkful in mid-air. "Look, buddy," he said, "I wasn't thinkin' very good when I throwed my old cloze in the river yesterday mornin'. It wouldn't look right . . . us bein' all dolled up like that . . . and old Shiftless lookin' . . . I should ought to have saved them old duds till I got her stripped down clean and painted."

"Don't worry about it," I told him. "That's just a cheap shirt and pair of jeans you've got on. You wear those to work on Shiftless. While I'm talking to the old gentleman at the bank this morning you can pick yourself up a pair of Levi's and a two-dollar shirt. We can afford that much whether we get any more jobs around here or not."

Lonnie gulped the rest of his breakfast and had Shiftless warmed up for the trip before I'd finished the dishes, and on the way to town she acted as if she'd turned over a new leaf herself. She didn't boil all the way.

14

Leave Me Try It!

I WAS a little nervous when I carried the clay model into the bank, and I grew more nervous as the old banker looked it over. "Well," he said at last, "it's me all right, but doggoned if I don't have kind of a naked look. Guess I'm used to seeing that old picture with the beard. Wasn't much of the time, back there fifty-sixty years ago, when I didn't wear one."

I swallowed a couple of times and made my best pitch. "Did you leave your mustache on when you shaved your beard off?" I asked.

"Yep! Yep!" he said quickly. "Left it on ten, maybe twenty years."

"Let's try putting a mustache on," I said, "and see if it looks more natural to you."

He looked at me as if I'd said I'd grow a mustache on the model, and asked, "Could you do it without spoiling what you've got now?"

That was enough to let me know I hadn't muffed the job entirely, and my fingers were steady when I reached behind the V of the uniform for a bit of clay. I rolled it into a pigtail between my palms, with one end tapering off a little, stuck

the heavy end under one nostril of the model, then pressed it
down till it extended below the edge of the lip. The old gentleman had his face right at my elbow, watching me like a coyote
watches a prairie dog he's about to pounce on, so I said, "You
could help me a lot if you would. Of course, I don't know how
big your mustache was, or just how you wore it. If you take
hold here with your fingers you could show me. Smooth it out
and twist it just as you did with your own mustache, and if
there's more clay than you want just pinch it off."

The old fellow was a bit too gentle with his fingers when he
started, but he picked up the feel quickly, curved the pigtail
down past the corner of the lip, flattened it with his thumb,
and turned up a little duck-tail at the end. It wasn't a very good
mustache, but he was as tickled as if he'd created a masterpiece.
"Now we got it," he chuckled. "Lord sakes! All these years and
I never knew I was a sculptor. Mind if I try the other side?"

I didn't. I scooped out a bit more clay, rolled another pigtail, and passed it to him. He had a little trouble in trying to
make that side match the other, but I was able to straighten
it out fairly well when I marked the hair on. While I was doing
it I asked, "Did the girl who called you about this tell you it
would take me two or three days to make the marblelike
casting?"

"Yep. Yep. Mabel told me," he said. "Understand you're going to stay around for a couple of weeks. She tells me most of
the bankers this side the state line want their likenesses made."

I was careful not to let the banker see how excited his news
had made me, and tried to act as casual as I could while I
drew the carrying sack down over the model. "Yes," I told him,
"you people in this part of the country have treated us so fine,
and we like this climate so well, that we've decided to stay
over for a couple of weeks. I doubt we can make busts for most
of the bankers between here and the state line, but we'll do
as many as we can." Of course, I was thinking, "can get," but
I said the last word only to myself. Then I thanked the old
gentleman for the help he'd given me on the mustache, and

left.

When I came out of the bank I noticed a little knot of people standing in front of the general store, and Shiftless parked at the side of the street just beyond them. Lonnie wasn't in her, so I expected he'd be in the store buying his new shirt and jeans. I stepped right along, with the intention of going in to find him and hurry him along. If we were going to get as much business as the old banker thought, we'd have to drive right to Safford for more supplies. I'd have to get some better materials for making armatures, tell the man at the building material yard to order in three or four more sacks of fired gypsum, and buy shellac and alcohol for hardening and finishing the plaster busts. And, somewhere, I'd have to get hold of a lot more modeling clay.

I was so busy thinking about the things I'd need that I didn't notice Lonnie until I turned out to pass the knot of people in front of the store. He was the center of attraction—leaning one shoulder against the building, his back half toward me, hat pushed onto the back of his head, a bundle under his arm, and his feet crossed in a nonchalant manner. As I stopped at the edge of his audience he was saying, "My partner, he does the temp'rary clay stuff and cleans out the insides of the molds. My part o' the artist business is makin' the castin's—the finished produck, you know. We don't make 'em for ordinary folks—only for bankers and suchlike."

It seemed a shame to break in on Lonnie's enjoyment, but I was afraid that if I let him go on he might get us into a tangle, so I started around the outside of the crowd, stopped as though I had just noticed him, and called, "Oh, partner! We'll have to be moving along. We've got a lot to do today."

When I spoke, the people looked around at me, and Lonnie was quick in doing the honors. "Folks," he called out as if he were selling patent medicine, "this here's my partner—the man I was tellin' you 'bout—cowboy artist o' the Southwest!"

He sauntered over to Shiftless, climbed in behind the wheel, and reached for the goosing wire while the cowboy artist o' the

Southwest twisted her tail.

Lonnie gunned Shiftless down the street as though he'd been Barney Oldfield out to set a new world's speed record. We were a mile out of town before he let her slow down to twenty-five, then without looking toward me, he said, "Look, buddy, I was only tellin' them folks how you make faces out of clay . . . and make molds on 'em . . . and how I pour in the stuff to make the castin's."

"Fine," I said, "but I wouldn't tell them too much. You know, a man that tells all his secrets doesn't stay in business long."

"Oh, I wasn't givin' away no secrets, buddy," he assured me, "only tellin' 'em how we done a few things. You know, the folks in these small towns don't see artists every day, and you can't blame 'em for bein' curious like. Where we bound for, back to camp?"

Our trip to Safford took all morning and part of the afternoon, but I found most of the things I needed, and the man at the building material yard said he'd order the gypsum for me right away. The one thing I couldn't find was the one I needed most—clay that was fit for modeling. The nearest I could come to it was a few shovelfuls of adobe mud that some Mexicans were using for making brick. I think Lonnie was still worried for fear I'd heard more than he wanted me to when he'd been talking to the crowd that morning. He didn't have much to say, either going or coming, and he didn't pester me to let him buy stuff for Shiftless.

After we got back to camp he kept busy till dark, scrubbing away at her speckled layers of paint. I kept busy enough myself. I made three new armatures, with good heavy bases, two-foot pieces of pipe for pedestals, and heavy wire rings at the top. Then I pressed a mass of adobe onto each one of them—about the shape of a man's head, but only two-thirds as large. By letting it harden and bake in the sun I was sure it would make cores that I could use over and over, and it would let me stretch my clay far enough that I could have three or four

busts in the molds at the same time. I'd simply have to wet
the core each time I reused it, and work a half inch or so of clay
over the outside to make my models.

Our little canyon was ideal for my work. There was never
a time of day when part of it wasn't in bright sunshine and
part in shadow. I changed into my working clothes and was
starting on the first armature when it come into my mind that
there had never been a time since I'd come to Arizona when
I could do as Dr. Gaghan had told me—get as much sunshine
as possible on my body. It seemed to me that if we were going
to be in that canyon for a couple of weeks it might be a good
time to start. Before I went on with my work I pulled off my
shirt and undershirt, then took out my jackknife and cut the legs
of my jeans to about six inches long. I'd finished the second
armature and was working on the third when Lonnie came and
asked to borrow my knife. He didn't mention my having
stripped down and cut the legs off my britches, and I didn't
think to tell him why I'd done it.

I'd forgotten about Lonnie's having borrowed the knife and
was working with my head down when he laid the jackknife by
my hand and asked, "Ain't there some kind of funny caps
artists wears too? I seen pi'tures of 'em."

When I looked up Lonnie stood there, stripped to the waist,
and with the legs of the britches I'd given him for Christmas
cut even shorter than mine. I had to bite my tongue to keep
from laughing, but I couldn't let myself, because he was as
serious as if it were a matter of the greatest importance. "Oh,
those are berets," I said. "Only the professional artists wear
them."

He looked down at me in a rather puzzled way for a moment
or two, and said, "Well, buddy, we're professionals, ain't we?
We're doin' it for money."

I had to stop and do a little thinking before I could answer
him. He was certainly right about a man's being a professional
if he earned his living through some form of art. But my work
was terribly amateurish as compared to Ivon's or the busts I'd

seen in museums. Then too, if Lonnie was going to talk his head off every time he could scare up an audience, I knew I'd have to be awfully careful what I told him.

"You see, it's like this, Lonnie," I said. "There are two kinds of art: fine art and commercial art. The kind they have in museums is fine art—carved in marble or cast in bronze. Our kind is commercial art. . . . you know, we make ours out of plaster. It's only the artists who do fine art who wear berets."

"Oh, I see," Lonnie said. "Never did know before there was so many different kinds of art. Suppose it's like horses and cattle—different folks likes different kinds." Then he went back to scrubbing paint off Shiftless.

When I'd finished with the armatures I cleaned the isinglass sections, put the dividing dam carefully onto the clay model of the second banker, and mixed a pan of plaster for the mold. I'd tossed a couple of dollops onto the eyes and ears when Lennie called, "Hey, buddy, ain't you goin' to leave me sling some of that stuff at the old buzzard?" He slung so hard that he splattered plaster back against his own chest, but he was having too much fun to pay any attention to it. With each fistful he'd hoot and laugh, but as soon as all the clay was covered he lost interest and went back to his first love.

After supper I brought Mabel's little horse head from the ledge where it had been drying all day in the sun, took mallet and chisels from the car, and sat down by the fire to chip the mold off. I was a bit nervous, for I'd never before tried using Castile soap to keep the casting from sticking to the inside of the mold. If it hadn't sealed all the pores in the mold tightly, I couldn't break it away clean. The casting would, of course, be ruined, and I'd have to do the whole job over from scratch.

I cut the burlap bands that bound the two sides of the mold together, ripped them off, and decided I'd better start at the crest of the neck, where there would be the least chance for any binding. I stood my chisel edge close to the crack left by the isinglass dam, tapped it gently with the mallet, moved it along a bit, and tapped a little more. It didn't take much tapping till a little half circle of the brittle mold cracked free. When it lifted out freely and I could see the smooth, clean plaster of the casting, my nerves went jangly—the way they will after a near-accident. I let my arms hang loose till my hands stopped trembling, then went on with the chipping. Piece after piece, the mold cracked free, uncovering more and more of the casting.

Lonnie sat across the fire, watching me until I had half of the neck exposed, then he got up and wandered away toward Shiftless. I was too busy to pay any attention to him until I heard a clanking as he sat down at the fire again. When I looked over, he had the mold, with the casting of the banker's bust inside it, perched on his lap, face up. In one hand he held the old carpenter's hammer he used for fixing Shiftless, and in his other hand a half-inch chisel. "I can do this stuff all right, buddy," he told me. "It's kind of like shellin' nuts, ain't it?" I managed to stop him just as he swung the hammer up to wallop the chisel.

I must have shouted at him, for his voice had an injured tone when he said, "Jeepers Creepers, buddy, I wouldn't do it no hurt! I was only goin' to shell off some of this moldin'."

I tried to explain to Lonnie that breaking away the mold was a real ticklish job, and that I'd ruined three or four castings before I'd learned how to do it without marking or cutting them with the edge of the chisel.

"Jeepers, buddy," he told me sadly, "you won't leave me do nothin' exceptin' to pour in the stuff for the castin's. How'm I goin' to be an artist if you won't leave me do some of it?"

It seemed to me that maybe I was being a little rough on him, and it wouldn't make too much difference if he did scar the back of the head a bit. I'd have to trim the parting place in the hair of that one anyway, to make up for the ridge he'd scraped out with the mixing spoon. It wouldn't take much extra work to fill in a couple of chisel marks, and the patches wouldn't show in the hair anyway.

"All right," I told him, "I'll let you try your hand on the back of his head—after I've made a starting place for you—but you'll have to learn to do a perfect job before I let you touch a face."

"Look, buddy," he said earnestly, "I've used a hammer and chisel ever since I was a little kid. We was homesteaders, and my old man used to leave me help him make chairs and tables and stuff."

Lonnie's feelings were hurt enough as it was, so I laid the horse head down, got up and went around to sit beside him. I took the big mold onto my lap, turned it face down, stripped away the burlap bindings, and picked a spot that I thought would be right above the damaged parting place. After Lonnie had passed me his hammer and chisel I marked out a half circle at one side of the isinglass crack—no bigger than a half a silver dollar. "That's as big a chunk as you want to take at one time," I told him, "and you don't try to chop it out with the chisel. You just crack it loose and pick it out."

As I talked I stood a corner of the chisel edge on the mark I'd scratched, and tapped it with the hammer. "You don't really hammer it at all," I said. "You just sort of bounce the hammer on it—as if you were bouncing a marble. Then you follow on around, tapping it a little more. It's that bouncing tap that cracks it loose, not the cutting."

"I get you, buddy! I get you," he told me anxiously. "Leave me try it."

I didn't let him try till I'd cracked out half a dozen chips. Every one of them came away clean, but I'd started a bit too far back to uncover the damaged parting place. And Lonnie was becoming more anxious with every chip that cracked away. I put the mold back into his lap, passed him the hammer and chisel, and told him, "Just take it slow and easy. It doesn't make a bit of difference whether or not we finish taking these molds off tonight. I've told them it might be two or three days before the finished pieces were ready. Suppose you crack a little chunk out, just above the last one I took."

Lonnie clutched the hammer and chisel as though he were

afraid someone would steal them. And instead of laying the chisel for a little chunk, he laid it for a big one. Then he tapped it—as if it had been a railroad spike.

I was lucky. The casting had been drying only a single day, and even in the Arizona sunshine it hadn't dried enough to become brittle. But it's lucky that old banker's head was only a plaster cast. A chunk of brittle mold flew past my face, I ducked, and when I looked back there was little more than the handle of the chisel sticking up through the top of the old gentleman's pate. Lonnie was sitting and staring down at it, the way a hypnotized cow will stare down at a coiled rattlesnake. "Jeepers, buddy!" he whispered, "I've ruint it."

That's one time I believed him, but when I examined the casting there wasn't a single crack running out from the chisel. It had gone through as cleanly as it would have gone into a bucket of lard. And, best of all, it had gone lengthwise of the damaged parting place.

That was the last of Lonnie's active practice at his new profession—except for pouring the casting plaster and heaving a handful or two of mold plaster into the face of "them old buzzards."

Those first castings came out better than I'd dared to hope they would. When I'd trimmed and sanded every rough spot— and closed Lonnie's brain incision—they looked reasonably near professional. The coating of shellac and alcohol took off the stark white look, and though they didn't look like marble to me, they did to Mabel and the banker.

Mabel must have nearly bankrupted her boss with long-distance phone calls, but she certainly saved Lonnie and me from bankruptcy—and if she wasn't the best salesman in the world she was close to it. Right from the beginning she was anxious to see how I did my work, so one afternoon Lonnie and I brought her out to our little canyon. She kept as quiet as a hidden fawn as she sat for a couple of hours, just watching me shape the clay with my fingers. And I had to be a bit of a hypocrite while she was there. The tintype I'd picked up that morning was a particularly poor one, but the banker's face had been a strong, well-chiseled one. I knew exactly how it must have looked in his early thirties, and all the work I did was from the picture I could bring up before my mind, but every few minutes I'd take the tintype up, act as though I were studying it, and make some little change in the clay.

After that first time Mabel came to our camp almost every day, but she never came alone. She always brought along some nice old gentleman with a tintype in his pocket; a few of them had come more than a hundred miles to have me make likenesses of their youth. Each one of them came back when I had the clay model ready, liked it, and came for the finished bust when I had it completed. It saved me days of traveling time, and by working early and late I could just about finish one bust a day.

My biggest trouble was with Lonnie. With nothing to do but scrub paint off Shiftless, he wanted to sit around and talk all the time, and his talking nearly drove me crazy. After I'd stood it a couple of days I gave him twenty dollars and said, "We can afford it now; why don't you drive Shiftless to Safford where you can get a garageman to help you put her into first-class shape?"

Lonnie grabbed the twenty and was away within three minutes. He always came back to camp every evening, and I know he spent all the money I gave him on Shiftless, for he had some new part on her every time he came back—but it cost me just about ten dollars a day to keep him out of my hair.

Lonnie and I lived in our little canyon for more than three weeks, and when we pulled out for the last time no one could have guessed we were the same two boys who had pulled in there—or that Shiftless was the same old flivver. Really, she wasn't, and she'd cost me about fifty dollars more than if I'd bought her brand new. Lonnie had put so many new parts on her that there was little of the original jalopy left—except for the chassis. He'd done a cracking good job of painting her, and he kept her polished till she shone like patent leather. But it had hurt his feelings when I wouldn't let him letter her front doors, THE COWBOY ARTISTS OF THE SOUTHWEST.

We'd been living "high on the hog," according to Lonnie. Steak, baked potatoes and dessert for him every day, and for me chicken, eggs, plenty of milk, and canned salmon. At the end of our first week we'd gone to Safford and bought whole new outfits of clothing. Levi's, shirts, underwear, boots, and hats. Lonnie wouldn't pick out either boots or hat till I bought mine, then took exactly the same thing—only that his hat was two sizes larger, and his boots two sizes smaller. He even insisted on buying Levi's that were six or eight inches too long, then folding the cuffs up the way I did mine. His were only so we artists might look as much alike as possible, but I had good reason to keep mine folded up. There were three fifty-dollar bills and two twenties in one of them.

I'd still been a little pasty-looking when we settled down in the canyon, but when we pulled out I was as brown as tanned calfskin—except for a white band around the middle. I'd been to see the doctor every week, and had mailed the report cards to Dr. Gaghan. Each of them had been almost exactly like the sample one I was still keeping, just in case I might have to take another one sometime. If I wasn't a lot stronger than I'd been when I left home, I certainly felt as though I was, but I couldn't seem to gain an ounce, no matter how high we lived on the hog.

Every bust I'd made had been from a picture—usually an old faded tintype—but I hadn't let myself become confused by trying to copy them. For me it was better to study the old gentlemen's faces while I visited with them for half an hour or so. In that length of time I knew all I needed to know about the shape of a nose, the size of an ear, type of eye, breadth of forehead, and general shape of the face and head. But I knew a lot more than that; I knew exactly what sort of man he was in his old age, so it wasn't hard to guess what he must have been like as a young man—for a man's character doesn't change after he's thirty. It only becomes more firmly set, and is more deeply marked in his features.

In shaping the clay for the first two or three busts I'd had to close my eyes and bring back to mind some young face of the same type—one I'd known well—but from there on I didn't have to close them at all. As soon as my fingers began shaping the clay I could see the man I'd been talking to that morning, but I'd see him as he used to be before the lines of his face had deepened and set. And with each one I made, it was easier to see, and easier for my fingers to make the clay say what I wanted it to. The busts weren't fine art, and I didn't try to claim it for them, but they made a good many old gentlemen happy, and they made Lonnie and me a right good living. When we crossed the line into New Mexico I had a dozen letters tucked away in my toolbox, letters that I knew would get me a customer in almost any town with a single banker.

15

City Slickers

WHEN we left Arizona I had three jobs lined up ahead of me. I'd promised one kindly old banker that I'd make a bust of his son-in-law who, he told me, was a very prominent El Paso attorney. And I'd promised two others to stop on our way and make busts of friends of theirs; one at Lordsburg, and one at Deming. We stopped three days in both towns, because it took that long for the plaster to dry, but we weren't fortunate enough to find a little canyon where we could hide away for our work, so I thought it would be best to take hotel rooms.

It wasn't.

The trouble was that Lonnie didn't have anything to do. With Shiftless all fixed up he couldn't spend more than an hour a day on her—polishing the body, the brass on the radiator, and even the engine. He never read, not even the headlines in the newspaper, so it was hard for him to amuse himself when I was too busy to talk. He got along pretty well our first forenoon in Lordsburg, because he was able to round up a couple of little audiences on the sidewalk and tell about his being an artist and making the finished product—the actual marble busts we made for bankers only.

But Lonnie didn't have too much imagination; he was never able to expand his original story, and it wore out quickly in a town the size of Lordsburg. When he could no longer scare up an audience he slouched around our room, wanting me to talk to him, and nearly driving me out of my mind. It wasn't hard to do, for the light in the room was poor; it wouldn't reflect off the moist clay as it should, and I was having trouble in bringing out the expression I wanted.

The money I had stashed away in the cuff of my new Levi's was my own personal savings account, but I had about forty dollars more, along with some change, in one of the pockets. I'd worn the Levi's when I went to see the banker that morning, but when I got back to the room I'd stripped down and put on the cut-off pair before starting on the clay model. When Lonnie had pestered me for nearly an hour I lost my patience a bit, went to the closet where my Levi's were hanging, rammed a hand in the pocket, and said, "Here's some change, Lonnie. Why don't you go see a movie?"

I'd intended to give him a handful of change, but there were only a few small coins in the pocket, so I peeled what I thought would be a dollar bill off the roll. Lonnie was standing right behind me when I jerked it out, turned, and passed it toward him. I wouldn't have noticed that the bill was a five instead of a one if Lonnie hadn't brightened up when he took it. He hurried out of the room like a little kid who's been given a nickel and is bound for the store to buy candy.

With Lonnie out from under my feet the poor light didn't bother me as much as it had—but not for long. He couldn't have been gone more than fifteen minutes before he was back, looking more sad and lonesome than before. "The movie don't open till six o'clock," he told me.

I should have had better sense, but I wanted to be rid of him while I was working on that clay, so I said, "You're a pretty good looking guy, and you've got a pretty fancy automobile. I'd think you could find yourself a girl you could take for a ride. Take her for a good long one. Buy her some supper and take her to the movies when you bring her back."

Lonnie's face lit up like a mountaintop that's just been touched by the morning sun. "Honest-a-God, buddy, would it be all right?" he asked excitedly.

"Sure! Sure, it would, Lonnie," I told him. "You've got a five there. That ought to do the trick."

Lonnie was out of that room in less than two seconds, and I thought I'd seen the last of him until time for the movie to let out, but I hadn't. In about twenty minutes he was back, smelling like a dance hall girl who has passed her prime. He must have been to the dime store for perfume, and stopped at the bathroom down the hall to plaster it all over himself. His face was scrubbed till it shone like copper, his new hat was cocked on one side of his head, and his new boots were sparkling. He strutted back and forth across the room a couple of times, stopped squarely in my light, and asked, "Say, buddy, shouldn't a man ought to buy a lady a box o' candy when he takes her to the theeater?"

It sounded to me as if he were leading up to make a touch beyond the five I'd already given him—by mistake—so I said, "Not if he's going to take her to dinner first. Either way is fine, but I wouldn't do both."

Lonnie was never under my feet again when I had to work in a hotel room—but it cost an even five dollars a day for gas, oil, dinners, and movies. The only reason it didn't cost more was that I made five his limit. With three days in a town to make a twenty-five-dollar bust, we could just about break even. It took most of the other ten for room rent and meals—the ones we had when Lonnie wasn't entertaining a lady.

Between Las Cruces and El Paso there were nearly a dozen towns along the Rio Grande where I believed I might find jobs, but we didn't stop at any of them. In the first place, I was almost out of materials, and El Paso was the only place within hundreds of miles where I could find the right kind of plaster of Paris, real modeling clay, and the kind of clay and plaster tools I needed for doing a good job. Then too, I knew there would be a letter from home waiting for me there. But the thing I was most anxious about was making the bust for the very prominent attorney. From what his father-in-law had told me I knew there would be no chance of my getting a picture, then hiding away to make the clay model in some little canyon. I'd have to make it with the attorney sitting for me, and I'd never tried one from a live model without Ivon right there to tell me where I was making a mistake.

I worried about it all the way from Deming to El Paso, and the more I worried about it the more nervous I became. I didn't know whether the old banker had written his son-in-law that I was just a cowboy artist, and I didn't know how to act as any other kind. Before we reached the city I'd made my mind up to two things. I was going to buy myself a suit of clothes before I went to see the attorney, and I was going to rent as good a room as I could get in the best hotel I could find. I'd pay whatever I had to for a corner room with big windows—on the northwest corner if I could get it—so I'd have just the right light, and a dignified place to take the gentleman for his sittings.

As we were pulling into El Paso I changed my mind again, and decided it would be better to rent a suite—a corner one that had a door from the hall to both the bedroom and the parlor. Then if Lonnie couldn't find anything to do he could stay in the bedroom while my client was sitting for me in the parlor. And I'd buy my suit first, and a suitcase, so I wouldn't look too much like a hick when I went into the hotel to rent the suite.

The more I thought about it the more it seemed the right thing to do, but there wasn't any sense in diving right in and renting the suite the first day. It would be better to take just an ordinary room in a reasonably cheap hotel for one day. That would give me time to buy the supplies and tools I needed, and to have the suit of clothes altered if it didn't fit me exactly right.

On second thought I made up my mind that it would be only sensible to keep the room in the cheaper hotel for all three days we'd be in town. We couldn't leave our saddles, bedrolls, and all the rest of our stuff in Shiftless safely, even if we put her in a garage. And it seemed to me that we'd look terribly silly if we went lugging that sort of stuff into a suite in a top-notch hotel.

To save one night's hotel bill we camped eight or ten miles outside El Paso, and drove into the city early in the morning. We found a fairly good room in a respectable hotel for two dollars a day. And after we'd moved into it I told Lonnie to go see the town while I went to find the tools and supplies I needed. I didn't tell him anything about my going to buy a new suit; not that I wanted to keep it from him, but just because I didn't think about telling him. When everything had been carried up to the room I peeled him a five from the dwindling roll in my pocket and said, "Have a good time. I'll see you back here at noon."

I'd expected that I'd have to hunt all over town to find the tools and supplies I needed, but I didn't. I found them all in a combination store that sold books and stationery and artists' supplies. It didn't take me more than half an hour to pick out the tools I wanted, and the storekeeper sent a couple of boys to lug the plaster of Paris and clay back to the hotel for me. I went along to let them into our room, then started down the street to find myself a suit of clothes. That was easier than I expected, too. At the first clothing store I went into I found a slim-jim suit that fitted me pretty well, except that the arms and legs were too short, and it was only $22.50. Then I got a tailor, a few doors farther on, to lengthen the arms and legs for a dollar. He said he'd have the suit ready for me by eleven o'clock.

While I was waiting for my suit to be altered I went to the post office and found a letter from Mother waiting for me at the general delivery window. The first part of the letter just said that everybody at home was well and that Dr. Gaghan was very much pleased with my report cards and the regularity with which they were coming through. Then there were two or three pages telling me how delighted and proud she was that I'd been able to find myself such a fine job with a big cattle company, one that fully appreciated my worth and was sending me all around the country to look after their herds. Over and over again she cautioned me to be careful about riding rough horses in my condition, or spending too many hours in the saddle without rest. And she was worried for fear I was sending home so much of my pay checks that I was keeping myself strapped. She said there was no need at all for it, that they were getting along nicely, and that she wanted me to keep a few dollars by me for a possible rainy day.

The farther I read, the more ashamed of myself I was for all the lies I'd written her, but I couldn't write her the truth. Of course, she'd known that I'd whittled horses ever since I was big enough to carry a jackknife, and she knew that I'd roomed with an artist while I was at the munitions plant, but a preacher couldn't have made her believe I'd been earning as much as twenty-five dollars a day as a portrait sculptor. If I ever wrote her anything of the kind she'd be positive it was a lie, she'd be worried sick for fear that in desperation over my health I'd turned to banditry, and she'd never believe another word I wrote as long as I lived. There was only one thing I could do, and that was some more lying.

I bought a stamped envelope and a pad of paper, then stood at one of the high desks in the post office and wrote her a bunch more fairy tales. I told her our boss was very much pleased with the job we'd done, had raised both my partner's pay and mine, and was sending us north along the Rio Grande River, probably as far as Santa Fe. I wrote that we expected it to be late spring before we got there, because we'd have to move the cattle slowly, and much as I liked my bosses I planned to quit my job at Santa Fe. That would leave me within less than three hundred miles from Littleton, and I'd promised to be there in time for the Fourth of July roundup. I added a few lines about going to see all our old friends as soon as I reached Colorado, then bought a fifty-dollar money order, folded it inside the letter, and mailed it.

On the way back to pick up my suit from the tailor, I bought myself a white shirt and sort of conservative necktie, then I thought about buying a pair of dress shoes, but there didn't seem to be much sense in it. My boots were almost new, and the pants legs would come down far enough to cover the tops. It seemed better to spend what spare time I had getting a haircut and shampoo. I hadn't had one since we left Phoenix, and was getting a little ragged around the edges.

Of course, I knew my hair had bleached out a bit from working bareheaded in the sun, but when the dust was scrubbed out of it, it looked nearly as white as snow, probably because my face and neck had tanned so dark. Then too, it had dried out so badly that it stuck up like the fur on a scared cat's back. I had to have the barber put some oil on it, and I guess he took me for a back-country boy; he charged me a quarter for no more than a teaspoonful of oil tonic. Maybe I got my money's worth out of him anyway. While he was cutting my hair I asked him where I could buy a fairly good suitcase without spending too much for it. "Juarez," he told me. "Leather goods are cheap on the Mexican side of the line. Watch out for the pickpockets over there. They're thicker'n fleas."

It was about half past eleven before I got back to the hotel, but Lonnie wasn't around, so I went down the hall and took a bath, then put on my new clothes to surprise him. He might have been surprised when he came in, but he wasn't happy. "Jeepers Creepers, buddy," he said. "I'll look like a bum . . . us travelin' 'round with you all slicked up the likes o' that— and me in overhauls."

"I won't be wearing these clothes when we're traveling around," I told him. "The only reason I bought them is that I'm going to make a bust of a fine gentleman, and we're going to take a suite in the best hotel so I'll have a dignified place for the sittings."

Lonnie looked sorrowfully at his reflection in the mirror, and asked, "We're goin' to take it, or you're goin' to take it?"

Lonnie wasn't *trying* to look sorrowful—he never could look any way other than he felt—but anyone would have thought he'd lost his last friend on earth. "*We're* going to take it, Lonnie," I said. "You're my buddy, aren't you? If you want a city-slicker suit there's no reason you can't have it. Wait till I hang up these working duds and we'll go see what we can find."

As I said it I picked up my Levi's—with two fifties and one twenty still folded inside the cuff. I fiddled around in the closet till I'd fished the money out, then we went to buy a suit for Lonnie. It wasn't an easy job. He wouldn't even try a jacket on till he'd found a suit almost exactly like mine—light gray, with a dark pencil stripe—and that was in a fancy store where they charged $27.50.

It was the middle of the afternoon before the tailor had Lonnie's suit altered to please him, and as soon as he'd put it on we crossed the bridge into Mexico. I'd only intended to buy a suitcase in Juarez, but the shops were full of hand-tooled leather goods, and with a little haggling the prices were a lot cheaper than in the United States. While I was dickering for the suitcase Lonnie found a real nice tooled-leather handbag that he wanted to buy for his sister in Wyoming. It was a good bargain, so I told him to go ahead and buy it. Then I bought one just like it for Mrs. Larsen, one for Mabel, and some little trinket for everyone at home.

We mailed everything from Juarez, so the packages would have the foreign postmark on them, but I didn't notice the address Lonnie wrote on the one for his sister. I couldn't forget what the barber had told me about pickpockets, and was too busy trying to address my own stuff while I kept one hand on my roll. I made up my mind right then and there that I'd never let myself be caught that way again. If the money had been left right in the cuff of my Levi's, hanging in the hotel closet, it would be as safe as if it were in a bank. No thief would ever steal a pair of jeans the size of mine, and nobody would ever think to look in the cuffs.

I had only one fifty and a ten left when we got back from Juarez, so I didn't want to pay an extra night's rent on a hotel suite. Still, I couldn't phone the attorney and tell him where to come for his sittings till I knew the number of the suite. The only thing I could do was to go and make a reservation. The clerk said I'd need only a sitting room, not a suite, but even at that the price was eight dollars a day.

As soon as I'd made the reservation I called the attorney, but I didn't like his voice or what he said. When I told him who I was he snapped, "Oh, the artist fellow. You may call at my office tomorrow morning at ten sharp." Then he said, "sharp," a second time, gave me the address of his office, and hung up.

After supper Lonnie wanted us to go out and do the town, but I got him to settle for a movie instead. The one he picked was a rip-roaring cowboy-and-Indian picture, and there were some pretty good horse falls in it. They were in two short strips, spliced into a half-hour film, but they were taken at the Wickenburg movie lot. I recognized the location the instant it was flashed on the screen, and a couple of the Hollywood cowboys' horses, but I couldn't be positive about any of the fall riders. Lonnie swore that one of them was me, so we stayed to see the picture a second time, even though I knew he was wrong. Both runs had been made on the flat set, and I took all my falls on the one that plunged down the mesa side.

The next morning Lonnie helped me carry an armature, the clay, and my new tools over to our sitting room, then I gave him five dollars and told him to enjoy himself while I was busy with the attorney.

16

Two of a Kind

THE Arizona banker who had given me the attorney's name was a kindly old gentleman, but his son-in-law was no gentleman in any sense of the word. His name was painted on his office door in big gold-leaf letters, and under it COUNSELOR AT LAW. Then, down in the corner of the frosted glass panel, was the smaller word ENTER.

I did. We looked straight into each other's eyes for the barest fraction of a second, then he looked down at his desk. In that bare fraction of a second I took a dislike to the man, and if I'd had the amount of sense given geese I'd have left in a hurry, but I didn't. I'd promised the old banker I'd make his son-in-law's bust, and just because I hadn't fallen in love with him at first sight was no reason for running out on my promise.

The office wasn't in the best building in town, and it wasn't a very big one, but three-quarters of it—the part with any windows—had been walled off to make a private office. It was through the open doorway that I caught a glimpse of the attorney. Half the space not taken up by the private office was cut off by a heavy railing, with a settee at one side and a couple of straight chairs at the other. Beyond the railing a birdlike little woman of about fifty sat at a typewriter desk. She looked up nervously when I came in, rather as though she expected me to be cross with her, and she didn't answer when I said, "Good morning." Then when I told her my name and that I had a ten o'clock appointment, she acted as if she didn't know what to do with the information. She glanced around toward the open private-office doorway, back at me, and toward the doorway again. Without saying a word to me she moistened her lips with the tip of her tongue, fidgeted them a bit, got up as if she weren't yet fully decided, and went to the open doorway— just as I'd have gone to the one in the lions' den if I'd been Daniel.

She didn't go in, but I heard her mumble something, half under her breath. With her in the doorway I couldn't see the attorney, but I couldn't help hearing him say, in a voice that sounded as if he were holding it deep in his throat, "Oh, it's that artist fellow. Let him come in."

She did. And I went. But I still don't know why. I, too, stopped in the doorway, because the pompous little man didn't look up at me for at least two minutes. He was sitting behind a huge golden oak desk which was covered with a sheet of plate glass, and seemed to be studying a long, closely typed page in front of him.

He was a little man of about forty, with pig eyes, cheeks as round and smooth as an apple, a wrinkleless forehead, and a chin that faded away in shapeless waves till it joined his fat neck and was lost in the V of a wing-tipped collar. A carefully trimmed little mustache bristled between his characterless mouth and equally characterless nose. He wore oval-shaped glasses with heavy gold rims, the lenses held together by an ornate spring the size of a quarter. One of the lenses had a little handle at the side, from which a pair of black ribbons dangled down across the man's chest and looped around his neck. I didn't need anyone to tell me he'd just had his hair cut and prettied up to look like Francis X. Bushman's—one of the waves was scorched a bit by the curling iron.

Between the two small windows beyond the desk hung a terribly poor oil painting of my prospective client. It was at least three by four feet, and I had to be careful not to grin when I caught sight of it. It wasn't a painting of a man; it was a painting of a pair of glasses with bright yellow rims and a flowing black ribbon, a mass of wavy golden-brown hair, and a pair of rosy cheeks.

At either side of the room there were two heavy, straight-backed, leather-upholstered oak chairs. At one side of the room two children—a girl about eight and a boy about ten—sat on a single chair; spilling off a bit over each side, but looking very prim, with their hands folded in their laps. The little girl peeked up at me; but she didn't smile when I winked at her, just looked down at her hands again. A rather pretty woman—not much more than thirty—sat straight on the other chair, hands folded on her lap, eyes down, and looking as though she might be waiting out a long, dry sermon at church.

I'd just glanced around at an elderly couple, sitting at the opposite end of the room, when the attorney ahemmed loudly, and said, "Come in, young man!"

I did—foolishly—and walked to the front of the desk. The man let me stand there another minute or such a matter while he played at studying the long typewritten page on his desk. I knew it was some kind of a legal document, because every paragraph began with a long word or two in capital letters.

If the little man's pomposity hadn't been so ridiculous as to be comical, I'd have become furious, told him for the benefit of his wife, children, and parents that he was a fourflusher, and got out of there. But it suddenly occurred to me that the paper was a contract—and that the contract was for me. For some reason I couldn't even be furious with myself for having been such a fool as to spend most of my money in getting ready to make one twenty-five-dollar bust. Instead, I had to hold my tongue tight against the top of my mouth to keep from laughing out loud. Here we were—two of a kind—both holding four-card flushes and trying to run a bluff. While I'd been standing in the doorway I'd made up my mind that I wasn't going to make the little man's bust, but it seemed to me it would be fun to play the hand out.

After giving me plenty of time to become impressed with the seriousness of the proceedings the little attorney took a fountain pen from his breast pocket, unscrewed the cap without looking up from the document, and marked an X before the second of two blank lines at the bottom of the page. With an air of finality he flipped the paper around so the blank lines were toward me, pushed it across the desk, held the pen out at arm's length, and demanded, "Sign there, young man!"

I could either call his bluff or raise. I decided to raise. I didn't reach for the pen, but let him sit there holding it out for about the same length of time he'd kept me standing in front of his desk. In the meantime I picked up the contract and put on the same kind of an act he had, but all I did was to glance down the WHEREFOREs and WHEREASes till I came to the NOW THEREFORE. I read that paragraph all the way through, and wish I could remember it all, but I can't. It started off with, "The said party of the second part shall execute in durable material which shall closely emulate carrara marble, a true and faithful reproduction of the countenance of the said party of the first part."

I stopped when I'd gone that far, and said, "This isn't written in proper form."

The little man took off his glasses, waved them languidly, sighed resignedly, and said, "Quite proper, young man! Quite proper! I have perused the instrument diligently."

"So I noticed," I told him pleasantly, "but Carrara is generally spelled with a capital C. It's a city in Italy, you know."

For a moment he looked as though he might explode. His face turned scarlet, he gasped for breath, then bawled, "*MISS BEGGS!*"

"No need to call her yet," I told him. "So far, it seems to be full of mistakes, but just hold on a minute till I finish reading it."

"Preposterous! Preposterous!" he barked, but it had the

sound of a dog that's run back into his own yard before turning
to make his challenge.

I knew I had him where I wanted him right then, and though
I didn't look up from the paper I knew he was watching me, so
I let myself smile as much as I wanted to as I read on to the
bottom of the page. There were a dozen more "said parties"
and "without recourses," but what it amounted to was that
he'd pay me twenty-five dollars after I'd made a reproduction
of his countenance to his complete satisfaction, with as many
sittings as he deemed necessary, and at such times and places
as he might find convenient. The best part was the last. It said
that if I breached the contract in any manner whatsoever it
would "constitute a confession of judgment," and I'd owe him
for whatever time and inconvenience my failure had cost him.

I pretended to go back and begin reading the whole thing
again from the top, but my prospective client snapped, "Come,
come, young man! I can't waste the whole day on this little
matter."

I kept right on—running my eyes back and forth across the
page, but not reading a word—for another minute or so, then
I tossed the contract on the desk and said, as if I'd just made a
big discovery, "Oh, I see what the main trouble is. You've got
your parties of the first part and parties of the second part
twisted around. A man's apt to do that when he has so many of
them."

His face turned fire-red again, and he made a grab for the
paper, but caught himself and pulled his hand back. It took
him a few seconds to get back into his act, but it must have
been an old one, for he knew it by heart, and I never saw a
man who could get a more perfect sneer into both his smile
and his voice. He took his glasses off, with one pinky lifted
gracefully, waved them, and said, "My dear young man, it is
apparent that legal terminology confuses you."

"That's right," I told him, "but you've still got your parties
turned around. You see, it is I who will decide what material
the bust is to be cast in, the competence of the workmanship,

the price, how many sittings will be required, and when and where it will be convenient for me to have them. It is you who will sign a confession of judgment agreement to make good any loss of time or inconvenience you may cause me. The price will be fifty dollars, in advance, and before you make up your mind about so large an investment you should understand that the finished bust will neither emulate nor simulate Carrara marble. It will be plaster of Paris, just as your father-in-law's was. Now, sir, if you would like to draw up a contract saying exactly that, and nothing more or less, I'll be happy to sign it. If not—Good morning."

All the way through I had kept my voice at the same tone I'd have used if I were telling the little boy he must be good or Santa Claus wouldn't come. And before I was finished that attorney wasn't a bit sure but what he was the little boy. That's why I put the "Good morning" on the end. I knew as well as if he'd told me that he'd bragged to everyone who would listen, telling them he'd engaged a famous artist to come to El Paso solely for the purpose of executing his portrait bust, and I knew he'd eat whatever amount of crow he had to before he'd let me get away.

Before I'd finished he was sitting with his mouth open—like a newly-caught fish gasping for air—peeking nervously, first at the old folks and then his wife. But I'll have to give him credit for being a cracking good little actor. He caught himself before I could turn away from the desk, put on his best synthetic smile, and burbled, "Let's not be hasty. Good business should be done in good humor. I'm afraid the legal verbiage may have been upsetting to you. We in the profession sometimes forget that . . ."

"Oh, I didn't mind the verbiage," I broke in, "it was only the order in which the words were arranged that I objected to—and the price."

He ha-ha-ha'd as mirthfully as if he'd lost his best client, waved his glasses, and said, "Possibly it would be as well to forgo the formality of a contract to cover so small a transaction, but I believe there is a slight misunderstanding. I was informed that the . . . ah . . . the emolument . . . ah . . ."

"Would be twenty-five dollars," I finished out for him, "but that's my rural price. If you want one it will cost you fifty dollars, cash in advance, and you can have a contract or not, just as you please."

He pleased not to have a contract, and I pleased not to accept his check—not because I was afraid it would bounce, but just to make him eat a little more crow before I had to take him for a sitting. It was probably a kiddish thing to do, but an ornery nag will usually handle better if you give him a taste of the spurs before you start out on a difficult trail. The hardest part of our meeting was finding something to say while Miss Beggs was out getting the check cashed. Just as I left I reminded him to be at my hotel suite at two o'clock sharp. Then looked back and added another, "Sharp," just as he had done on the phone.

The little man didn't try to bluff at all when he came for his first sitting—or any other—but he couldn't get it through his head that he wasn't posing for a photograph. I'd blocked out the shape of his head, the V of his coat collar, his hair, and the general features of his face before he came the first time. He seemed quite amazed that I should have been able to do any part of it without his being there, looked at it from one side, then the other, touched the clay with a fingertip, and said, "I fancy you superimpose the glasses as . . . ha-ha . . . sort of the finishing touch."

"I don't superimpose them at all," I told him. "In bronze, I could do it. In stone, they could be simulated. But in a plaster of Paris casting I wouldn't attempt it. Just put them in your pocket and sit over there by the window while I try to catch the expression of your mouth and eyes."

For half a minute the little man looked almost sad enough to weep, but he was a genius at pulling himself together after a disappointment. He went over to the chair, sat as bolt upright as though he had a crowbar for a backbone, threw his shoulders back, straightened his tie, patted his hair, and put on his professional smile.

"Just relax," I told him. "Try to think you're all alone in your office—maybe thinking about where you'll go for lunch."

He gave it too much consideration. Either that or lunch was a lot more important to him than to a man on a diabetic diet. Anyone might have thought he was Chief Justice of the Supreme Court, considering an infringement upon the rights of Man.

When I found that wouldn't do, I tried half a dozen other tacks, but none of them worked. Acting was so much a part of him that he couldn't stop, and I'd never had a chance to look at his face for a single minute when he wasn't either scared or acting. After wasting half an hour I told him he might go, then come back again at four—sharp.

When I'd taken that eight-dollar sitting room I'd planned that I'd need it for no more than two days, but I had to keep it three, and I must have had the attorney up there a dozen times. With his applelike cheeks, smooth forehead, wrinkleless eyes, and nondescript nose, I could have modeled him without having him up there at all, except for his mouth. Try as I might, I couldn't shape it so it didn't come out with either a smirk or a sneer. The worst of it was that he'd have been satisfied with any one of a half dozen smirks I came up with, but I couldn't make myself leave them alone. That was one time when I was as eager to heave plaster at a model's face as Lonnie had ever been, but I could no more leave that mouth alone than I could fly to the moon. I must have made it over a hundred times before I gave up, took the clay model to our cheaper room, splashed on the mold, dried it, and let Lonnie pour in the plaster for the casting.

Altogether we were six days in El Paso before that bust was finished and ready for delivery, and it didn't help my feelings a bit that the little attorney liked it. He had a regular reception at his office for the "unveiling," and the last thing I saw as I left was that durned plaster face with the mouth smirking at me. I delivered the bust at five o'clock in the afternoon, and an hour later Lonnie and I were rolling out of town, where there was plenty of space to sleep without paying hotel bills.

17

Ladies' Man Lonnie

THE cuff of my Levi's was empty when we left El Paso, and the roll of bills in my pocket was just about as big around as my thumb. But I thought I'd learned one lesson I'd never forget: big cities were places to go broke in, not to make money in—particularly since Lonnie had become a Beau Brummel and ladies' man. It had cost me five dollars a day spending money just to keep him out from under my feet. I'd foolishly established the rate that first day in Lordsburg, when I'd given him the five by mistake, and once he'd ascended to that standard of living I couldn't cut him down without breaking both his pride and his heart.

I had another lesson to learn, and it didn't take me long to learn it: isolated towns weren't too good for my new business either. The smaller the town—so long as it had a banker—the surer I was of getting a job, but if I took them one at a time, I'd be all winter in rebuilding the treasury in the cuff of my Levi's. From constant working with clay day after day, my eye had become sharp enough, and my fingers deft enough, that I could knock out any ordinary model in five or six hours. But even though I was lucky enough to have bright sunshine and a dry breeze, it required at least two more days for the mold and casting to dry enough that I could finish the job. Worse still, there was nothing for us to do—except to clean our saddles, practice throwing our ropes, or something like that—while we were waiting for the plaster to dry.

I made the mistake of doing an isolated job like that at the first town we struck north of El Paso. After his week of high living in the city, Lonnie was a pest. We were still within an hour's drive of El Paso, so he thought I should give him a fiver every day and let him go back to entertain his girl friends. Of course, I wouldn't, and I tried to ignore his pestering while I was shaping up the clay model, but it finally got on my nerves and I lost my temper.

"Your trouble is that you need work, and if I hear any more of this pestering you're going to get it," I told him crossly. "I'll sell Shiftless and take in some old rattletrap in trade, then you'll have something to keep you out of my hair."

Lonnie couldn't have been any more shocked and bewildered if he'd been listening to a judge pronounce his death sentence. "Jeepers Creepers, buddy!" he whispered. "You wouldn't do nothin' like that! She's our . . . . She's our . . . ."

"Our nothing!" I told him. "She's my flivver, and I'll do whatever I please with her. Since we struck Lordsburg you've blown in more than sixty dollars, playing big shot and ladies' man. I'm not squawking about the money; you had it coming to you, but I am squawking about your blowing it on the dames. It was your money; I wasn't going to tell you what you could do with it, but if you'd turned part of it on Shiftless you could say *our* flivver. As it is, you've nothing to say about what happens to her."

Lonnie didn't get right down on his knees, but I was afraid he was going to. "Honest-a-God, buddy! Honest-a-God," he told me; "I'd of turned every dime of it in if you'da said the word. Look, buddy! Look! I'll get me a job . . . washin' dishes, or anything. Honest, buddy, I ain't goin' to ask you for another dime out o' the business . . . not for nothin' . . . even makin's.

Look, buddy, gi'me just one more week, will you? I'll promise you I'll . . . ."

Nobody could have stayed mad at Lonnie long, I least of all. "Okay," I told him. "I won't sell her till you start pestering again, but the minute you do she's a goner. Why don't you go for a good long walk? This would be a cracking good day for a hike."

Lonnie took off as though he were afraid I'd change my mind again, and when I went back to work on the model I couldn't help feeling sorry for the way I'd jawed at him. A walk for Lonnie would be just about as entertaining as pounding mud into a rat hole. And with all his talk about getting a job, how could he if we were going to keep running around from town to town while I hunted out bankers who would be flattered to have a marblelike bust of what I thought they might have looked like in their youth?

Although I'm sure Lonnie spent most of the day sitting in the shade of some bush, not more than half a mile from camp, he didn't come back till late afternoon—just soon enough to drive me into town for my client's okay on the clay model. But by that time I'd had a chance to do considerable thinking, and on the way back I told him, "We're going back to doing our business the way we did it in that little canyon west of Safford. We'll make camp at some place where there are at least half a dozen towns within twenty-five or thirty miles, then we'll spend a day getting jobs, and I'll have the customers bring their pictures to camp, and come back for the finished busts. In that way I'll have clay models to work on while the plaster molds and castings are drying, and if we can get orders enough I could turn out one a day. Your part of the business will be to tend camp, do all the cooking—except the gluten bread—and to drive me wherever I have to go. Then you'll get five bucks from each job. You can pay half the gas and grub bill, and do whatever you like with the rest of it. Is that a fair deal?"

Lonnie nearly let Shiftless run off the road as he hugged an arm around my neck and told me I was his buddy, but I couldn't help feeling guilty, for he thought we were going straight fifty-fifty. I'd never told him I got more than ten dollars for a bust—and I didn't have any intention of letting him find it out. If I did, and we split even, he'd only spend the money on girls, then we'd go broke if the bottom should fall out of our business.

Of course, I hadn't told Lonnie all my plans, but there was no need of that. No one had to tell me that we'd been lucky in the area around Safford. There I hadn't had to do any selling at all. Mabel had started the ball rolling for me, then one banker had told another, and all I'd done was to visit with my clients when they came to see me, collect twenty-five dollars and a tintype from each one, show him the clay model when it was ready, and deliver the plaster bust when he came back for it.

I couldn't expect that sort of luck everywhere we went, and I couldn't expect bankers to fork over twenty-five dollars before they'd seen my work, no matter how many letters of recommendation I might show them. I'd have to have a sample of my work to show, and I'd have to tell them there would be no payment required unless they were well pleased with the finished marblelike bust. There would be some risk that a finished piece might be refused, but I felt I could afford to take it, for I'd never made a likeness that didn't please my client. Even if I did have one or two finished busts refused, the lost time would be much more than made up by that saved in travel.

The thing that bothered me most was what I'd use for a sample. The first time I'd used a little horse's head, but it didn't seem like a good plan to show a banker a horse's head and tell him, "I could make one just like that of you."

It wasn't until I began putting the mold plaster on the model I'd made that day that I got the right idea. I'd just put the first couple of flecks over the eyes and ears when Lonnie came hurrying toward me, calling, "Aw, buddy, leave me sling some of it at the old buzzard. I ain't had a chance to sock one of 'em since we left Safford."

He socked to beat the band, and his face lit up like a sunrise as he whanged on one handful after another. I just watched his expression and let him keep right on until there wasn't a speck of clay showing, and by that time I knew I had just the right model for my sample—that is, if I could catch that expression a few times more, and was able to work it into the clay.

During the time we'd been in town Lonnie had seldom got up before ten o'clock, but the next morning he was up by sunrise. He had a fire built and the coffee water on to boil before I was up, and for the first time since I'd known him he washed the breakfast dishes. I didn't offer to help, but set an armature up in Shiftless's shadow, got out a big lump of clay, worked it pliable, and began blocking out a head and face. After Lonnie had finished with the dishes he spent an hour polishing Shiftless, but being very careful not to get in my way. Then he began scouting around through the brush and lugging in armfuls of firewood. By ten o'clock he had as much as we could have used in a week. He knew it as well as I did, but he was so anxious to show me he was carrying out his end of our deal that he kept right on lugging.

I didn't even look up at him when he passed me with an armful of wood. I didn't need to. I knew his face so well that I could almost have made a model of it with my eyes closed. And he didn't pay any attention to what I was doing either, until I'd gone about as far as I could without him. Then he called, "Jeepers, buddy, I didn't know you had another job ahead. Where'd you get it?"

"I found it last night," I called back. "Come on over here."

When Lonnie came over to see what I wanted I told him, "You're working too hard, buddy boy. Sit down and rest yourself awhile; I just had a bright idea, and we can talk about it while I'm fiddling with this thing."

I knew better than to let him see the face I was working on, because he'd have recognized it as his own, and I knew better than to tell him I wanted him to pose for me, because I'd get everything in the world except the animated expression I wanted. The only way I could get that would be by keeping him entirely unself-conscious, and by telling him whatever was

necessary to make him bubble with happiness at the time I
needed it. So, as he slumped down in the shade of a bush near
me, I turned the back of the model toward him and moved the
box I was sitting on so I could see his face right beyond that of
the model. I managed to get the animated expression every
time I needed it, but sometimes I had to go nearly overboard
to get it. The worst mistake I made was in telling him that if
he could pay in the eighty-five dollars I'd originally paid for
Shiftless before we reached Santa Fe, I'd have her taken out of
my name entirely and registered in his.

When you're busy on something you like to do, or when
you're listening to things you like to hear, hours go by as if
they were minutes. When I'd started on the model that morning
I'd told myself I was going to make the best sample I possibly
could, but I forgot all about its being a sample as soon as
Lonnie came over there. It couldn't have been more than half
an hour before I noticed that the clay face was beginning to
come alive—as Ivon's always were. I don't know where the
time went from then on, but we never thought about lunch,
and the sun was way over toward the western mountains when
I said, "Take a look here, Lonnie, and see how you'd like to
sling plaster in this old buzzard's face."

We couldn't have had a better salesman than Lonnie's happy
likeness. He was so proud of it that the animated look always
came back to his face whenever I had him bring it in to show a
banker, and I never failed to get an order after he'd shown it.
Of course, I had to work out a system where he brought his
bust in, showed it, and took it back out to Shiftless. Then I
went on and made my deal with the client. They were all the
same: a marblelike bust made from a picture taken at any age,
and a payment of twenty-five dollars if it was satisfactory when
completed.

There was only one part of my original plan that didn't work
out. It wouldn't do for me to let two or more clients come to
see me on the same day. I could do a good job only if I had my
client come to see me in the morning, visited with him till I

had every detail of his features and expressions in my mind, then went right to work on the clay model while the memory was still sharp and clear in my head. I never had but one refusal, and that was when I tried to carry three likenesses in my mind at the same time. I always took the pictures, but I looked at them only enough to be sure I was right on the combing of the hair, and whether or not to put on a mustache.

There were a dozen towns within thirty miles of our first central camp—between El Paso and Las Cruces—and there were three fifty-dollar bills in the cuff of my Levi's when we broke camp and headed on up the Rio Grande. Besides that, Lonnie had turned in forty dollars toward his ownership of Shiftless. For the next two days our road was on the west side of the Rio Grande, parallel to the Jornada del Muerto on the east side of the river—the Journey of Death on the Old Spanish Trail. We passed through four or five towns before we reached Socorro, one of them good sized, but we didn't stop because they were all isolated. We did have a little excitement though.

About halfway between Hot Springs and Socorro we saw a small band of horses grazing through the brush, over toward the San Mateo Mountains. They were less than a quarter mile from the road, and Lonnie and I got the same idea at the same time. We'd had our saddles and cowhand outfits for more than two months, but had never had a minute's use of them and—with the way things were going for the cowboy artists of the Southwest—it didn't seem as if we were apt to for some time. We'd barely come in sight of the horses when Lonnie let out a war whoop and shouted, "Let's go ride 'em, buddy!"

"One's enough for me, you ride the rest!" I yelled back, and Lonnie pulled off the road.

We'd been traveling in our cut-off jeans, so we had to change into our cowhand duds, but we put everything on, bandanna and all. While we were changing Lonnie told me, " 'Member, buddy, how we caught that old cow Christmas Day? It'll be a cinch to catch horses the same way, only easier, 'cause this brush ain't so tall, and I can drive right on over it."

If we hadn't yelled so loud when we first spied those horses we might have had better luck with them, but by the time we'd changed our clothes they'd drifted on another quarter mile. With me perched on the running board and lashed to a top iron, Lonnie took off across the desert with Shiftless bucking like a Brahma bull. He didn't turn out for anything until we were closing in behind the little band of racing horses, and I had to hold on so tight I could neither build a loop in my rope or get a decent look at the horses. When I got it I thought for a few seconds that it was going to be my last look at anything on earth. The band took a sudden turn to the left, and Lonnie forgot he was mounted on Shiftless instead of a horse. He turned her right on the heels of the frightened mustangs.

Shiftless sort of hunkered down on her off forehand, the way a horse will when he tries to make too sharp a turn on the wrong lead. But she didn't go end over end, as a horse often will. She rocked toward me till I'll swear my face wasn't a foot off the ground. Then Lonnie jerked the wheel in the opposite direction and Shiftless went into a dance—about the kind a drunk might do on a pogo stick. On the first eight or ten hops I don't believe she ever touched more than one wheel to the ground, but lunged and tipped—from side to side and front to back. By the time Lonnie got her back under control the horses were long gone, and I'd had all the bronco busting I wanted for one day.

We finished out February and the first half of March in two central camps—one between Socorro and Albuquerque, the other between Albuquerque and Santa Fe—and we did better than I'd dared to hope. The only trouble was that, skinny as I was, I nearly froze to death. We'd come far enough north and high enough that the nights were often bitter cold, and there were lots of days when my hands would get so numb I'd have to stop every ten or fifteen minutes to warm them. Of course, I couldn't work in my cut-off jeans, and I couldn't do my best work, because the clay stiffened too much to handle well.

I think it was a combination of the cold evenings, Lonnie's

not having enough to do to keep him from being bored, and curiosity that made us into movie fans. Ever since we'd seen that movie in El Paso with the horse-fall strip in it, I'd been anxious to see another—hoping I might see one with me in it. If, on an evening that was too cold for me to work—and often on ones that weren't—we found there was going to be a cowboy-and-Indian picture in one of the nearby towns, we'd hide our stuff away in the brush, wind Shiftless up, and go to see it. With two exceptions I think we saw every cowboy-and-Indian picture that came within fifty miles of us—and those two exceptions were Albuquerque and Santa Fe. I'd learned my lesson about Lonnie and big cities when we were in El Paso, and though I had to get a bit tough a couple of times I kept him away from both cities till I'd finished the last job in our second camp.

As I'd written Mother, I'd planned that we'd be all spring on the way from El Paso to Santa Fe, and that I'd go on to Colorado from there. But while we were in our second camp I changed my mind. There were several reasons for it. In the first place, it would be colder in Colorado than in New Mexico, and it would be too early for the spring cattle work to have opened up. In the second place, I was having too much fun and making too much money to quit the plaster bust business. It seemed to me that if our luck held out—and we kept away from big cities—I might have nearly a thousand dollars tucked away in the cuffs of my Levi's by the end of June. Then when I went to meet Ted Hawkins and my old Colorado friends at the Littleton roundup on Fourth of July, I wouldn't be going just as a cowhand looking for a job. There was plenty of good grazing land in Colorado that could be bought for five or six dollars an acre, and I'd be able to start out as a small rancher—with maybe a quarter-section of good pasture land near the mountains and a dozen or two head of young stock.

At first I thought about taking Lonnie into partnership with me, and then I decided that might be a mistake. It would be better to sell him the idea of going back to his folks in Wyoming. I was sure he'd never willingly give up Shiftless, and without the bust business I couldn't afford to support both of them.

Of course, I didn't tell Lonnie all my plans; it would only have hurt his feelings. Instead, I kept dangling the ownership of Shiftless before his eyes, to keep him away from Santa Fe and Albuquerque, and from spending all his share from the business on girls. I promised him, though, that we'd go into Santa Fe for just one day, to register Shiftless in his name if he had her paid for, then we'd head south again where the weather was warmer.

With my having taken Lonnie to the movies nearly every evening, and threatening to drive Shiftless myself if he left camp without my say-so, he hadn't had much chance to blow money on the girls. Soon after we'd moved to the camp near Santa Fe he cleaned up the last of the eighty-five dollars that I'd promised would make Shiftless his. From then on he was as restless as a caged coyote, begging me every day to lay off so we could go to town and have the registration put into his name. I knew well enough what would happen if I did it, so I wouldn't go till the last job was finished, and even then I made him promise that he'd leave without any argument after we'd spent one day in the city. When we did go, I had nearly a hundred dollars in my pocket, and eight fifties folded into the cuffs of my Levi's. It didn't take much figuring for me to know that Lonnie had a pocket roll almost as big as mine. If he'd swiped as many chickens as I suspected, his share of the gas and grub bill hadn't been more than ten dollars for all the time since we'd left El Paso.

It was early in the forenoon when we drove into Santa Fe, but Lonnie insisted on going straight to the Motor Vehicle office and having Shiftless registered in his name. The minute the clerk gave him the ownership paper he forgot that he wasn't a millionaire. While I was registering at the hotel desk he tipped one bellboy a dollar to lug our stuff up to the room, and gave another a dollar to have his suit pressed in a hurry. By the time I got upstairs he had shucked off his shirt and Levi's, left them where they had fallen, and was taking a bath. He called to me above the splashing, "Listen, buddy, I aim to keep that promise I made you, but you know a day don't end till midnight."

"Yes, I know it," I called back, "but you'll be broke long before suppertime, and don't come trying to borrow from me, because I'm not going to lend you a dime. If you had a thousand dollars you'd blow it on the floozies in a couple of hours."

"You're wrong, buddy! You're dead wrong!" he shouted. "Ain't you took note how I been savin' my dough lately? This time I don't aim to spend more'n a fiver. Just ride around a little to look the town over, and maybe take in a movie. I'll have old Shiftless waitin' outside the front door at straight-up midnight. Is that fair enough?"

"Fair enough," I told him, "but don't wait for me down there. I'll be sleeping. All I care about is getting away early tomorrow morning."

While Lonnie was getting dressed and away I sent my own suit down to be pressed, then hung up the clothes he'd shed, and straightened up the stuff the bellboy had dumped in the middle of the floor. I put our bedrolls in a far corner, laid the saddles and outfits on top of them, then set my armatures, supplies, and toolbox at one side. When my suit came back I changed into it, put the loose change and small bills in my pocket, and hung my Levi's in the closet beside Lonnie's. Even by feeling of the cuffs, no one would have guessed that mine weren't as empty as his.

It was a warm, sunny forenoon so I went out to order an additional supply of clay and plaster of Paris, then wandered around the streets sort of aimlessly, and just by chance I found the post office. Since I'd written Mother that I wouldn't reach Santa Fe till late spring I didn't expect to find a letter waiting for me at general delivery, but there was one there. If I'd used my head I'd have known there would be; that Dr. Gaghan would have known where I was every week by the report cards from doctors I had gone to for check ups, and that he'd have told her. He had, and she was worried sick. She wrote that she was afraid I'd lost my good job with the big cattle company, or that I'd had to quit because of my health. She was frightened because I'd slipped to 101 pounds instead of gaining, and she was even more frightened because I'd sent sixty dollars home at the end of February. She said she must insist on a full and honest explanation as to how I was getting hold of any such large sums of money.

I'd written Mother so many lies that I wasn't sure I could remember them all, so when I'd sent her the fifty and ten at the end of February I'd written a very short note, just saying I was feeling fine, and that the weather was nice, and asking about each one at home. Then I'd crossed the river and mailed the letter from Veguita, a little town about thirty miles north of Socorro and so small I was sure she wouldn't be able to find it on a map.

Before answering the letter I took it back to our room and thought about it for awhile. It was certain that Mother was already suspicious about what I'd been writing her, but if I should come a quarter of an inch nearer the truth she'd be even more suspicious. There was nothing to do except to make up some more fairy tales, but I tried to make them sound as reasonable as I could. After a few paragraphs about the great confidence our bosses had in my working partner, Alonzo, and me, I wrote that we'd been sent ahead of the herd again to buy more cattle, and that the extra money was from bonuses we were being paid when we made exceptionally fine bargains in our buying. Near the end of the letter I said that our bosses' only disappointment was with the scarcity of good cattle, that they wanted to gather a much larger herd, so were sending us back into southeastern New Mexico to do more buying. I didn't dare put any money in that letter, but said I'd write again when I got my pay check at the end of the month, adding that I had hopes of a real good bonus that time.

There wasn't much to do after I'd written the letter, so I spent the afternoon around the Plaza, looking through the old buildings that still remained from the early Spanish days. I'd just come out of the museum late in the afternoon when I caught a glimpse of Shiftless. Lonnie was tooling her through the Plaza as proudly as if she'd been a Rolls Royce. He had a gaily dressed black-haired señorita beside him, and two more on the back seat. They were all laughing and merry, but didn't seem a bit rough or coarse.

After I'd found a restaurant with food I could eat, I went to a movie and didn't get back to the hotel until nearly midnight, but Lonnie had been there ahead of me. His saddle and outfit were gone from the top of his bedroll, but everything else was just as I'd left it. I don't know when he sneaked in, but he was asleep in a chair when I woke up the next morning. I let him sleep till I was shaved and dressed. Then when I shook him awake he looked up sheepishly and said, "Honest, buddy, I didn't . . . ."

"Never mind the excuses," I cut in. "Just get into your old duds and lug this stuff down to Shiftless. But you'd better give me the pawn ticket before you change. I'll redeem your saddle and outfit on our way out of town."

18

End of the Trail

WHEN I'd written to Mother I'd planned that we'd drive right on south to Roswell, then try our luck in the southeast corner of the state, but it didn't work out that way. It was the middle of the afternoon when we reached the little town of Moriarty—accent on the *i*—east of Albuquerque, on the main highway running east and west. I'd known Lonnie was out of makings before we'd left Santa Fe, but I thought it might be a good idea to let him suffer a bit for his sins, so I never mentioned it till we were pulling into Moriarty. Then I passed him a quarter and said, "Why don't you stop here and get yourself a sack of Bull Durham?"

Lonnie was gone long enough to have bought all the Bull Durham in town, but I didn't mind. It was a nice warm afternoon, so I just slumped down in the seat for a little siesta. I didn't more than half wake up when he came hurrying back, took our sample from the back seat, and hurried away again. Ever since I'd made it he'd taken great delight in showing it to any audience he could scare up, telling them we were the Cowboy Artists of the Southwest, and that he was the one who made the finished produck. I couldn't see any harm in his catching himself a little glory in Moriarty. But Lonnie wasn't out for glory that time. He was anxious to hurry us back into business, so he could make good on the twenty-five I'd had to pay to get his saddle and outfit out of hock.

I don't know how long Lonnie was gone on the second trip, but when he came back around the corner his face was all aglow. "Hey, buddy," he shouted to me, "I got a job for us! And I collected in advance." He came hurrying up to Shiftless, poked a limp ten-dollar bill out to me, and babbled, "Keep it all, buddy! That makes a fiver on the hock ticket. I told you I'd get it paid off 'fore you knowed it. You can start right in on the old buzzard; here's a pi'ture of him. I had to wait while he went home to get it."

I was licked and I knew it, but there was no sense in scolding Lonnie when he was so happy about having put over a big piece of business. But I did suggest that in the future he let me make the deals, and that he stay and watch Shiftless while I went and had a talk with our new client.

The talk was a lot easier than I'd expected. My new client was one of the nicest old gentlemen I ever ran into, and he knew exactly what had happened. He said he'd been over to Albuquerque two or three times while we were camped near there, that he'd seen several of my busts, knew what they cost, and had planned to come and see me about making one for him. Of course, I told him that since Lonnie had made the deal at ten dollars I'd do the job for that price, but I explained about its taking three days to dry plaster, and that I didn't usually plan to stop unless I could get half a dozen jobs in the same area. He understood perfectly, laid another fifteen dollars out on the desk beside my hand, and told me he'd scare me up some more clients. He did. Six of them. And when I'd finished my work at Moriarty he asked me if I'd do him the favor of going to Santa Rosa and making a bust for a friend of his there. He'd been so nice to me that I wouldn't have refused if he'd asked me to go to the North Pole to make one, but our going changed the whole shape of my plans.

The banker at Santa Rosa had five jobs lined up for me—one from forty-five miles away—and when I was finished there, he asked me if I'd do some for friends of his near Tucumcari. With it being early April the nights were becoming warmer, so I didn't mind going farther north, but we needed a day to catch up with our housekeeping. Ever since we'd left Santa Fe I'd been busy every minute I could keep awake, modeling faces in clay, making molds, or chipping out and finishing busts. With the exception of our suits, every rag of clothes we owned was dirty, and our dish towels looked as though someone had scrubbed floors with them. We'd done our Santa Rosa work at a little pocket in the hills beside Pecos River, so I decided that we'd take a day off to do our washing there where we'd have plenty of water. While it dried, we'd just be lazy and lie in the sun.

When I told Lonnie what I'd planned he didn't think much of the idea. "We ain't no washerwomen, buddy!" he told me. "We're artists, and artists shouldn't ought to do their own wash. It ain't fittin'! And besides, our time's too dear. Ain't we makin' ten bucks a day? A tenner would buy the both of us brand new cloze, right from the hide out, sox and all."

"Go ahead and buy yourself new duds if you can afford it," I told him. "I can't. But we're going to take the day off anyway. Besides the washing, I've got a couple of letters to write, and my tools and armatures to clean."

Next morning Lonnie spent an hour polishing Shiftless while I washed the breakfast dishes, scoured our pots and pans, and put a dishpan of water on to heat for my washing. When he'd finished the job he took our suitcase from the back seat, came to the fire for a basin of warm water, and went down to the river edge without saying a word. After he'd shaved, he peeled off his dirty shirt and jeans, tossed them into the river, and put on his city suit. Then he came back to the fire and asked, "Say, buddy, how many jobs have we did since we left Santa Fe?"

"Twelve," I told him. "The hock ticket for redeeming your outfit was twenty-five bucks, you've drawn ten, and your share of the grub and gas has been five, so there's twenty dollars coming to you."

As I stripped two tens off my pocket roll Lonnie seemed a bit embarrassed. "Look, buddy," he told me, "I wasn't pressin' you none. It's only that . . . well . . . what with buyin' new cloze and all . . ."

"Sure enough. I know how it is," I told him. "You've found some dame in Santa Rosa who will let you ride her around in Shiftless and buy her ice cream. Have a good time, but get back here early. We're going to be on the road by sunup."

I don't know when Lonnie came back to camp, but he must have done his shopping before he picked up the girl, and it must have been late enough that he thought it best to get ready for an early takeoff before turning in. He was snoring like a fat sow when I woke up at dawn, and laid out beside him were a new blue shirt, sox, and a pair of Levi's. As always, he'd bought the Levi's six or eight inches too long, but had folded the cuffs neatly, and put a rock on them to make the creases sharp. I let him sleep till I had breakfast ready, then woke him just before sunup.

We were a week at Tucumcari, and from there were sent on to Dalhart, nearly a hundred miles to the northeast, across the line in the corner of the Texas panhandle. When I'd sent Mother the end-of-March money order from Santa Rosa I'd stuck to my story about going into southeastern New Mexico to buy cattle, but I had to get another letter off before we left Tucumcari. I couldn't have doctors' cards going to Dr. Gaghan, showing me headed northeast, while I was telling Mother I was going southeast.

There was only one thing I could think of, and after I'd mailed the letter it was too late to change my mind, my story, or my direction. I'd racked my brain to think of any reason why our bosses might be sending us to the northeast, and could think of only one, so I'd written it. I said our bosses had decided to divide the great herd, cut out the best steers, and have my working partner, Alonzo, and me drive them to market at

Kansas City. To make it sound more reasonable, I wrote that we'd be driving them over the old Santa Fe Trail—hoping no one would tell her the old trail had been out of use for more than a quarter of a century.

From there on there was no way out. We stopped to make camp wherever I could get four or more jobs within a radius of twenty miles, and followed fairly close to the route of the old trail. There was never a time when I wasn't busy, and I never had to spend much time in hunting for work. I don't remember our ever breaking camp when I didn't have at least one bust to make for some banker farther on. The only thing I had to watch out for was that we didn't get sidetracked. Some one of my clients was always wanting me to go north, south, or west to make a bust for a friend of his, but I'd make promises only for jobs that would keep us moving to the northeast.

When I'd written Mother from Tucumcari I'd made up my mind to work things out so we'd reach Kansas City at the end of June. Then, if I'd been able to save a thousand dollars, I'd get out of the plaster bust business, go to Littleton for the Fourth-of-July roundup, and find myself a little place where I could get started in the cattle business.

By late June we had worked our way to within thirty miles of Kansas City, I had only one more bust to finish, and I'd saved a little more than the thousand dollars I'd planned on. I had eleven fifty-dollar bills in each cuff of my Levi's, more than a hundred and fifty dollars in smaller bills in my pocket, and my last job still to be paid for. I didn't worry a bit about the money when we were in camp, because I was always wearing my Levi's or sleeping with them rolled up for a pillow. But ever since the barber in El Paso had mentioned pickpockets, I was nervous about taking a lot of money into a big city. It bothered me all the time I was working on that last bust, and the night I finished it I sat up long after Lonnie had gone to sleep, writing a letter to my older sister, Grace.

Ever since we lost our father, Grace and I had sort of worked as a team. She'd never believe some of the fairy tales that I could sometimes palm off on Mother, but she'd believe me if I told her the straight-out truth, no matter how fantastic it sounded. Besides, she knew I could recognize the kind of a bush nickels grew on, and had a knack for shaking them off. Then too, she was more or less the treasurer of our family.

Right after Father died I'd made some pretty good money by riding at the racetrack in Littleton—something Mother would never have let me do if she'd known about it. But it was money that we needed, and I'd made it honestly, so Grace slipped it, little by little, into the grocery bill, and Mother never found out about it. That night after Lonnie had gone to sleep I wrote Grace a long letter and told her the exact truth about the plaster bust business, and that I was sending her a money order for five hundred dollars. I told her to work any of it that was needed into the family, and that she should keep whatever wasn't needed till I came home or wrote for it.

Of course, I couldn't mail the letter directly to Grace, since everyone at home would want it read aloud if it came to the house, so I had to write a little note to Dr. Gaghan. In the first paragraph I just wrote that I was feeling fine, was going to Littleton, and that he'd get his next report card from there. Then I told him I was enclosing a letter which I would appreciate his giving to Grace privately, because it was about a family matter with which I didn't want to worry my mother. Next I wrote a letter to Mother, telling her we would reach Kansas City in a couple of days, then I was going right on to Colorado. I said we'd be getting an extra bonus when we delivered our cattle at the stockyards, so I'd have plenty of money for the trip, and was enclosing a money order for sixty dollars. Then I filled in the rest of the letter by asking about all the others at home, and telling her that I'd look up all our old friends as soon as I reached Colorado.

The next morning Lonnie drove me into the town where I had to deliver my last bust. After I'd collected for it, I asked the banker if I could use his washroom, but all I used it for was taking five fifty-dollar bills out of each cuff of my Levi's. From there I went to a doctor, got a report card, and went to the post office. I bought my money orders, mailed my letters, and went back to camp feeling happier—and more proud of myself— than I had ever felt in my life.

On the morning of July first we broke camp for the last time, threw out all my armatures, what was left of the clay and plaster, and all our working clothes with the exception of the blue shirts and Levi's we were wearing. Then we lined our dishes, pots, and pans up along the roadside where someone would find them. Our days of being the roving cowboy artists of the Southwest were over, and I didn't want to reach Kansas City with a bunch of junk we couldn't take into a first-class hotel.

We didn't stop on the Kansas side of the river, where the stockyards were, but drove right to the downtown section of Kansas City, Missouri. Then I asked a policeman to direct us to the best cattlemen's hotel in town. He sent us to the Dixon, on Twelfth Street just off Main, and I took a four-dollar front room on the third floor. It wasn't that I wanted to put up in style, but I did want to be sure we would be in a hotel where my Levi's would be safe in a closet.

From the time Shiftless had been transferred to Lonnie's name I'd lost a little control over him. I couldn't threaten to sell her if he didn't do as I said, and it would have been silly to tell him he couldn't take her away from camp evenings to give the girls a ride. I knew he must have spent considerable money during April, May, and June, but it was rolling in so fast that I was sure he couldn't have spent it all. I didn't realize he had until we'd checked into the hotel, had our city suits pressed, and were changing into them. Then he asked to borrow twenty dollars so he could go see the town.

I told him I wouldn't lend him a dime, and lectured him like a Dutch uncle. For the past month he had known we would reach Kansas City and go out of business at the end of June, so he'd had plenty of time to save himself a good fat roll. I'd planned to stay in town only one day, then take the train for Colorado, but Lonnie planned to stay a couple of days longer, then drive Shiftless home to Wyoming. He should have had sense enough to know he couldn't do it without money enough to live on and buy gasoline and oil.

When I found he was broke I told him he had no more business owning an automobile than a five-year-old, and that if he had a grain of sense in his head he'd sell Shiftless, buy a railroad ticket home, and get out of town as fast as he could. Lonnie didn't say a word while I was bawling him out—just stood and looked down at the carpet like a spanked puppy. He let me get all through, then peeked up at me under his eyebrows and said, "Look, buddy, I ain't makin' no excuses, but I ain't done nothin' wrong with none of them dames . . . just ridin' 'em around in Shiftless . . . and buyin' 'em suppers . . . and little trinkets . . . and ice-cream sodys . . . and stuff like that."

"I didn't say you had," I told him. "Whatever you did is your own business, not mine. But from now on you're going to have to paddle your own canoe, and you're not going to paddle Shiftless very far without gas and oil."

Lonnie looked back at the carpet and thought about that for

a couple of minutes, then he peeked up again and asked, "Look, buddy, didn't you say you had gave me the saddle and outfit? You know, that time when we was in . . ."

"Sure I did," I told him. "It's yours and you do whatever you like with it, but with jobs as scarce as they have been since the war you'd have trouble finding one without an outfit. And even if you hock it you won't get more than twenty-five bucks this late in the season. The way you spend money that wouldn't last long enough to get you past the first skirt you saw after leaving the hockshop."

Lonnie didn't try to defend himself, just stood looking down at the carpet, so to break it up I said, "Oh, don't let it get you down, Lonnie. Tomorrow's another day, and maybe we'll figure something out. Get your glad rags on and we'll go find some supper and see a movie."

Lonnie always changed clothes faster than I because he let the ones he took off drop wherever he happened to be. While I was putting on my tie I could see his reflection in the mirror, standing sorrowfully by the door and waiting for me. "Oh, don't feel so sorry for yourself, Lonnie," I called to him. "The world hasn't come to an end. We're going to go first class to-night—no greasy-spoon grub and dime movie. Go on down for a newspaper, and we'll hunt up the best restaurant and show in town."

Even that didn't do anything for Lonnie's gloom, and he slouched out of the room like a little boy sent for an armful of firewood. I didn't want the newspaper; we could find the best restaurant and show by just wandering around the streets for half an hour. What I wanted was to get rid of Lonnie for a few minutes. I had nearly a hundred and twenty dollars in my pocket roll, and I knew better than to trust myself out with Lonnie while I was carrying that much. Somewhere along the line I'd turn chickenhearted, lend him half of it, and he'd blow it on a bunch of girls before daylight. If I took along only enough for supper and a show I couldn't fall for his pleading, he'd get a good night's sleep, and if he wouldn't part with

Shiftless I'd give him money enough to buy gas and oil for driving her home.

As soon as I heard the elevator door slam, so I knew Lonnie wouldn't pop back in at any minute, I stripped everything but the singles from my pocket roll, turned down one cuff of my Levi's, and laid the tens and twenties in with the fifties. Then I folded the cuff again, rubbed it flat so it would look perfectly empty, and hung the Levi's in the closet. I'd just hung Lonnie's beside them when he came back with the paper, dropped it on the dresser, and slouched into an easy chair. I tried to cheer him up a bit and get him to help me pick out the best show and restaurant, but Lonnie was beyond cheering. All he'd say was that one joint was as good as another, and when we went out through the hotel lobby anyone might have thought I was his mother, making him go to school when he didn't want to.

When I'd looked over the paper I'd picked Wolferman's $2.50 dinner as the best meal in town, and Pantages as the best show—mostly vaudeville, with a cowboy-and-Indian picture we hadn't seen. Lonnie trailed a half step behind me all the way to the restaurant, but he perked up a little as soon as they brought the food. Before the meal was over he seemed to be his happy, carefree self again. Then he began telling me what a good buddy I'd been—and made the touch he'd been leading up to all the time. It was a cracking good one, because I knew Lonnie honestly meant what he'd been saying, and if I'd had my whole roll in my pocket I'd surely have divided it with him.

For a minute or two I was stumped as to what I might tell him. I couldn't say I was broke; he knew better than that. And I certainly wasn't going to tell him about the seven hundred I had stashed away in the cuffs of my Levi's. Besides that, I didn't want to lie to him. In all the months we'd been buddies I'd never told him the whole truth, but I'd never told him an out-and-out lie either, and I wasn't going to do it when we were about to separate, maybe forever. What I did was what I'd always done; I told him just enough of the truth to mislead him.

"Why didn't you tell me you were broke before I wrote

home?" I asked him. "You know I've been buying a money order and sending it to my mother at the end of every month. I could have cut down a little on that one I sent yesterday."

"Jeepers, buddy," Lonnie said sadly, "I never thought o' that. You always had dough when we needed it, and I guess I reckoned you always would have."

He sat for a minute or two, staring down at the tablecloth, then looked up, smiled happily, and said, "Jeepers! I'm glad I didn't think of it. Buddy, I wouldn't take no money off'n your ma, you know that."

"I know you wouldn't, Lonnie," I told him, "but you can't go on being a little boy all the rest of your life. You've blown in enough money during the past six months to have set yourself up with a little cattle outfit of your own. You could still do it. The shape Shiftless is in, she'd bring enough here in Kansas City to pay your railroad fare home and leave you a couple of hundred dollars in your pocket. The only sensible thing you can do is to sell her tomorrow morning and catch the next train for Wyoming. Two hundred bucks would buy you a dozen heifer calves, and if you took good care of them you'd have a nice little herd started in three or four years. Then you could get married and have a home of your own, instead of bumming around the country broke and barefooted."

Lonnie sat with his head down till I'd finished, then he looked up pleadingly and said, "But, Jeepers, buddy, we ain't no more'n got to town, and I couldn't leave old Shiftless go noways."

"Use your head, Lonnie," I told him. "The longer you try to hold onto her the worse off you're going to be. Remember, your girl trouble didn't start till you had Shiftless to ride them around in. Even if you could leave the dames alone you'd be licked. You can't drive Shiftless unless you've got enough money coming in to keep her in shape and buy gas and oil. And what good is she to you if you can't drive her?"

Without looking up, he said, "Well, buddy, I could hock my saddle and outfit, couldn't I?"

"Sure, you could," I said, "and how long do you think it would

be before you were flat broke again? Not long enough to get
you from here to Wyoming. And what do you think would
happen if Shiftless broke down or you had a blowout on the
way. You'd have to sell her for whatever anybody'd offer you,
and it wouldn't be much. You think about it overnight, Lonnie,
and you'll see that I'm right. But don't fret about it now;
we've been in a lot tighter spots than this and come out alive.
Let's go see that show; it ought to be a good one."

I hoped I'd convinced Lonnie to sell Shiftless, but I doubted
it, so I decided what I'd do if he was still holding out to keep
her when morning came. It wasn't much over five hundred
miles to Littleton, but that would put Lonnie more than halfway
home, and with Shiftless running the way she was we could
make it in two days. If we started early next morning we'd get
there the night before the Fourth, most of my friends would
be in town, along with Ted Hawkins from the Wickenburg
movie lot, and we'd have a grand celebration. It seemed to
me that would be exactly the right time to drop the word,
sort of offhand, that I was looking for a nice little ranch I could
buy at a right price, and that I'd like to pick up some young
heifer stock from an outfit that was running purebred Hereford
bulls on its range. When we reached Littleton I'd give Lonnie
fifty dollars to get home on, but I wouldn't do it till I had him
at the edge of town and headed toward Wyoming.

We hadn't been out of the restaurant two minutes before I
knew I'd wasted my time in trying to talk sense to Lonnie. I'd
almost forgotten he was with me, and was still thinking about
the old friends I'd soon be seeing at Littleton, when he suddenly chirped, "Chick-chick-chick-chick-chick," as though he
were a farmer boy calling the hens at feeding time.

I snapped out of my woolgathering at Lonnie's first chirp,
and noticed a couple of fancy looking girls about our age,
walking down the sidewalk a hundred feet or so ahead of us.
Just as I looked up they glanced back, giggled, and walked on,
but not very fast. That's all it took to make Lonnie forget his
troubles. "Jeepers Creepers, buddy!" he crowed. "Wisht I'd

hung onto some of that dough we made off'n our business! Them little chickadees is slowin' down and waitin' for us."

"You forget about 'them little chickadees,'" I told him. "That kind wouldn't waste five seconds on you if they knew you were broke. Your days of being a Romeo are over for a while."

All the way over to the theater Lonnie seemed as happy as if he hadn't a care in the world, but when we got to our seats he didn't pay any attention to the show. For as much as ten or fifteen minutes he sat looking down at his fidgeting fingers. Lonnie wasn't a fidgeter, so I knew he was doing some deep thinking, and I was pretty sure I knew what it was about. I wasn't a bit surprised when he leaned toward me and whispered, "I got to go to the can, buddy." And I wasn't any more surprised when he whispered, "So long," before he sidled out to the aisle.

I'd have bet half of all I had that his saddle and outfit would be in a pawnshop within twenty minutes, and that before an hour was up he'd have those two girls or some others out for a ride in Shiftless. Really, I was more pleased than not. He might as well enjoy his last fling. I'd redeem his outfit the next morning, then when I started him for home from Littleton I'd take the cost of the pawn ticket out of the fifty I'd planned to give him.

19

So Long, Buddy

THE show was a good one, and I stayed through to see the cowboy-and-Indian picture twice, even though I wasn't in the horse falls. It was about midnight when I got back to our room, and I chuckled out loud when I noticed that Lonnie's saddle, outfit, and bedroll were missing. It hadn't occurred to me that he might hock his bedroll, because it wouldn't bring much more than two dollars, old as it was. I'd started to take off my tie before I noticed a sheet of hotel writing paper lying on the desk. I knew I hadn't left it there, and Lonnie had never written a letter in all the time I'd known him, so I was a bit curious—but not for long. In printed letters, big enough that I could read them at six feet, Lonnie had written,

"SO LONG BUDDY.
I COULDENT LEEVE SHIFLESS GO
SO I HAVE TOOK OFF. LONNIE"

I couldn't help laughing aloud when I read it. No wonder Lonnie had been fidgeting in the theater; he'd been sitting on the horns of a dilemma and trying to decide which way to jump. For weeks he'd been looking forward to a big time in Kansas City, and those two chickadees he'd chirped to had almost set him afire. But I'd probably frightened him a little more than I'd realized at supper, and he was afraid I'd put the pressure on even harder when morning came. In his childish way he'd figured that his only hope of saving Shiftless was to pawn his outfit and head straight for Wyoming on the money he got for it.

But Lonnie had made lots of good resolutions before, just as he did in Santa Fe, and they'd lasted only long enough for him to see a skirt flapping in the breeze. He'd have done well if he'd gone a block after pawning his outfit without chirping, "Chick-chick-chick," at some chickadee. Before daylight he'd be tip-toeing into our room—dead broke and full of excuses.

I was still chuckling as I undressed, hung my suit coat over the back of a chair, and started to lay my britches out smoothly on the dresser. It was only then that I missed the bust I'd made of Lonnie as a sample to show prospective customers. Next to Shiftless, it was his most prized possession. He usually took it with him when he went to ride the girls around, and he always claimed to have made it himself because he'd poured the plaster for the casting. For a month he'd been talking about taking it home to show his folks, and he'd had it standing on the dresser when we went out to supper. I was glad he had taken it along, for I was sure he could never resist the temptation of finding some girl to show it to and brag of its being a self-portrait. When I went to bed I left the light on in the bathroom and the door open a couple of inches, so he wouldn't stumble over a chair or something and wake me when he came in.

I hadn't slept in a bed since leaving Santa Fe, and I must have gone to sleep the moment my head touched the pillow. It was broad daylight when I woke, and a stream of sunshine was pouring in through the window. For a minute or two I just lay there, yawning, stretching, and enjoying the softness of the mattress. Then I realized that Lonnie hadn't come back. Everything was just as I'd left it when I went to bed, and the light was still on in the bathroom.

I didn't believe for a moment that Lonnie had left town, but I wished I hadn't been quite so rough on him at suppertime. I might have frightened him enough that he didn't dare come back after a night on the town, for fear I'd force him into selling Shiftless. I was just a little bit ashamed of myself—and disappointed. Of course, we'd planned to split up in Kansas City anyway, but I did want to say good-bye to him, and wish him luck, and get his folks' address so I could write to him. Then, too, I didn't want to go away and leave him stranded— and he certainly would be after an evening of playing big-shot for the girls. The only thing he'd have left to pawn would be his suit, and that wouldn't bring more than two or three dollars —only enough to buy his breakfast and one tank of gas for Shiftless.

For maybe ten minutes I lay there in bed, wishing I'd told Lonnie my plan for having him drive me to Littleton, and try- ing to figure out what he'd probably have done, and how I'd better go about finding him. Just as soon as he'd picked up a girl to take riding he'd have taken Shiftless out of the garage where we'd parked her. But if I'd frightened him enough that he didn't dare come back to the hotel he wouldn't risk putting her back in that garage. He'd park her some place where he could sleep in her till noon, then he'd hock his suit, blow in whatever he got for it, and go hunting a job.

When I'd figured things out that far the rest seemed easy; I'd find him at the stockyards. That's where he'd always hung out before we teamed up and bought Shiftless, that's where he'd have to go to hunt a job, and that's where he'd be sleeping in her. There was no need of rushing right down there; he'd sleep until I woke him, and if we didn't get started for Littleton before noon it would be all right. We could easily make up the lost time by driving late into the evening.

I lay in bed a few minutes longer, spent half an hour soaking in a warm bath, scrubbed myself with a rough towel until I was tingling all over, and went to the closet for my blue shirt and Levi's. There would be no sense in wearing my good suit down to the stockyards. I was thinking about Littleton and the roundup, and didn't notice that the Levi's weren't mine until I'd stepped into them and hauled them up. They were at least four inches too big around the waist, and the bottoms of the cuffs reached only to the calves of my legs.

For a second or two my mouth went dry as ashes, then I couldn't help laughing. Poor old Lonnie! He must have been afraid I'd smell a mouse when he failed to come back from the men's room, and that I might catch up with him before he got his stuff out of the hotel. He'd probably never turned the light on when he came into the room, but left the door open while he snatched the first shirt and pair of Levi's he got his hands on, then grabbed up his outfit, bedroll, and bust, and got out of there as fast as he could. There was little doubt that he'd been playing big-shot for some girls all evening, and had finally had to tell them he was broke, while all the time my britches—with seven hundred dollars in the cuffs—were lying on Shiftless's back seat.

Small as the doubt was, it was still enough to make me uneasy. I wasn't a bit worried for fear Lonnie had taken my Levi's intentionally, but I was worried for fear someone else might have done it. While he took girls to a show, or into some shop to buy them presents or ice cream, he'd have left Shiftless in the street. And if he were asleep in her down at the stockyards I could be in real trouble. There were always a lot of down-and-out bums hanging around the yards, and any one of them would swipe a shirt and pair of jeans if he could get away with them. And Lonnie wouldn't wake up if they swiped the hat off his head.

My hands weren't too steady when I took all the money I had left—$2.85—from the pocket of my suit britches, hauled the belt out of the loops, reefed Lonnie's Levi's around my waist, and turned down one fold of the cuffs.

On my way out of the hotel I stopped at the desk and left word that Lonnie should wait for me if he came in while I was away. Then, after I'd caught a streetcar for the stockyards, I knew that stopping had been a waste of time. Even if Lonnie should discover that he'd taken the wrong pair of Levi's he wouldn't bring them back and exchange—not after my having scared him about Shiftless. He'd never guess there was anything in the cuffs, so he'd simply throw them away, or trade them off to some bum who had a pair that were too big for him.

All the way to the stockyards I told myself what a fool I'd been for putting the pressure on Lonnie. And I told it to myself at least fifty times more as I spent the day searching every alley around the cattle pens, and enquiring at every office and weighing shack. But nobody had seen either Lonnie or a 1914 Ford of Shiftless's description.

By late afternoon it occurred to me that Lonnie might have got in over his head the night before. If he'd picked up a couple of girls like those chickadees he'd spied when we came out of the restaurant, they could have led him into enough trouble that he might have been arrested. He wouldn't have any better sense than to let them take him to some gyp joint and run up a bill he wouldn't be able to pay. The more I thought of it the more it seemed to me that it might be all for the best. If he were in jail I could find him easily enough, and the cost of bailing him out and getting him squared away would be small as compared to the amount in the cuffs of my Levi's. Then he couldn't raise any objection to leaving town and driving me to Littleton. By driving straight through we could still make it in plenty of time for the roundup.

I'd already spent fifty cents in calling the hotel to find out if Lonnie had shown up, and by dusk I had only a quarter left. I'd spent all the rest of my $2.85 calling every police station in both Kansas City, Missouri and Kansas, but there was no record of either Lonnie or Shiftless anywhere. I'd called the last station before I'd admit to myself that I might have misjudged Lonnie right from the time he left me in the theater; that he might actually have headed for home as soon as he pawned his outfit. If he had he'd certainly left me stranded worse than I'd thought he would be. I already owed an eight-dollar hotel bill, and if I pawned everything I had it wouldn't leave me enough to buy a railroad ticket to Littleton.

On the way back from the stockyards I thought of something I should have thought about the first thing that morning. There was a pretty sure way of finding out whether or not Lonnie had really left Kansas City. If he had been alone when he went to the garage for Shiftless he'd probably driven straight out of town; if there had been a girl with him he'd still be hiding out somewhere in the city and I could find him.

I went right to the garage from the streetcar, and got there just as the night man came on duty. When I asked him if he remembered Lonnie's coming in, and whether or not he was alone, he said, "Yep! He was alone—lugging a bedroll and a statue rolled up in a pair of blue jeans. Only the hair was sticking out of the end. That's how come I remember him so well. Seemed to be in an awful hurry. Asked me the best road to St. Joe, and how to get onto it."

"What did he do with the statue?" I asked.

"Laid it on the back seat, right careful," he told me, "and wedged it into a corner with his bed roll, so's it wouldn't jiggle off and get busted. What had he, stole it some place?"

"No," I said, "it was his. Did you notice what time it was when he came in?"

"About an hour later'n this," he told me. "Not long after I come on duty. Why? Wasn't the flivver his? He had the claim check for it."

"Yes, it's his," I said. "He's a friend of mine and I just wondered if he'd left town yet." Then I got out of there before he could ask me any more questions.

It appeared certain that I'd frightened Lonnie out of Kansas City, but knowing where he was bound for made me positive that I could overtake him. I'd never before known him to leave a city with as much as a dime in his pocket, and I didn't believe he could do it twice in a row. Without me to watch after him in St. Joe, he'd be bound to get mixed up with some chickadee and go broke. Sooner or later he'd probably mooch enough gas to go on, but it might take him two or three days, and if I got up there soon enough I'd find him around the stockyards.

From the garage I hurried right back to the hotel, picked up my saddle and outfit, and wasted an hour lugging them to half the pawnshops on Twelfth Street. Every pawnbroker knew the saddle for an off-sized Oregon half-breed the moment he saw it, and the best I could get for the whole outfit was ten dollars.

Much as I'd wanted to go back to Littleton looking prosperous, there was only one thing I could do. I had to go back to the hotel, pay my bill, and take everything else I owned to the pawnshop. I didn't have any better luck with the rest of my stuff than I did with the saddle. The suitcase had been scuffed up a little from jouncing around in Shiftless, my suit was too small for anyone but a skinny boy to wear, my bedroll looked a bit tacky, and the pawnbroker didn't even know what my sculpturing tools were. All I could do was to keep the best and smallest tools, and take five dollars for the rest of the stuff.

I couldn't afford to waste time in trying to hop freights, so I went to the depot, struck up an acquaintance with some of the boomers hanging around, and asked when there would be a mail train going to St. Joseph. They said the Denver mail train pulled out at eleven o'clock and St. Joe was its first stop, but there was no use in trying to hop the blind baggage on any mail train leaving Kansas City. They all left from the main depot, and the railroad police watched the front end like bloodhounds.

One of the boys said he'd help me by making a run for the front mail car just before the train pulled out. Then, while the cops were chasing him away, I could duck underneath and climb up onto the rods. To me that sounded ten times more dangerous than riding horse falls, so I decided to buy a ticket and ride an earlier train, but all it left me was a pocketful of small change.

I wanted to reach St. Joe early enough to check the stockyards, then if I didn't find Lonnie there, make a round of every

garage, movie theater, and ice-cream parlor that evening, but
the only train I could get out of Kansas City was a local that
stopped at every flag station along the way. The Denver mail
train went zooming past us at the last flag stop, and was standing
in the St. Joseph depot when we pulled in. It blocked my way
to the stockyards, so I hurried up the track to go around it.
I'd nearly reached the engine when a railroad cop with a
revolver slung at his hip stopped me. He made me stand where
I was, and watched me like a weasel until the train was pulling
out so fast that I couldn't have flipped it if I'd wanted to.

When I got over to the stockyards it was easy to see that
cowhand jobs were as scarce in the North as they had been in
the South. There were three or four down-and-outers sleeping
around every little feed pile. None of them had saddles, and
less than half of them had bedrolls. I waked a boy at each feed
pile, asked him how long he'd been around the yards, and if
he'd seen a Ford like Shiftless or a boy who might have been
Lonnie. No one had, and I knew it must be nearly two o'clock
before I'd searched out every feed pile in the yards, so I lay
down by one of them for a few hours sleep.

I was out before daylight, and by eleven o'clock that night
I'd been to every garage and gasoline station from one end of
St. Joseph to the other. I hadn't missed a single movie theater,
ice-cream parlor, or restaurant, but no one had seen a sign of
Lonnie. Even though I'd been living on peanuts and canned
salmon, I was down to my last dime, so there seemed nothing
I could do but to go down to the depot and try my luck at
flipping the midnight mail train for Denver. If I made it I could
still reach Littleton before the roundup was over, and once there
I knew I wouldn't have any trouble in finding a job.

To kill a little time I stopped at each garage I came to on
my way to the depot, just in hope I might find some night man
who hadn't been on duty when I made my first round. I found
the right one when I had only a couple of blocks left to go. He
was an old fellow, sitting in front of a little garage on a side
street.

"Yeah, I seen 'em," he said when I'd described Lonnie and Shiftless. "Kind of a chunky set boy, wearin' a light gray suit with a dark pencil-stripe? He was driving a 1914 Ford that looked close to new. Arizona license plate. Stopped here to gas up night before last . . . about midnight as I recollect. Lost his way comin' into town is how he got way off over here. Asked how to get back onto the road for Sioux City."

"Was he alone?" I asked.

"Yeah, alone," he told me. "Nice friendly sort of a boy . . . clever too. Cowboy artist, he said he was. Had a likeness he'd made of his own self . . . spittin' image of him."

"Did he have it wrapped up?" I asked.

"Yeah. Yeah. In a blue shirt and pair of overhauls. He was takin' it home . . . present for his ma. Is he kin o' yours?"

"No," I said, "just a friend. I'd hoped to meet him while he was in town."

"Don't reckon he stopped over to see nobody," the old man said. "Told me he had nigh onto eight hundred miles to make and aimed to do it in three days. Ought to be close to home by now."

"Did he say where his home was?" I asked.

"Not that I recollect. Didn't ask him."

"Hope he makes it okay," I said. "Didn't seem short of cash, did he?"

"Wouldn't know about that," he said. "Paid for his gas out of a ten, so he couldn'ta been too hard up."

"Did he have a saddle and cowhand outfit in the flivver?"

The old man shook his head. "None that I seen. Not lest it was on the floor in back. All I seen was a bedroll and the likeness I was tellin' you of."

There was no sense in asking any more questions, and even less sense in trying to follow Lonnie any farther, so I headed for the railroad tracks. I didn't go to the depot, but circled around a couple of blocks to the north, crossed the tracks, and hid in a ditch a hundred yards beyond the place where the engine of the Denver mail train had stopped the night before.

It was nearly half an hour before the train pulled in, and as I waited for it I had a chance to do some of the thinking I should have done before getting into any such fix. There was nobody to blame but myself. I'd thought I was pretty smart when I'd been sitting there in the restaurant and putting the pressure on Lonnie to sell Shiftless. If I'd stopped to do a little thinking before passing out all my wise advice, I might have known what would happen. Lonnie had been in love with old Shiftless ever since the first day he'd seen her. And his affection had never cooled for a moment, not even when we discovered how worn-out and worthless she was.

As I lay there in the ditch I could almost see him again, up there in the mountains when we'd sheered off the half-moon key. Lazy as he was about everything else, he'd started off the next morning for a new key—knowing he might have to walk eighty miles to town and back—rather than run the risk of my abandoning the old wreck. I might have known that he cared more for that old flivver than for all the girls in the world, and that his taking them to ride had been more for a chance to show off Shiftless than for any other reason.

Even though Lonnie had taken my Levi's by mistake—seven hundred dollars and all—I hadn't really lost anything yet. There wasn't the slightest doubt but that he was headed straight for home—wherever that might be. Unless he ran into a lot of bad luck on the way, the money he got for his outfit would be enough to see him through. And when he got there my Levi's would still be wrapped around the plaster bust I had made for him. He might throw britches away because they were too small for him or needed washing, but his mother wouldn't, and she wouldn't wash them without unfolding the cuffs. I might not know where to find Lonnie, but he knew I was going to Littleton, and that I had plenty of friends there. He might swipe chickens and mooch a little money to spend on the girls, but I knew him well enough to know that when my seven hundred was discovered he'd get it back to me, one way or another.

The more I thought of it the more I realized that I wouldn't have lost anything, even though my seven hundred were never found and returned. Less than eight months ago the specialists at the Boston hospital had given me only six months to live, but I was still alive, and had never felt healthier in my life. In the past two months I'd gained five pounds, and Mother had written that Dr. Gaghan was very pleased with my reports.

More than that, in a time when thousands of stout, healthy men were out of jobs and having to queue up in soup lines, or to take charity in order to feed their families, I'd been making money so fast I didn't dare let my mother find out about it. With what I'd sent to Grace the family would be safe for a year, even if I didn't send home another dime. But there was no fear of that; I had my sculpturing tools in my hip pocket, and my eye and hand were well practiced in the way to use them.

The mail train pulled in while I was still thinking back over the months Lonnie and I had spent together. I lay flat, and didn't even let myself think until the mail sacks had been tossed aboard, the conductor swung his lantern, and the wheels began turning. I jumped to my feet and made my run at the instant the engine headlight passed me, and I was running at full speed when I grabbed the hand bar on the front end of the first mail car and flipped aboard. There was nothing to slow me down, for all I was carrying was one dime, the little Bible that had been my father's, and my sculpturing tools.

The railroad cop who stopped me the night before was on duty again. He must have been in the service, and couldn't have been out long enough to forget his army training. He shouted, "Halt!" before I'd taken five steps, and I heard the whiz of a bullet before I heard the bark of his gun. The shot was either wild or intentionally high. It didn't even hit the train, but it did make my nerves jumpy for a few seconds. The mail train had picked up full speed before I could settle down comfortably in the deep, blind doorway of the mail car, knowing that no conductor or brakie could reach me—and that there was no danger of the train stopping till it was far, far along the rails toward Littleton and the Fourth-of-July roundup.

About the Author

RALPH OWEN MOODY was born December 16, 1898, in Rochester, N. H. His father was a farmer whose illness forced the family to move to Colorado when Ralph was eight years old. The family's life in the new surroundings is told from the point of view of the boy himself in *Little Britches*.

The farm failed and the family moved into Littleton, Colorado, when Ralph was about eleven. Soon after, the elder Moody died of pneumonia, leaving Ralph as the oldest boy, the man of the family. After a year or so—described in *Man of the Family* and *The Home Ranch*—Mrs. Moody brought her three sons and three daughters back to Medford, Mass., where Ralph completed his formal education through the eighth grade of grammar school. This is the period of *Mary Emma & Company*. Later, Ralph joined his maternal grandfather on his farm in Maine—the period covered in *The Fields of Home*.

A new series of books, about Ralph's experiences as a young man, starts with *Shaking The Nickel Bush*.

In spite of his farming experience, Ralph Moody was not destined to be a farmer. He abandoned the land because his wife was determined to raise her family (they have three children) in the city.

"When I was twenty-one," he writes, "I got a diary as a birthday present and I wrote in it that I was going to work as hard as I could, save fifty thousand dollars by the time I was fifty, and then start writing." True to his word, he did start writing on the night of his fiftieth birthday.

—Adapted from the *Wilson Library Bulletin*